Unbreakable Chains

Shaanchuong mu-Fohnpah

Langaa Research & Publishing CIG
Mankon, Bamenda

Publisher
Langaa RPCIG
Langaa Research & Publishing Common Initiative Group
P.O. Box 902 Mankon
Bamenda
North West Region
Cameroon
Langaagrp@gmail.com
www.langaa-rpcig.net

Distributed in and outside N. America by African Books Collective
orders@africanbookscollective.com
www.africanbookscollective.com

ISBN-10: 9956-552-34-8

ISBN-13: 978-9956-552-34-4

About the Author

Shaanchuong mu-Fohnpah is a Bantu-American, born and bred in the plains of the Upper Nun Valley located in present-day nation of Cameroon. He is the youngest of a very big family in which both parents were educators and storytellers. His mother, a great folk tales' narrator, his father, a magical teller of personal and historical anecdotes, nursed in him the love for storytelling.

After choosing to study Physics at the University right up to sophomore level, because academic obligations made it impossible for him to jointly study Arts and the Sciences, Shaanchuong mu-Fohnpah immigrated to the United States of America. The curriculum of American universities which allows for fundamental Arts and Science courses in every major permitted him to reconnect with college level writing while studying Electrical Engineering at Prince George's Community College—Largo and University of Maryland—College Park.

Today with a Masters in Electrical Engineering from Tuskegee University in Alabama, ten years of practice in the domain, many years of teaching as an Adjunct Professor at Gulf Coast State College, and an ongoing Masters in Systems Engineering at Florida State University—Panama City, Shaanchuong mu-Fohnpah is happily settled in Panama City with his lovely and supportive wife and children. Galvanized by the advent of their children in his life and need to pass on to them the beauty of their history, he has used *Unbreakable Chains* as a way to reconcile his *seven* lives: an Engineering professional, a literature lover, member of a royal lineage, a family man, a pan-Africanist, and an African immigrant. These lives collide and morph into the pages of *Unbreakable Chains*; a collision which hopefully is the Big Bang leading to more works from the spirits.

Dedication

I dedicate this piece of work to my father Prince Ghghmu Fɔɔŋpah muun-Fɔ'ɔshɛ, my mother Aboul me-Nkeuya, my granny Mamma Mabangɔ, my wife Haoua Koulama, and to my inexhaustible pride and joy Bébbé Naantɔnɔ and Shaachuoŋ Mbɔrɔnwi.

I am eternally grateful to Minwi the creator of all, especially thankful to Clarice P. Williams, Ndi Andham Nangha, and Dr. Hassan Mbiydzenyui, and honored by the unconditional affection of Prince William Fohtaw Ndi, Pulera Adamu, Ŋkwanwi muuŋ-Fɔɔŋpah, and Ndombuɔ muuŋ-Fɔɔŋpah.

Thank you to all my Fɔɔŋpa'a family and friends.

Shaachuoŋ muuŋ-Fɔɔŋpah

Table of Contents

Chapter 1

Upper Nun Valley, Kamerun 1897

The golden light from the oil lamp danced to the beat of the night breeze and under the gaze of the night's darkness. As seconds crawled by, as the darkness grew intense, the flame grew tired and shy, and gradually its brilliance faded away. This was not the first time the flame had grown weak and dim in the course of this night. Earlier that evening Mahbangoh had noticed that her oil lamp was running out of fuel. So, she had then decided to borrow some oil from her sister-wife, Nahshieh; just enough oil to last her while she fetched some more fuel from one of the village's oil merchants.

Nahshieh was a very young woman and so too was her union to Tahkuh. As the leaves of this fresh marriage budded off its stalk Mahbangoh made sure that the dead leaves were trimmed off and fertile ground gathered beneath the growing plant. Seasons of joy and seasons of pain were to be expected, but there was not much to be afraid of. Tahkuh was a man who respected the tradition, the tenets of having a long-lasting marriage; and Nahshieh was a young bride who loved the idea of being someone's wife –like most girls of her age.

Apart from being Nahshieh's sister-wife, Mahbangoh was also Nahshieh's mentor; she taught Nahshieh the secrets of a good marriage-life—what it took to keep her man, every man, happy: a filled stomach, a warm bed, and a controlled tongue. Behind closed doors, along riverbanks, and underneath shadows cast by the leaf-stuffed branches of tall trees of the kingdom, the village women asserted that it was Mahbangoh who led a group of women some full moons ago as they accompanied Nahshieh from her parents' home to her husband's home. This was the reason why Nahshieh was at times referred to as Mahbangoh's wife.

1

Memories of that day when Mahbangoh had gone to take Nahshieh from her family were still carved in Nahshieh's mind, even though the beautiful exotic body paint patterns that had covered the smooth brown skin of the young bride's arms, legs, and face on that day had long faded away. It was not only this captivating beauty of the wedding day that had faded with time but the pain of parting from family as well; indeed, as time went by Nahshieh remembered the pain of separation from her parents lesser and lesser. This rapid emotional recovery was in part thanks to Mahbangoh's loving and motherly care towards her husband's new wife, Nahshieh. In every polygamous home, it was the duty of the senior sister-wife to mentor and treat all the other wives with love and respect--just as Mahbangoh had been treating Nahshieh. Thanks to this positive energy, the relationship between these two ladies blossomed day by day, and so on this particular day, the junior sister-wife did not mind lending some lamp oil to her mentor, amongst the many other items that they borrowed from each other.

Mahbangoh had been so busy diligently performing her motherly, wifely, and senior sister-wifely evening chores with the oil borrowed from Nahshieh that she had forgotten to go get some more oil from the oil merchant. Chicken gone home to roost, goats regurgitating the earlier meals in the pen, and owls hooting behind leafy branches meant it was now late to go knock on anyone's door for some oil. Too late; especially on an extraordinary night like this one, a night when the border between the ancestral spirits' world and the physical realm was nonexistent. Even a traveler going through Mighang kingdom's Grassfield vegetation for the first time could deduce that this particular night was not an ordinary one: there were no drumbeats, no celebratory songs, no joyous shout, and no laughter-infested games came from the moonlight-illuminated and feet-battered red ground of the kingdom's arena and playgrounds. Tonight, silence reined in absolutely authority, simply because most people had retired into their huts and stretched out their sleeping mats.

Lying on her sleeping mat Mahbangoh contemplated for a short while the darkness in the room as it was growing greedier and swallowing more of the lamp's flame. Grunting faintly, she rose from her sleeping mat, walked towards the lamp made of clay and poured the last drops of the oil she had gotten from Nahshieh into her lamp's reservoir. The flame at the tip of the lamp's wick gallantly grew bigger and brightened the single-windowed hut. The brightness revealed the quasi-rectangular shape of the hut, the spatial arrangement of its content, and the position of its occupants.

Covering the door of the hut was a mat made from dried bamboo slats tied to each other thanks to strings pulled off the leaves of raffia palms. If one stood at the door and looked into the hut from that position, it was obvious to them that Mahbangoh made the most out of the corners of her hut. The front left corner accommodated a big old clay vase resting on three big stones and containing fresh water in permanence. The rectangular floor space located at the base of the mud wall lounging from the door to the corner with the clay vase was about four meters wide and was perpendicular to the mud wall opposite to the door. This floor space was occupied by calabashes and clay pots. These receptacles were turned upside down and laid on recently harvested fresh plantain leaves. Diagonally across from the water-containing clay vase was a bamboo ladder leaning against two walls, which formed a right angle between them. This ladder led up to the attic where all sorts of foods items and medicinal plants and herbs were preserved and stored. At the center of the hut was a fireplace made of big stones, the stones were covered in thick layers of soot and firmly seated on the hut's floor. On the hut's slightly red and dusty floor, the space located between the front right corner of the hut and the door was covered with sleeping mats. These colorful mats, made tender and robust by the interweaving of soft cotton silk threads and cellulose-based fibers made from tree barks, were presents offered to Mahbangoh by Nahshieh during the latter's wedding. Three days after Nahshieh had moved into Tahkuh's home, Mahbangoh had worked with her to make her hut as well organized as hers. Today the only treasure missing in Nahshieh's hut was a child and that was certainly going to come in no time. That was why Nahshieh's hut was built as wide and large as Mahbangoh's.

The entire decor in Mahbangoh's hut was barely visible now, as the recently provoked brightness of the flame from the oil lamp had begun diminishing anew. This time Mahbangoh did not have any extra oil to feed her voracious lamp. Mahbangoh quickly glanced at the sleeping mat on which her boy slept; he was sleeping peacefully, the recent inhale and chewing of an empty mouth by the boy were proof of his transition into a deeper sleep phase. She laid back, moved her body from side to side, rolled and yawed, in search for a more comfortable position in which to resume her sleep, and then she thought for moment of waking up the boy. She wanted him to go out and answer nature's call even before lady nature called for him in the deepest phase of his sleep. But, she immediately recalled that this was no ordinary night.

Earlier that evening the town crier had visited every nook and cranny of the kingdom. He had announced that the *Ngumba* was to come out of its sacred house later that night, thereby imposing a curfew going from early dusk to early dawn over the entire kingdom. Due to this curfew, Mahbangoh could not take her boy out of the hut that night. She therefore concluded that in the event of any pressing need to release toxic body contents there was an old clay pot and its lid, and some natural deodorizer that she could use for the boy and herself.

Ngumba was the secret sacred society of the kingdom; it was made of men who were more than mere mortals. It is said that its members had powers that allowed them to be transformed into animals, and that they were the agents of ancestral gods.

4

The name of this secret sacred order was not uttered in trivial conversations, its members where quasi-unknown and its decisions irrevocable. Nobody ever directly referred to a mortal as being part of the *Ngumba*, instead if one needed any information they inquired on what the *Ngumba* would have told the mortals who were part of the order--making it sound as if the *Ngumba* was a person of its own and not a mystical order. Mahbangoh's husband, Tahkuh, was a member of the *Ngumba*. Whenever he and other members of the order met to fulfill the task of the gods, they lost all of their mortality and became inhabited by the spirits of the gods. Nobody, not even the bravest of mortals, dared look at them in that transfigured state or else the person was going to drop to ground and begin an agonizing journey to the land of no return. That person's death was going to be preceded by the rapid painful coloring of their skin; their skin would turn red--as red as red-hot coal.

The kingdom's oral history mentioned few people, not more than three, that had survived the sight of the *Ngumba*; that was the case with Ngwangong who, while pregnant with her third child, had unintentionally crossed path with the *Ngumba* during one of her business trips to Foumban the economic hub of the Bamoun Sultanate. She had survived only because she had respected the laws of the land. The law prescribed that in the event that a person inadvertently saw the *Ngumba* that person had to be rushed to the sacred quarters of the King's palace for purification within eight hours after the incident. If this purification was not done in time the person was going to eventually die. In Ngwangong's case the unique rituals performed during the purification rites impacted the destiny of the child in her womb. From birth this child was considered a priestess and was given the name *Fousseh* and the title *Mahbangoh*. The former name meant the riches of the land, she was considered the priestess of the goddess of land fertility, and the latter name meant enthroned matriarch of the Bangoh sub-clan.

Back in the hut where the little boy slept peacefully, Mahbangoh visually verified the last details in the hut while she was progressively engulfed by the impatient voracious darkness, that very darkness she had fought against. Forsaken by the light from her oil lamp, Mahbangoh knew that with Tahkuh gone for the night the family's safety was her responsibility, so she quietly and carefully glided across her mat towards her son, clutched her boy close to her, and closed her eyes. Her eyes closed, she reminisced on how much honor and respect she had amongst her people because she was a priestess, her husband was a member of the *Ngumba*, and her younger sister was the bride to the young and handsome king of the Mighang Kingdom. As long as the kingdom flourished so would the status and privilege of her family. It was even known, within the *Ngumba* circle and beyond, that Tahkuh had a very special relationship with the King. His loyalty and respect towards the King and the traditions were known all over the mainland and islands of *Láah Mighang* (Home of the Mighang People).

Earlier that evening before the first tongues of flames had been lit on the wick of Mahbangoh's lamp, and as the sun dove behind mount *NgohMuhntaw* the town crier navigated through every dusty path of the kingdom, and his powerful and deep voice disturbed the family friendly cool evening atmosphere descending on the Mighang Kingdom. The town crier announced the *Ngumba*'s procession, mapped out its itinerary, and reminded the mortals of the dos and don'ts by using a unique sense of exaggeration bounded by terrifying warnings about the outcome reserved to those who will not heed to his advice. His voice and the sound of his trumpet carved out of elephant tusks went like this:

"Toot! Toot! Toot!"

"Mortals of Mighang, the gods are honoring you with their presence. But remember no one should laugh at his father, even when he sees his father's sagging testicles hanging loose. If you dare peep at the gods your eyes will burn, and all your

6

descendants will be plagued with generational leprosy, barrenness, and impotence!"

"Tooooot! tooooot!"

"If you dare look at the gods you skin will turn red like red-hot coal."

"Tooooot! tooooot!"

"If you just dare see them you will know a painful and long death. Your guts will spill out of your corpse before you are buried in a shallow grave uphill where the vultures will feast on your remains."

"Tooooot! Tooooot!"

"The river dwindled because her mother did not warn her about the obstacles. The gods have warned you."

"Tooooot! Tooooot!"

Hearing the town crier's voice that evening Mahbangoh instinctively knew that there was no need for her to over-prepare herself to go spend the night in her husband's hut, as it was the habit on every seventh day of the week. Dashing in and out of her smoke-filled hut, which served as kitchen too, she prepared supper for their husband. While the contents of her clay pot fused by means of an endothermic process, the dedicated mother of the family also prepared an aromatized bath for her husband. She delivered the clean fresh aromatized bath water in a roofless hut made of four wooden poles forming the corners of a cubicle whose sides were covered with palm fronds. This roofless and three and the half-walled hut was located behind Tahkuh's hut and served as his bathroom whenever he chose not to go and bathe himself in the stream running a mile away from the back yard of his residence. The bath water delivered, Mahbangoh returned to her kitchen chores and later served Tahkuh's supper. The one thing, usually part of her routine, which she did not do on this extraordinary day, was to ask her son to get ready to sleep in his stepmother's hut.

Having showered herself and served supper to her husband, Mahbangoh sat by her fireside shelling peanuts in anticipation for a future meal. A task her son intermittently joined in, not because it was effortless but because he fed his restless mouth with some peanuts every now and then. Once her husband was done eating, he called out her name from his hut, "Mah! Mah!" It was the cue for her to know he was done eating. she rose from her stool, loosened up the rope serving as waistband to her skirts made of leaves and then tightened it back. The she walked out towards her husband's hut. She announced herself at the door of his hut by clapping twice, he in turn acknowledged her claps by loudly clearing his throat and Mahbangoh immediately walked in. She gathered the dishes in which she had served him supper and while still in her squatting posture she bade him good night.

"May we see each other tomorrow, our husband," Mahbangoh bade as she picked up the leaves that contained the remains of p'nah and the calabash that had *kehkhung* stew and placed them on her wooden tray.

Standing upright with the tray in hand, the beads of her necklace slipped down into the cleavage formed by the cloth wrapped around her torso and covering her two slightly saggy breasts. She had made herself just beautiful enough for her husband thanks to the camwood paste rub all over her feet, the homemade eyeliner displayed in a concave semi-ellipsoidal contour above her cheekbones and just under her eyes, and a modest amount of body paint reinforced by a proportional amount of *manyaga*, palm kernel based body lotion. She had left out the most intimate aspect of being beautiful, this included the intimate bath using the white rock, the full body scented vapor bath, and the wearing of *jigidah*, colorful beads around her waistline. This one-man beauty parade was a reminder to the couple that even though the night was not to be exploited as planned she remained the first of his life partners.

"The meal was very delicious, and the cook is very beautiful" Tahkuh expressed his appreciation to both the tasty food and the beauty of his wife.

Mahbangoh and Tahkuh were more than just partners they were teammates in every sense of the word; even though Tahkuh was both team captain and coach. Most villagers did not know the reason why the *Ngumba* was to come out of their sacred quarters on this particular night, yet Mahbangoh knew she was going to be one of the first citizens, outside the *Ngumba* circle, to be informed. Experience guaranteed that the next morning her husband was going stop by her hut and exchange on the purpose of the *Ngumba's* meeting with her just before she leaves for the village market. It was this relationship of trust that had strengthened their bond during the unforgettable tragedy and that had pushed Tahkuh to seek Mahbangoh's opinion about taking a second wife. A tragedy still spoken about in the Tahkuh family to this day.

After bidding good night and right before walking towards the exit of her husband's hut Mahbangoh paused and carefully adjusted the positions of the still almost full food-recipients on her tray, the same tray carrying her oil lamp. She rapidly visually examined the leftovers to know if her husband her eaten enough. She carried the tray, made of woven bamboo peels, and walked out of her husband's hut. Her husband did not only seem preoccupied by the curfew, he was indeed worried and Mahbangoh knew this because he had barely eaten his supper even though he had complimented her on the quality of the meal. A great deal of the smoked tilapia stew and corn fufu which she had served him was still untouched. The Mighang people believed a happy man feasted on his wives' meals. Like most other women, Mahbangoh could not dare to directly ask her husband what was on his mind. Such a reaction would have been perceived as a sign of disrespect. So, without a rationale to her husband's loss of appetite Mahbangoh walked to her hut. As she walked away, a timid early night breeze put off the flame on her lamp's wick after a short-lived epic wrestle between the two elements. Nonetheless, she calmly navigated through the darkness by placing her feet on the ground with very little pressure and slowing down her pace while her eyes

9

widened in the process of visual accommodation. She knew the locations of most bumps and potholes on the battered ground leading to her hut, her home till death. Playing the role of a lighthouse, the fire from the fireplace in her hut also helped her find her way in the dark. She easily walked towards the bamboo mat covering the door of her hut because it glowed faintly as light rays from the fire flames crept through the slits of the doormat made of bamboo slats. By the time she got into her hut, her son was done with his meal and was licking his fingers and smacking his lips.

"Wash those hands of yours before the mice eat them while you are asleep," Mahbangoh warned her son. Following the warning, Mahbangoh placed her tray on the floor and helped her boy wash his hands. Then she tucked him to sleep with songs and tales about prodigious men and women of Mighang. This bedtime routine this took place earlier that evening when the oil borrowed from Nahshieh was not yet finished and the darkness had not yet dominated the hut.

Engulfed in dense darkness and stretched on her mat Mahbangoh was reliving all these events of the early evening and gradually fell asleep as her body and that of her son, curled up together underneath a cloth, reached thermal equilibrium. Their noisy breathing, the chirping of the crickets and the croaking of the toads conquered the silence of the night. A sky deprived of moon and stars hung above the land and the river stretches that formed the Kingdom of Mighang. The mortals were asleep while the immortals were awake. Alone in her hut Nahshieh had also fallen asleep comforted by the thought that having Tahkuh as husband meant she will be promptly informed of the reason why the *Ngumba* had been summoned. In the oral history of the Kingdom of Mighang the *Ngumba* had never been summoned for a pleasant reason.

The morning sun of the next day brought with its glimmering and blinding beauty the ambiance of an eighth day of the week, the market day in the Kingdom of Mighang. The suspense about the previous night's unexpected call to duty of the *Ngumba* still floated in the air, but the attention of every villager had drifted to the market day's activities. The *Ngumba's* outing was the headline of most discussions, but this was obscured by the village's market day spirit. The village on market day was comparable to a beehive at its busiest hour. Everyone had something to do, something to say, somewhere to go, and someone to meet. It was a moment when the lower and middle classes of the society got together with very little class-related segregation, while the folks of the higher class maintained the myth about their status and savored the power bestowed on them by society. The Mighang people had a saying that: "if hunger was a woman, then her weeding will be on the market day and her bride price will be all of the marketed goods"; it was their way of describing the inestimable value of market days in the community's survival.

The marketplace could easily be mistaken for one of the many community god's shrines; it was so because the sacred rock of Mighang, the sacred artifact on which everybody swore, stood tall at the heart of the market. Shooting outward from the same heart of the marketplace were eight evenly spaced wide footpaths that made up the marketplace's transportation network. On either side of this footpaths wooden stands occupied by sellers stood shoulder to shoulder. The market itself was not too far from the King's Palace, thus it seemed as though the market and the sacred rock were a sacred place built in proximity to the King's Palace.

Tradition did hold the market day as a special day; no hard field labor was permitted on this eighth day of the week. The day did not only encourage social interaction amongst the citizens of Mighang, but also promoted inter communal relations as merchants from other neighboring kingdoms converged to Mighang's marketplace. Even more than any other thing, the market day ultimately honored the goddess of land fertility which had given much and needed a day off her provision-duty.

Most village roads, whether official or improvised, led to the Market. In part because it was the venue of regular gatherings, but mostly because it was the exchange center *par excellence*. Sellers and buyers met at this venue, used cowries as currency or simply engaged in trade by batter. On these roads and on every market day one watched with much amusement the comedy of goats reluctantly pulled and sheep naively guided to the marketplace. It was also common to come across kids preceding their parents to the market; they carried their parent's merchandise on their heads from home to market. The unfortunate parents had very playful kids who often got carried away by games and social interaction with their peers, and the kids either made it late to the market or lost part or all of their parents' merchandise.

On this particular market day after the *Ngumba*'s convening, the palm wine harvesters had delayed in bringing out the fresh and appetizing white stuff, the refreshing and spell-biding sap from palm trees, as early as usual. This lagging in delivery time was due to the curfew that had lasted till sunrise had impeded the very early morning harvest of palm wine. Nonetheless, the other products at the market arrived early and quite fresh, almost alive one would say. The farmers were used to the restrictions put on field labor on the eighth day of the week and so they always prepared their goods the afternoon of the day before the weekly commercial jamboree.

Miles away from the already noisy and crowded marketplace was Mahbangoh; she had her son strapped to her back because he was too young to trek to the marketplace. Then she lifted a basket filled with peanuts and bundles of smoked fish which she placed on a *kata*, a cradle resting on the top of her head serving as a stabilizer for her head-borne luggage.

The *kata* was a toroidal-shape cradle and was made of dried plantain leaves wrapped in a circular form. Once placed on the

12

head it was held in place by a string. The string originated from the cradle on top her head, ran down along her right jaw, passed under her chin, and finally ran up along her left jaw and back to the cradle.

Picking up an additional luggage, a sack of yams, with one hand, Mahbangoh headed towards her sister-wife's hut. On one hand tense muscles stuck out creating contours mapped out by the weight of the sack of yams, and the other arm swung freely with very little muscle sticking out, as Mahbangoh started what was always a long day at the market.

Mahbangoh walked, her steps gently landing on the firm ground beneath her bare feet, her swinging hands far off from the basket on her head, her neck muscles twitching on and off as she coordinated her head's posture in order to keep the head-borne luggage in balance. The capacity of maintaining balance with a load on the head was something every Mighang child learned after their first steps. Few steps away from her hut and a little bit more before the village road, Mahbangoh paused and made a 45-degree angle turn to her right. Facing the door of her sister-wife's hut she called out her name and asked her to hurry up.

"If she is being lazy again, she will have to take not only her merchandise out of this home but her belongings too!" Tahkuh roared, as his anger and voice echoed from his hut. It was the angry voice of a once very hungry man.

Earlier that morning Nahshieh had forgotten to serve breakfast to her husband on time. It was not until Tahkuh had given Mahbangoh skewers filled of very big smoked mudfish to take to the market that Nahshieh had stepped out of her hut with Tahkuh's breakfast. Moments before the stepping out she had just remembered that it was her turn to serve breakfast to their husband--it was a tricky thing for a newlywed to keep track of the schedule of marital tasks drawn up by the senior wife. Could anyone blame her? Like most young girls of about thirteen, Nahshieh's mind was focused on going to the market instead of serving food to her quasi-newly wedded husband.

At her husband's roar, Nahshieh quickly stepped out of her hut with fountains of tears running down her cheeks. She did not want to be sent back to her parents' home--repudiation was an unfathomable disgrace for the bride and her family, one that negatively impacted both the married and unmarried siblings of the bride. Having angered Tahkuh twice in such a short span had made her fear that her repudiation was on his mind. But there was no need for Nahshieh to worry about being repudiated, after all her father was a friend to Tahkuh and in addition she had been offered in marriage to Tahkuh by the village King. Tahkuh had married her as a proof of his friendship, loyalty, and respect to the King—that was a different but long-lasting genre of love.

It was this friendship between these two sons of Mighang that had prevailed during extraordinary meeting of the *Ngumba* convened the night before at the village borders. News had reached the King that a white man and his troops were advancing, conquering kingdom after kingdom. The conquistador made slaves out of the dominated kingdoms' people and the kingdoms themselves were made into provinces of another kingdom. This other kingdom was already allied to the white man; it was the Kingdom of BaNyonga. The young enthroned King of Mighang had asked the *Ngumba* to perform a traditional ritual at the village borders to protect them from the invasion of the Dr. Eugene Zingraff's troops. The village council of nine, inspired by the big nine or founding fathers of the kingdom, and the *Ngumba* members had also come up with a contingency plan. This judiciary body of the kingdom, the big nine and the *Ngumba*, suggested that the king's beloved queen, amongst his many wives, and her son, the potential heir, were to seek refuge in the queen's homeland. On the other hand, the Mighang people geared up in anticipation of an eventual war--these two decisions constituted the contingency plan.

Without any surprise, Tahkuh was named scout of the Mighang Kingdom and dispatched to the Ngohmbi and

Mendenkye Kingdoms, allies to the Mighang Kingdom. Upon his return from the mission, the council of nine was to decide on which person was going to accompany the beloved amongst the queens, Queen Ndomboh, to her safe haven. This planned post-mission get-together of the big nine was more of a formality, because everyone knew in their heart who was going to set up and lead the group escorting the queen to her haven. There was no question as to whether Tahkuh was going to be part of this second expedition.

Tahkuh's bravery and loyalty was second to none. During the last village war against the people of Nyamfuka. Tahkuh had fought by the side of his friend and King. They had led the village to a historic victory against all odds. This bond between Tahkuh's family and the royal family survived for centuries and generations. Many generations down the road Muungo, a descendant of Tahkuh's family, grew up hearing about and benefiting from the legendary loyalty and bravery of his ancestor.

It was this pending war and the delicate tasks assigned to Tahkuh that had made him roar at his younger wife, Nahshieh. Soon afterwards he regretted; he felt bad after his threats had fled out of his mouth into the ears of his wives, and with a sigh he acknowledged the impossibility of taking back his words. Sitting in his hut and pondering on the importance of the tasks ahead, Tahkuh picked a piece of wood buried under the cold ashes in a central fireplace in his hut. He tapped the wood against one of the fireside stones, the small particles of the wood ash rose up in the air and those particles that floated into Tahkuh's nostrils caused him to sneeze. Like a little child without a playmate, Tahkuh scribbled on the floor of his hut with the stick from the fireplace. He made a quick count of the items he was going to need in order to perform a sacrifice at his family shrine before leaving for his trip as special envoy of Mighang. He had once vexed his ancestors but neglecting their input in his decision-making process and the results of his negligence had been disastrous, as the entire Tahkuh family was almost decimated. The burial ground behind his hut, mounts of dirt clustered behind his hut, was all his fault--that is what he had always thought and told himself. Like the reflux acid burning the esophageal lining during a heartburn, the thought of his mistake surged from the depth of his conscience interrupting his tally of items needed for the sacrifice. With his face staring down searching for something to lift his spirit, Tahkuh silently broke the stick in his hands as he dealt with this culpability.

In times of war, no warrior was allowed to kill children or women, or spill the bloods of a relative; that was part of the *worldwide* war ethics, or at least the war ethics that reigned amongst the kingdoms that crowded the banks of the River Nun. But during the last war fought by the Mighang Kingdom against the Nyamfuka Kingdom, the people of Mighang driven by revenge and led by an enraged Tahkuh had taken the art of warfare a little too far. Under the Mighang King's orders, Tahkuh had led a special unit into the heart of the enemy's camp where he committed the unforgivable.

The war was at its peak, every son and daughter of the Mighang Kingdom was busy. The men refilled the quivers, sharpened machetes and took rounds on the battlefield, while the women nursed the wounded, stock baskets of food transported carefully and expeditiously to the battlefield, and kept the children indoors. Tahkuh and other troop leaders had suffered a heavy blow from the Nyamfuka Kingdom. It was four days since Mighang warlords had sent messengers to Ngohmbi and Mendenkye Kingdoms asking for backup, but still no answer. The tweeting of birds, the rustling of grass blades, and clipping clopping sound of hooves in the bushes had been replaced by battle cries, machete clashes and war tactics' whispers. Even the smallest pinch of joyous shouts of children and the social gatherings had become non-existent as the women and children of families close to the Mighang and Nyamfuka Kingdoms' border line had gone to seek refuge in homes farther from the cursed land.

Tired of waiting for salvation, the King of the Mighang Kingdom held an emergency meeting with his warlords and councilors in the most sacred quarters of the palace. Of this meeting we know very little, but reliable rumors has it that one of the high-ranking warlords of Mighang returned dead, beheaded using his own machete, and the King dispatched Tahkuh and his unit to a special mission.

Tahkuh and his unit, after hours of crawling through the swampy raffia bushes and enduring the bites of mosquitoes and the attacks of poisonous snakes had discovered the worst of all horrors. They found a lonely hut in the bushes where tens of female virgins willingly offered themselves as sacrifices to the war god of the Nyamfuka Kingdom. This sacrifice supposedly empowered the Nyamfuka warriors. With godlike strength and Lucifer-like rage; Nyamfuka warriors marched into the Mighang Kingdom killing and burning anything and everything that had breath. The passage of these warriors of darkness was marked by bits and pieces of burned and charred human body parts, homes burned to ashes, and animals burned whole.

After hours of crawling in mud right up to the vicinity of the lonely hut, Tahkuh and his men quietly pulled themselves out of the swamp onto dry land, their bodies were covered in sticky black mud and were dripping wet with swamp waters. Suddenly, a loud jubilant voice babbling senseless phrases floated along the still night air and reached the ears of the Mighang warriors. The sound originated from the same direction as a group of feeble light rays that escaped through the door cracks of the lonely sacred hut of the Nyamfuka Kingdom. The hut was located about three hundred meters from the swamp-dry land border. The hooting of owls, the howl of jackals and the screams of hyenas joined the voice of the Nyamfuka Kingdom's priest in spreading a sadistic tune of horror that terrified everyone and everything. Even the air froze and hesitated to ruffle leaves hanging off the many trees that populated the space between the hut and the swamp.

17

Tahkuh exhaled as quietly as he could, flushing out the tiredness and pain that had invaded him after close to a week of war, he pulled out a gourd filled with oil made of boa constrictor fats. He and his men scooped the mud off their body and rubbed the boa fats oil all over their bodies. The stench of the oil presumably scared away any predator, and the intrinsic properties and mystical powers of the oil made the warriors invincible. The sound of Mighang warriors' breathing became more imposing as the reptile's oil made the warriors feel every strength of a boa constrictor - slick, swift, lethal, strong, and smart.

All instructions and attack tactics had been issued before emerging from the swamp; Tahkuh and his men squatted in the dark behind tree trunks and in the midst of the smell of wet bushes patiently waiting for right moment to make their move. The buzzing sound of bloodthirsty mosquitoes grew in amplitude around the Mighang warriors, but the metamorphosed humans cared less about the insignificant mosquito bites. No slap, not even a swift movement of the hand was made to deter the mosquitoes from approaching the warriors. Verily, the mosquitoes did nothing but hover over the unit because the boa-like smell deterred every bug from attacking its prey. But the Nyamfuka's Kingdom priest and his team did not know that they were potential preys to an elite unit from the Mighang Kingdom.

It was close to 9:00 p.m. when the drums resonated in the sacred hut, the voice of the priest and the clacking of bamboo slits joined the rhythmic effervescence. Unknown to the Nyamfuka cohorts, this mix of sounds was also the signal for the Mighang warriors to head for the sacred hut. The sounds of sticks breaking under the feet of Mighang warriors and the dry leaves crushed as they ran towards the hut were swallowed by the drumbeats, clapping, and banging of wood and gong in the hut. The three guards watching over the entrance of the sacred hut barely had the time to see six men pounce on them, when their screams were muffled by strong palms pressed against their mouths and noses; shot spears pierced through their back into their lungs. Strong arms held the guards down, even breaking their bones at times, while blood rushed into their punctured lungs. Repeated stabbing from their attackers slit the guards' carotid arteries, their jugular veins, their ventricles and auricles. While the drumbeats increased in pitch and intensity, the guards lived through their last muscle spasms as life fled their wasted bodies.

The effervescence in the sacred hut came to an abrupt stop; the priest had sensed a rival spirit in the vicinity and had signaled his orchestra to stop playing their instruments. The priest was turning towards the door when the bamboo slats that made up the hut's door came flying inside the hut as the Mighang warriors broke in.

One of the Mighang warriors picked up one of the drums, sprung up into the air with the drum in his hands and in a swift boa-like movement smashed the drum to pieces on the head of the drummer; spilling the drummer's grey matter on the floor.

Tahkuh performed a choke hold on one instrumentalist and once he was unconscious Tahkuh smashed his head against the altar found at the center of the hut. Tahkuh then headed for the priest, an old feeble man who had been instantaneously crippled by fear as he saw the superhuman strength of his attackers. Tahkuh passed his machete from his left to his right hand and with it landed heavy precise blows on the limbs of the old man who had cramped himself in one corner of the hut. Tahkuh's teammates had subdued the other musicians and ceremony officials except for a bunch of young virgins calmly seated in a corner of the hut, almost unperturbed by the horror that had just taken place.

Tahkuh and his unit had one plan, one instruction to obey: stop the main orchestrator of this ritual that empowered their enemies. After incapacitating the priest of the Nyamfuka war god, Tahkuh gave instructions to his men to take the girls captives. To his greatest surprise these young ladies were determined to die for their kingdom's victory. In the blink of an eye one of the girls rose and took the blade on the altar and began cutting through her torso as she leaned over the clay pot in which human blood was to be collected by the priest. The other girls got up and dashed towards the altar as well with the aim of doing the same. In the heat of the moment and frustrated at the thought of casualties endured by the Mighang Kingdom at the hands of the Nyamfuka warriors, Tahkuh picked up his machete swung it in all and every direction around the altar. Every swing of his trembling hand urged him to go for the next swing; with splatters of the girls' blood on his bare torso and the girls' screams in his ears Tahkuh proceeded with his killing spree— slaying every single one of the virgins in the hut.

This act of bravery and valor of this famous night had saved his people but had put a heavy burden on Tahkuh and his conscience. The King of Mighang and the other village notables had performed purification rites on Tahkuh to cleanse him of the curse that had befallen him following the summary killing of the virgins, but the expiation for this abomination had only come at the cost of Tahkuh's own blood. Months after the war his infant daughter had died in the forest killed by an unknown beast. The mutilated remains of the unrecognizable poor girl had been laid to rest in Tahkuh's home. Compounding the grief of the Tahkuh family, Tahkuh's pair of newborn twin sons died few months later of what seemed to be jaundice; but the village medicinal expert said it was a curse from the gods and not an ordinary illness. Tahkuh's ancestral gods had forbidden him from and explicitly warned him about killing children and women, but it seemed his love for his people had led him astray and he had paid so dearly for his headiness.

So, this time, for the oncoming possible war expedition, Tahkuh had chosen to consult and obey the gods before anything else. It could be the early morning sight of Nahshieh, the wife given to him after the victorious war against the

Nyamfuka Kingdom, or maybe it was the sight of his only child going with his mother to the market that had made him relive his blunder. In the depth of his dark memories about that famous night he heard vivid screams and shouts of terror, the kind of high-pitch and desperate screams and cries that preceded the presence of death. His victims screamed in terror while his unit members implored him by desperately shouting his name with the hope that he was going to realize he was committing an abomination.

So, on this market day, some five years after the war, Tahkuh waited for a while in his hut for the voices and footsteps of his wives to vanish into the joyous morning air, and then suddenly he rose from his stool, or better still, he uprooted his body from the stool. He stood up as if he was fighting against a force that was pressing him down. He leaned over towards the wall of his hut and plunged his hand in a basket, hung about five feet above his sleeping mat, from which he picked out some kola nuts and garcinia kola; eye-inspected them for quality and size and dropped the freshest and best in a semi-rigid bag made of tanned goatskin and containing other items. One could hear the nuts as they crash-landed on other items in the bag. He took the bag and walked to the door of his hut, looked far into the horizon with his chewing stick wiggling at one corner of his mouth as he vehemently chewed on it. Once outside his hut, he spat out a mix of saliva and bits of chewed wood, stepped on the spittle, and then headed for the shrine of his family's ancestral gods.

He placed his bag against the horseshoe shaped bamboo fence that enclosed the area considered to be the shrine. He handpicked few weeds that had established their roots next to the flat rock serving as the altar of the ancestral gods. Next, he brought out a gourd of palm oil, the garcinia kola and kola nuts from his bag. He was about to pour some palm oil and throw some kola at the feet of a fungi-covered and liquid-stained wooden statute when he heard the faint sound of approaching footsteps, and then the sound of someone clearing their throat

21

in an attempt to draw his attention. It was Nahshieh's father, a friend and the most renowned messenger of the King's army, standing next to Tahkuh's hut a few steps behind the graves, and clenching in his right hand a hollow helix-shaped ram horn symbolizing the voice of the King

"Did you rise up this morning my brother?" He greeted Tahkuh.

"Yes, I did and you, did you rise as well?" Tahkuh retorted as he struggled to let loose the wrinkles on his face that expressed his anger at the fact that he was interrupted during his ritual at the shrine.

"What brings you here on a market day my in-law?" he asked the messenger, knowing very well that the King had sent him as the horn in his right hand silently screamed out.

"The hen only gathers her chicks if the hawk is in the sky. His Majesty has summoned you my in-law to appear before him before his spittle dries out on the ground. The enemy is already heading in the BaNdop plain. May our ancestor and gods of this land protect us from the fury and fire of this people. " The messenger said.

The reference to the King's spittle drying out was a way of describing the urgency with which the King's orders had to be executed. Tahkuh stood frozen for a moment, he knew what this summoning meant. He was to leave for his mission right now. Leaving right now meant he had not said goodbye to his wives, his son, and had not consulted his ancestors.

"What have we done to the gods to deserve such misfortune?" He voiced while pondering on why he was put in the dilemma of completing his ritual or going to meet his king.

The messenger turned his back and headed for the palace. The king was expecting his messenger to return once the message was delivered. Upon the messenger's return the king was going to spit on the floor, multiple times if need be, in order to judge the urgency with which his subject, Tahkuh, was going to answer his call.

Chapter 2

Panama City Beach, Florida 2016

Mercy Lewis walked out of the break room located on the third floor of an office building situated at the heart of Panama City Beach; an industrial and tourist residential stretch of mostly reclaimed swampy land and sandy soil. This relief once covered by a forest of pine, was today transformed into an urban jungle. Over the years Panama City Beach, had seen high-rise buildings and all genres of businesses sprout out of the sand as the land had gotten showered by bank notes. The *Business Lighthouse* was the name of the magnificent building housing the company for which Mercy worked. It stood there among many other high-rise buildings of similar height and shape, but it gained its title of lighthouse because of its outside walls made of expensive reflective tinted glass.

The outside part of the tinted glass walls located on the south side of the building reflected the undulating blue ocean waters that washed up the white-sand beaches. These waves brought with them small amounts of colorful maritime weed and shells that covered the sand spread on the south side of the building. On the Northern, Eastern, and Western sides of the building the glass walls reflected the surrounding architectural diversity. A diversity defined by structures built to resist the assaults of hurricanes, colorful facades made to attract tourists, and open spaces for open-air dining by the raging ocean.

The third floor's break room had windows that gave a paradisiacal view of the Atlantic south side of the building; a view always enjoyed during lunch hour by the building's third floor occupants who, like Mercy, had offices with windows not facing south. Sitting by the south side's glass wall of the break room, its occupants would enjoy the performances of seagulls swiftly flying across the blue and white clouds and occasionally

23

diving downwards towards the blue waters' ever dancing moody tides. On some days when the ocean breeze is dominated by the omnipresent humidity of Panama City Beach, the building occupants would sit immersed in the cool air of their air-conditioned break room while admiring the emerald canvas. Looking out through the window they would savor the scenery and sounds of the waters' splashing and the birds tweeting. All these melodies blended to create an auditory sensation that aroused feelings of internal peace.

Today, just like most late morning hours of every workday, Mercy and Muungo, her coworker, left their shared office space and headed to the break room with its paradisiacal view. They sat on high breakfast stools lining up the lengths of a rectangular table made of faux marble. One of the table's width side was next to a vending machine and a fridge, and the other width side was jammed against the cream-colored dry wall. The breakfast stools occupied the table's lengths, with one length side opposing to the windows. Muungo and Mercy sat on the breakfast stools positioned on the table's length side opposite to the window, and from there they could admire the coastal relief bordering the south side of the building. In between short conversations, the sound from the break room's TV, and the humming of the fridge one could hear the sounds of Mercy and Muungo chewing on their lunch. The difference in the content of their lunch boxes was almost a perfect illustration of their divergence in opinion over many issues.

Mercy's lunch box contained what she called a *Garden of Eden sandwich*. It was a slice of ham and a fish filet separated by a slice of goat cheese with all three trapped in between two identical tri-layers of lettuce, tomato slice, and slice of wheat bread. Bite after bite Mercy enjoyed the crust off the edges of her sandwich before going for the more tender part of the sandwich. Muungo's meal was a spicy broth of goat meat accompanied by boiled ripe plantains. A culinary delicacy which Mercy, and everybody else in the break room, had witnessed a few other times. Muungo ate with appetite and nostalgia. Forgoing his fork and picking up pieces of goat meat with his fingers, to better unleash his appetite on the meat, he sank his teeth into the meat. Muungo shut his eyes, as if opting for sensory deprivation, sucked up the broth dripping off the meat, tore the meat apart, and then licked from off his fingers the lucky drops of broth that had survived the serial munching of the meat. Of all their differences in opinions, their most significant point of divergence was not in their meal types, it was their perceptions of the importance of blacks' ancestral African heritage.

Mercy always felt as though her African heritage was not of the greatest importance given that it was more than 500 years since her ancestors were forcibly brought to the Americas. This was an opinion not shared by Muungo. Muungo was more than convinced that it was important for Mercy to find out and hold onto her African Origins. This issue was their most recurring and widest divergence of opinion. It was a divergence that was made conspicuous by the wrong, but popular, idea that because they both were blacks they certainly shared the same cultural background. In reality, the only thing they had in common was that in White America they both were blacks in America; African American and African Immigrant—same Genus different Species.

Miles away from their divergence in opinions, the two coworkers shared a strong bond of friendship. After a few years of working together they had developed a chemistry that allowed them to collaborate smoothly on every project they laid their hands on. Mercy had the undeniable networking ability and understanding of the American maze, while Muungo had the unmatched resilience and work ethics of someone who knew that as a black immigrant he had to work double to gain half the recognition. In the words of one of his idols: "He had to work like a slave in order to live like a King." Their complicity, complementarity, and efficiency had earned them the nickname "M&M," referring to a popular and successful American candy's brand. So much so that, restless tongues at work suspected that they were more than just friends—that they were friends with benefits.

On that afternoon, after lunch, as they walked along the corridor covered in rectangular beige colored ceramic tiles, they rounded off a discussion which they had been having regarding the influx of college students in Panama City during the college spring breaks. It was at the epilogue of their conversation that Muungo felt his phone vibrate in his pants' pocket. He gave that look and twisted facial expression that translated into "sorry, but I need to look at this one," then he lagged as he typed the password to his phone in order to access a recent text message. He halted, paused for a few seconds, and then replied to the text. All the while Mercy kept walking; she even slowed down her pace waiting for Muungo to catch up with her once he was done responding to the text.

As she walked forward at a slower pace her train of thoughts headed in the opposite direction, taking her all the way back to the first topic she explored during their lunch break conversation with Muungo: African-Americanism and African heritage. She was American and proud to be one, yet there was something that had always bothered her; something which she had never even mentioned to Muungo in all their multiple discussions on the topic of origin and heritage. This thing was her opinion on her peoples past and the way forward.

The history which Mercy was taught concerning people of color was one that began under the dark stormy clouds of the transatlantic slave trade--the middle passage; a history that continued into the turbulent depths of the bloody waters of slave labor and the Jim Crow era. Events in the recent past years had added new lines to this history. Lines written in ink made of blood, sweat, and tears. Lines which retriggered memories of, and actions inspired from, the civil rights movements. The present-day effects of these events inspired from civil rights movements were visibly the social network proliferation of the hashtag Black Lives Matter and photo captures of people kneeling on one knee during the execution of the American anthem. Black Lives Matter was either a desperate cry calling for the end of what most blacks saw as an open *black hunting season* manifested in recent years, or maybe it was the reaction of the people to the media's long overdue exposure of an ever existing and painful *black hunting season* dating far back as the exploration of Africa.

All alone, while waiting for Muungo, Mercy slowly shook her head from side to side in moderate denial and in a deep emotional struggle as she navigated through these African-Americanisms. She hated those words which said: *when born under a thick dark cloud it is easy to desire but hard to admire the sun, because the sun's glare can be very uncomfortable to the eyes.* The blacks in America who looked above their dark cloud of years of institutionalized oppression knew it was an uncomfortable, yet necessary, effort to give a *new* story and a different history to those who will come after them. Embracing a refocused, but true, history of transatlantic slave trade and slavery, a narrative which concentrates more on survivors' stories than on stories about the oppressors and the oppressed, was analogous to looking at the bright sun above the dark clouds. It meant temporarily and willingly relegating the debates and the reminiscences of slavery, though intimately and collectively painful, in favor of establishing and celebrating a black elite inspired rivaling the elites of other races. But this approach was not a universally endorsed approach. In other words, overcoming this history of oppression in a subtle and apolitical way, by shooting for the great social goals and perks like people of all other races did, could easily earn an African American the label of a *white wannabe.* Moves such as moving into nice neighborhoods, partnering with rich nonblack investors, sending one's children to ivy league schools and expensive summer programs where they could network with potential future leaders of the world were not always applauded, especially if done at the expense of paying the *black tax.* Mercy could not say on what side she was when it came to this debate on racial elevation. Her indecision over the personal definition of black success was not strictly associated with her thoughts around human servitude, alienation, and dehumanization of African American.

Just like the case addressing the horrible crime of human servitude, Mercy also believed that picking up the political quill to rewrite the black history could easily be considered a subtle way of embracing racism—the perspective of racism embedded in politics. Becoming a politician, with a compulsory soft diplomatic tongue, in order to impact the future of black history could easily be considered as embracing the racial history of a given political entity—Democrats or Republicans.

While Muungo did not suspect Mercy's stance on political affiliation and personal success, their debates were most often centered on the dos and don'ts of African Americanism. According to Mercy, approaching the topic of African Americanism from a heritage perspective spelled trouble. A similar conundrum plagued the resolve of blacks in America regarding the right way forward with respect to their relationship with the African continent. Some African Americans often wondered if the idea of going back to Africa, Africanizing themselves, or simply De-Americanizing themselves was the way out of the hovering dark clouds. Others who knew about the story of freed slaves becoming slave masters when African Americans returned to Africa in the created nation of Liberia were totally against a remaking of what they considered an unsuccessful experiment.

"Oh Lord... you already dreaming of good African spicy soup." Muungo chuckled as he tapped Mercy on the shoulder waking her from her daydream.

"You've decided to brainwash me with this *African roots* thing all day today. For your information it is a waste of time." Mercy replied as her steps regained in stride length and speed. Mercy stacked her views on politics and personal success in one distant corner of her very active brain and limited her conversation to African heritage as they walked to their office while glancing at their watches to make sure they did not exceed their time allocation for lunch.

It was almost 1:00 pm when the two friends sank in their seats in their shared cubicle. The workday was almost over, but the day's work was yet to be over, the ringing of phones, and walks to the photocopying machine, and the clicking sound from fingers tapping on keyboards took over from the morning and lunch hours' discussions.

On this particular day, few minutes before noon after their conversations on spring breakers, Muungo had taken their usual discussion about Africa to an ever more serious level. Muungo and his family were planning a trip to Cameroon in the next 6 months and he asked Mercy if she would like to come with them. It was hard to tell if Mercy was interested in the idea, the look on her face was not one of much expression; horizontal and unperturbed lips, slightly raised eyebrows above which, on her forehead, wrinkles ran across and were stacked from bottom to top as she listened to Muungo's proposition.

Nobody could blame Mercy for this lack of enthusiasm; the media had always portrayed Africa as a modern-day Colosseum where the uncivilized African savages gave themselves to bloody battles and power struggles. The colorful and vivid painting of Africa which Muungo had in his mind was the opposite of the blood-filled canvas which was engraved in Mercy's mind by images from television and movies. Mercy did not offer an immediate answer to Muungo's proposition, six months was far off and an alibi not to go or a motivation to tag along was the last thing Mercy was going to lack in the next six months.

Later that evening, after work and away from the effervescence of beachside nightlife, Mercy was walloped in her comforter watching TV. Time after time, her eyelids slowly weighed down for a few seconds and rapidly rose back up at the command of a reluctant central nervous system. She had missed snippets of the documentary she was watching on TV; this was not as a result of her degree of concentration. In fact, like a long musical note, the documentary narrator's voice was monotone and the story not very captivating causing Mercy's brain to drift slowly into sleep before spiking back to awareness. The quasi silence in her room and the perfect room temperature made her feel even more tired than she really was. She needed to do something in order to stay awake until her traditional bedtime of 10:30 pm, else she would find herself losing sleep after the hour hand of her wristwatch lying on her bedside table strikes 4:00 am and her neighbor drives off in his noisy van. So, Mercy grabbed the TV's remote and started browsing through her cable channels, the television screen repeatedly flashed bright and then dimmed as she tuned the television from one channel to another.

One of the many cable channels was streaming information about a terrorist group terrifying the Nigerian-Cameroonian border. At the mention of Cameroon, Mercy suddenly shook off the sleep bug that had been crawling on her. She began listening to the news, trying to make sense on what was happening in Africa, this could be a good alibi to turn down Muungo's offer of a trip to Cameroon.

Back at her desk at the end of her workday, Mercy had resolved to come up with a great alibi not to accept the offer on travelling to Cameroon. Since she did not want to hurt her friend's feeling in the process of turning down the offer her excuse had to be one that had some irrefutable rational. And this one instability, one too many, in Africa could be a way out for her, she thought to herself. So, she watched the TV with even more focus than before with the aim of finding the right words for her excuse.

Precious minutes melted away slowly, forming a stream of irrecoverable time which flowed into the ocean of the past as Mercy watched the documentary and built her alibi. After a while, she fell asleep while her meninges spun around the idea of using the terrorist actions in Cameroon as an excuse not to travel with the Muungos. She somehow hated the thought of making up an excuse, but she hated even more the idea of vaguely turning down the offer of a good friend.

As the coastal sunrise remained faithful bringing with her a majestic morning view of the horizon from the Hathaway Bridge, Mercy also faithfully drove early to work, after her neighbor's noisy van woke her up. Her car's headlight, which had come on in response to the cloudy sky of that morning, automatically went off once the brightness of the sun created an acceptable visibility. A similar acceptable visibility would have greatly aided her clouded mind. Yes, she had made up her mind about not going to Cameroon with Muungo but she also recalled those college years when she read tons of books about Africa written by African authors. In the pages of this African literature her imagination took her across deserts and rivers, through them she visited the library of the great ancient University of Timbuktu, the Slave Market of Bimbia and the Island of Gorée, she discovered the taste of local dishes, and attended traditional African weddings and many of those colorful and rhythm-rich African festivities. From her imagination to her reality, here she was with a good friend, Muungo, offering her the chance to visit Africa, but new times and past events continued to cloud her mind. The condescending way a good number of African immigrants treated African Americans was a turnoff for her. It was that excessive pride bordering on arrogance of these few African immigrants towards African Americans that made her kill that college kid fantasy of going to Africa. But when you met someone like Muungo it was hard to generalize and develop stereotypes on all Africans.

The Florida Panhandle morning offshore breeze had pushed the clouds off the coast into the hinterland. The bright and rising sun casted an elongated shadow of Mercy's vehicle on the ground as she drove over the tarmac of the parking lot. Pulling the key out the ignition, Mercy broke the contact, silenced the roaring car engine, and opened her driver-side door. As she walked through the parking lot of her office building, alongside dead leaves tossed by the breeze, she noticed Muungo pacing back and forth on the concrete walkway on the side of the building. His left hand was buried deep in his pocket and was anxiously fumbling with his keys and producing a sound of metals rubbing against each other. His jaw muscle mapped out on his face each time his lips stopped moving and his upper molars pressed against the lower molars. Once she had gotten really close to the building Mercy realized that Muungo was on the phone. With his phone glued to his ear, Muungo paced at an irregular pattern--pacing slow when he was listening and pacing slower when he was speaking on the phone. Occasionally, he was pausing and frowning; these were moments when he seemed not to be sure if they could hear him clearly at the other end of the line. Muungo was so carried away by his phone conversation that he did not notice the presence of Mercy. Mercy tracked Muungo's movement with her pupils swinging between the canthi of her eyes. She kept walking with her gaze loosely glued to the moving talking *machine*. She was waiting and hoping to wave a good morning salute at the least eye contact. But even as Mercy walked pass the double glass door, slightly creaking as it swung open and close, Muungo still did not notice her. With one last quick turn of the head, then a look over her shoulder and through the glass door in Muungo's direction, Mercy could tell something was not right.

Indeed, something was not right. All had gone wrong, Muungo had spent the early morning hours calling his family in Cameroon. All this while when he paced back and forth and did not even notice his coworker's presence, he was dealing with some very bad news over the phone. The terrorist attack in the northern part of Cameroon had not gone unnoticed for Muungo's family. His older brother, a member of an elite military corps in Cameroon, had been killed by a suicide bomb attack while in the line of duty at the northern border of Cameroon. Like every form of pain and loss, no one ever knows how it truly feels until they have been run and rerun

32

over and flattened by the emotional asphalt roller of that pain and loss.

Mercy walked past the glass walls of the lobby, ascended the stairs and went to her office on the third floor just after stopping by the break room to make herself a cup of coffee. She got to her desk and grabbed a folder from the shelf, flipped through the pages in the manila folder, set the folder on her desk then picked it up again. Hesitation and confusion. For a moment she wondered as to why she had picked up the folder, then slowly, with the hope that the hesitation would help her regain her train of thought, she slowly placed the folder back on her desk. The folder landed an inch or so away from her coffee mug. She grabbed her coffee mug so swiftly that a small amount of her black Rwandan beverage spilled over the rims of the mug and landed on the manila folder. The splashes made by the lost drop of the precious coffee diffused through the cellulose material of the folder, leaving circular spots with spiky edges. With a multitude of clumsy gestures Mercy struggled to keep her composure.

Mercy's clumsiness persisted, even after Muungo had returned to his desk following a short meeting in his supervisor's office. The clumsiness lasted longer because she was waiting for the right time to find out from Muungo what the matter was. She had been unable to inquire when Muungo walked into the office for the first time because when he had walked into the office, he had grabbed some papers and had walked directly to his supervisor's office. There he spent quite some time with his boss.

During Muungo's time in their supervisor's office, only whispers and the sound of papers rustling escaped through the half-closed door of their supervisor's air-conditioned and antique-decorated office. Mercy, while working, looked in the direction of the supervisor's office time and time again as she fumbled with office supply on her desk. Finally, Muungo walked out of the office with his head barely held up by his neck. He whispered an almost inaudible good morning to

Mercy who replied with a slow response –a reply obstructed by genuine concern and a lack of social skills in times of anxiety around personal or almost personal issues.

Greetings offered, Muungo took place at his desk and got very busy revisiting folder after folder, replying email after email. Despite his very busy mood he did remember lunch time and asked Mercy if she was ready for lunch. Mercy answered almost unenthusiastically, but her answer was not a portrayal of the relief she truly felt when Muungo initiated the invitation for lunch. Instead, she was surprised and reassured by the fact that he considered inviting her to lunch given his earlier indifference to her presence. This surprise was expressed by what looked like an unenthusiastic answer. For the last four minutes or so she had followed the second hand of her wristwatch go through several lapses as the hour and minutes hands approached the hour of 11:00 a.m. During this time, she had rehearsed tons of ways to start the conversation with Muungo who was lost in his work like never. Despite thinking and rethinking the words, Mercy was yet to come up with the ideal method of initiating a conversation. Luckily enough, Muungo came up with the invitation, breaking this new and awkward environment between his close friend and himself.

Sitting in the break room Muungo briefed Mercy about his family's situation in Cameroon as they both pretended to eat their lunch. Mercy now understood Muungo's evasive attitude. As it happened to be, the family journey had been rescheduled to a closer date, Muungo and his family were to fly to Cameroon in one week. The family had to attend the funeral of Muungo's elder brother. This 40-year-old soldier had invested much of his money and effort in sending his younger brother to the U.S.A. Thus, to Muungo his elder brother was like a father to him. Emotions in Muungo's words and sporadic chuckles coupled with watery eyes revealed the strength of the bond that characterized the relationship between Muungo and Mingo, Muungo's older brother. Listening to this bittersweet narration of the love story between siblings made Mercy break down into tears. She too had a brother who had done so much for her, from paying her way through Tuskegee University to taking care of their mother's hospital bills and funeral. But a few weeks before Mercy's graduation from Tuskegee University's College of Engineering, her brother was killed by a rival drug dealers' gang.

The story goes that Mercy's brother was the head of a popular gang of drug dealers in Atlanta, Georgia and had on multiple occasions chosen not to respect the limits imposed on his gangs' territory. This simple problem of jurisdiction led to many deaths in the glorious city of Atlanta. Owen, Mercy's brother, was to Mercy what Mingo was to Muungo. Two persons that had never met each other and yet had almost the same stories except that their stories had different epilogues.

"I am going to travel with you to Cameroon for your brother's funeral," Mercy suddenly interjected while Muungo was still painting the canvas of Mingo's life story in words.

"What? You don't mean that Mercy!" Muungo replied. The air stood still, so it seemed. Muungo's red and teary eyeballs rolled up and stared into the brown iris floating in Mercy's eyes. Her eyes said it louder than her mouth had said it, and Muungo knew it was one of those decisions whose roots were buried in the heart.

Then the air seemed to start moving anew as Muungo exhaled heavily. Fondling with his fingers, he mustered the courage and the words to try to make her rethink her decision; but it was a waste of time. Mercy had found in this unfortunate situation an excellent opportunity for her to honor her own brother whose mutilated corpse had arrived piece after piece at the residences of his multiple business associates. This gruesome gesture translated into some sort of black spot sent by Owen's business rival to his associates. Owen's junior sister had not been able to give a proper burial to her *father* and brother. Maybe assisting at Mingo's funeral would provide closure and would fill this void she had had inside of her for over 8 years now. Eight years that felt like 8 centuries on days like this one. Muungo did not know much about Mercy's brother but he knew the picture of the guy on her phone's screen saver was the last picture she had taken of her brother.

At the end of that workday, Muungo and Mercy were seen standing over the copying machine in loud silence. A silence that sounded like a scream of pain and a cry of desperation. The only audible sounds were their breaths, the humming sound of the copying machine and the fluttering and squashing sound of papers rolling in and out of the copying machine. They were making copies of some of the documents which Mercy was going to need to fill out as part of her application for a visa at the Cameroon Embassy. The two engineers had not encountered any difficulty in asking Alonso Genevieve, their boss, for some time off. As it turned out the work on their ongoing contract could be done remotely and the earliest contract for which they were to work only from the office was only going to kick off in three months. Lifting the top cover of the copying machine, his eyes staring away from Mercy, Muungo said:

"You don't have to come to Cameroon with me this time, you know? We could always take a trip some other time Mercy."

Mercy kept her head down, almost pretending to be reading the information on the copied document. Yet, Mercy's silence spoke loudly enough for Muungo to understand that she was determined to go. She was determined to honor her brother's memory as well as assist her friend during this hard time. The duo stood silent for a moment; the only sounds perceived were the ticking of the second hand on Mercy's wristwatch and the momentary buzzing sound accompanying the light beam that swept back and forth on the flatbed of the copying machine. The scenario lasted for a couple more minutes until the footstep of a member of the cleaning crew approached the copying room and diluted the emotionally concentrated atmosphere of the room.

Once both friends were done photocopying, they walked out of the copying room and went pass the Janitor who was emptying the trash box in the alley. They picked up their belongings from their respective desks, headed down the stairs and out of their office building. The light beams from the streetlights in the parking lot made visible the moisture of the humid atmosphere. Muungo and Mercy chit-chatted while walking slowly across the almost empty parking lot and heading towards their cars. As she got to her car, Mercy turned around and told Muungo, who was heading towards his own car, that she was going to call her friend, Brianna, to inform her that she would be traveling to Africa.

"She will be able to provide information to the police in case you get kidnapped during your stay in Africa"; Muungo replied jokingly. An unexpected spark of humor that had an explosive impact on the morose atmosphere that had hovered over their heads for most of the day. Muungo heard Mercy roaring with laughter as she slid into her beetle; she sat idly in her car's driver seat for a few minutes trying to regain her breath.

Muungo had met Brianna for the first time four years ago at Mercy's birthday party. The slim girl with a polished ebony-complexion and blue-eyes, Brianna, had caught Muungo's attention. Muungo had engaged himself in a long one-year battle as he tried to convince Brianna to entertain a romantic relationship with him. Time wasted is the term that best describes that year for Muungo. Brianna had a thousand and one reasons why she could not be in a relationship with Muungo or any other African for that matter. After wasting almost one year running after Brianna, Muungo came to the conclusion that Brianna was not in any way different from the African American girls he had known from his school days. To Muungo, and most of his African male friends, most African American girls were considered disrespectful towards males, viewed as very lazy, classified as materialistic and believed to be horrible cooks with respect to African culinary standards.

37

Well, according to Muungo, Mercy was an exception to the rule. In the same way Mercy had repeatedly told Brianna that Muungo was not a typical African male. The typical African male was labeled as rude, listed as pompous, seen as pushy, identified as controlling, and categorized as too damn demanding. Flaws Mercy did not see in Muungo. Yet, these flaws, Brianna could read them off Muungo's forehead without Mercy's help.

The humming sound from the engine of Muungo's vehicle attenuated the sound of Mercy's laughter that had been reaching him in his vehicle. He had his windows rolled down to force out the warm, humid, and almost unbreathable afternoon air trapped in his vehicle. He sat still in his vehicle as the old air crawled out and fresher air rapidly and noisily oozed into the cabin via the AC inlets of the vehicle. Mercy's beetle drove by as she rapidly honked twice; Muungo honked twice in response to this drivers' code of "I see you!"

The air in the cabin was now fresh and delicious, Muungo closed his eyes and took big inhales of the refreshing cool gas molecules. The oxygen gas molecules and other gases were sucked up through his nostrils and made their way pass tiny erect nostril hairs. Under the effect of a relatively low air pressure in the thoracic cavity, created by the upward movement of the rib cage and the downward movement of the diaphragm, the oxygen molecules sped down the trachea through the bronchi to the bronchioles before ending up in the alveoli where they hopped on red blood cells that took them on a body tour. This was how detailed Muungo's experience of breathing fresh air was; the warm air always gave him this uncomfortable feeling of a pending nosebleed. A feeling he often had during his childhood when he rode in Mingo's air-conditioned –deprived vehicle. Fun memories of Mingo were all what Muungo was going to ride with now that Mingo was no more.

Life had thrown so many projectiles at Muungo, he appreciated the comfort of the United States of America, and yet preferred the social warmth soaked in materialistic discomfort of his home country. Every time he travelled back to Cameroon, he missed the comfort of the States and when in the States he missed the social life of Cameroon. It was a catch 22 situation imposing an undesired tradeoff between social warmth and comfort. But as the saying in Cameroon went: *The goat feeds off the grass closest to where it has been tethered.* Muungo slightly leaned ahead lifting his back from the leathered car seat's backrest, and then he turned the AC knob, releasing more of the fresh and delicious air—a delicacy in Panama City at this time of the year.

As he sunk back deep into the backrest of his seat, he noticed something among his belongings mildly scattered on the passenger seat. The papers in the manila folder had partially crept out of the folder. So, he leaned sideways to grab the folder and reorganize the papers; that is when he realized Mercy had left without giving him her visa-application papers. They had agreed he was going to mail them to his friend who worked at the Cameroonian Embassy in Washington DC so that he could use the influence of his family name to expedite their visa application process. For a moment Muungo thought of calling Mercy, but finally he decided not to do so. It could well be that the forgotten paperwork chapter was a sign that she was not meant to travel, he thought to himself as the humming sound of the engine isolated him from all other ambient noise. He decided he was going to remain quiet and if by the next morning she did not give him her application then he would conclude that the trip was not meant for her. The next day was the latest date for them to send in their applications if they wanted an expedited visa in time.

It was not Muungo's intention not to take Mercy with him, but he was worried about her stay in Cameroon. He knew how involved he will be in the preparation of the funeral and felt as though Mercy will feel abandoned and may even fall prey to people with devious intentions. Mercy had this particularity of becoming clumsy and irritated whenever she felt let down by friends. Had it been they had traveled on a less activity-intense trip, then he himself would have been her tour guide and ensured that she was taken care of and kept away from any sort of trouble. He gave himself all sorts of rationales as to why he did not have to take her with him, but, strangely enough, he knew this was the best opportunity for Mercy to discover the unadulterated Africa. The one where people shared the little they had, the one where borders and languages were obsolete, the one where humans and plants were considered creatures of the same creator. It was through this kind of situation bridging the world of the living and the dead, that the most precious and the richest traditions came to life. It was when one died that they actually came to life. It was when one died that their culture and beliefs also came to life. Even just for a brief moment, the deceased were seen just as a mere mortal and not jugged by impressions and choices. As his car stopped at a red light glowing amidst the darkness from the starless sky, Muungo glanced once more at the folder on the passenger seat, picked up his phone and paused for a moment trying to decide if he should call Mercy to remind her about the visa application or not.

From the East end of the ECP airport of Panama City Beach, Muungo could be seen pulling his luggage along, while his wife carried their one and the half-year-old baby girl. Overloaded with luggage on every side he looked more like a moving pack of luggage than a traveler pulling his luggage. Most Africans look that way when travelling back home.

Trips to Africa were never light because family, friends, and even strangers placed orders for the American versions of the things they already had in Africa. This gesture was one that perpetrated the illusion that Africa needed saving, when in reality Africa was the one saving the world. No Congo no affordable bauxite, no Niger no great source of Uranium, no Nigeria no enough oil, no Sierra Leone no affordable diamond, No Cameroon no Cobalt and the list went on and on.

But the debate on natural resources was not on the priority list in Muungo's mind, neither were the merchandises in his luggage. He had one thing on his mind: family; family in all its possible dimensions. Traveling to Africa with one's family, and most of all a baby, warranted a lot of luggage; it was this luggage that Muungo was struggling with as he walked along the shiny smooth tiled floor of the airport's departure hall. That means of transporting his luggage was a must because he was not able to lay hands on a service cart. Yet, heavier than this luggage was the reality of his brother's death. If his brother were indeed dead, then it meant he was the last surviving male of Nahshieh Tahkuh's lineage. The weight of this undesired thought pulled the commissures of his mouth downward while he clenched his teeth resisting an emotional choke that had sprung with the thought.

A vibrant and amplified female voice came through the public address system. The voice interfered with the sounds of travel cases' wheels rolling on the tiles, the scream of a crying kid lying on the ground and throwing his feet in the air manifesting a tantrum, and the light stumps and squeaks of the shoes of hurrying travelers. These interfering noises allowed Muungo to noisily swallow his saliva in order to overcome the emotional choke. But the same noises forced Muungo to speak at a louder tone each time he addressed his wife.

"Mercy is already here!" He said raising his chin as if that helped raise the pitch of his voice.

He had sighted Mercy from a distance and tried to notify his wife, but with all the noise from the human traffic she did not even hear him talk.

"Mercy is already here at the airport, honey!" Muungo repeated with a little more insistence as he slowed his pace, looked in his wife's direction and simultaneously inclined his head--leaning in Mercy's direction as a way of indicating Mercy's position to his wife.

His wife noticed the insistence with a slight delay, turned her head and looked in Muungo's direction. At the same moment Muungo turned his head and his eyes made contact with those of Mercy and he smiled. Muungo's smile while facing a direction other than that of his wife made her eyebrows rise out of curiosity. She swiftly turned her gaze and followed the trajectory of Muungo's smile. Tens of meters away, across from rental car agencies', she caught a glimpse of a familiar face in her field of vision even though this field was invaded by people walking in different directions. She recognized Mercy dressed in a pair of blue bootcut jeans, white t-shirt and a sweater wrapped around her neck. Mercy was not all alone she was with a friend who had her back turned towards Muungo and his family.

At the sight of her travel companions, Mercy interrupted her conversation with Brianna, smiled, and pointed in the direction from which Muungo and his family were coming. Brianna did not put on a smile, she was not too excited about this trip to Africa, but she had stayed true to her friendship with Mercy. A friendship that went as far back as their high school years but had gone through a rough ride during the period when Muungo had cast his macho nets in Brianna's direction.

"He has done well for himself." Brianna thought as she caught sight of Muungo's wife.

Muungo's wife was presenting a beaming face and a big smile to Mercy, the gap in the middle of her top teeth made the smile even more attractive. Her arms wrapped around the toddler, who seemed to enjoy sniffing the maternal aroma emanating from her mom's neck, made the beauty even more beautiful.

"When is he going to marry his second wife?" Brianna asked Mercy in a sarcastic tone and almost inaudible voice through her teeth.

"How about you becoming that second wife..." Mercy responded, keeping her eyes fixed in the direction of her friend's wife, in an attempt to keep a tight grip on the already establish positive vibe between her and Muungo's wife. Mercy had always diluted the wine of her friendship with Muungo each time she was in the presence of his wife. But with a long trip ahead, she was probably going to inadvertently ignore this safety guide and did not want Irene to over analyze any complicity between Muungo and Mercy—M&M.

"Hell No! Never girl!" Brianna responded more audibly this time as she raised her hand to her mouth, her lips and eyes squeezed in disgust to the idea.

Mercy let go of her hand-pulled luggage as she made a few steps in the direction of Muungo and his family. Brianna caught the falling hand-pulled luggage and shook her head in disapproval to Mercy's carelessness. Brianna pulled the luggage up and walked towards the others. A polite smile from Muungo caught Brianna by surprise, surprisingly she returned it with a genuine smile that stretched her thin darkened lips. After all, Muungo was a funny guy, at least his accent had always got her laughing back in the days when he did not want to give up on the spouse hunt. To Muungo, Brianna had not changed that much, her ebony complexion and blue eyes had been refined thanks to the right dose of makeup. He recalled how he used to tell Mingo about this African American girl who had caught his attention and how his brother showed very little interest to that particular topic, probably as a strategy to dissuade Muungo from pursuing his conquest. Every single moment of Muungo's life, past and present, reminded him of his brother.

After avoiding bumping into other people walking in all directions, the two groups met and exchanged greetings. Wilanne, Muungo's daughter, quickly became the center of attraction. The three ladies hurdled around the toddler while Muungo checked in the travelers' luggage. Every now and then he turned around and looked behind only to see the three ladies talking, examining each other's outfit, facial makeup, hair, hair style, or nail polish.

"You better learn some of those African braiding styles when you are over there." Brianna teased Mercy while

43

throwing her hand over Mercy's shoulders and pulling Mercy closer for a hug.

"I don't have to; Irene got my back now girl." Mercy replied, smiling at Irene pending a positive feedback from Irene.

"Sure, and I can always hook you ladies up. Provided our schedules workout." Irene responded with an accent that made it hard for the others to hear anything other than the word *sure*.

The other two ladies did not worry about the rest of the phrase, they just smiled back at Irene. Brianna continued with an "Oh my God, girl I love your accent." Compliment.

How time flies by when separation lands! About an hour later the group split with a tearful Brianna waving goodbye and blowing kisses to an emotional Mercy. Mercy's eyes were all watery and red, but she succeeded in staying calm, at the same time she was carrying Wilanne and struggling to wave back at Brianna. Mercy did not want to let tears roll down her cheeks, in part because of the black eyeliner she had adorned in order to reinforce the lower contours of her eyes, but additionally she stayed calm because she feared that crying over a momentary separation will be belittling the purpose of her trip—an everlasting separation. With rapid quick short breaths through her mouth Mercy attenuated the feverish urge of bursting into tears that was incinerating the nerves on her already blushed face. With feeble upward stretched lips that desired to drop downward, Mercy faked a smile and kept her gaze to the floor; any eye contact would have led to an avalanche of warm salty fluid gushing out the ducts of her pair of lacrimal glands and racing down her puffy cheeks.

Thanks to a piece of folded tissues in her hand, Brianna dabbed the tears on her cheek with just enough finesse to avoid dabbing away the light brown face powder that accentuated the tone of her ebony complexion. Brianna waited until *the travelers*, standing on the crowded escalator had disappeared from her visual field. Like a setting sun sinking behind the horizon, *the travelers* disappeared for an instant only to reappear on the second floor of the airport. Brianna turned around and walked towards the exit door of the airport hall. Before she reached the exit door, she stopped by the restroom to refresh her makeup. The Brianna who came out of the restroom had refreshed more than just her makeup; there was a new vigor in her stride as her legs crisscrossed over each other in her tight short skirt. A conspicuous composure displayed by her chin lifted upwards and head held up high accompanied her through the airport hall and out.

Happening in parallel, back at the airport's second floor, the group travelling to Cameroon had begun feeling more and more like family, especially Irene and Mercy. Wilanne was gradually rolling out of her majestic toddler morning sleepiness. Her little hands curled in fists rubbed against her eyes as they accommodated one last time to the brightness of the morning. The growling noise in her stomach announced time for a small bite. Wilanne had rejected the food offered to her earlier that morning by her mother. Seeing many new and busy faces at the airport did not help quell this temporary loss of appetite, but now that hunger had reached its zenith, her expression reduced itself to rapid breathing, progressively loud whining, and a slow side-to-side swing of the head.

"Ah eat?" Her mother asked in *baby language*.

A slow nod and more whining were Wilanne's answer. Mercy grabbed and raised the toddler by her underarms and offered to pass her back to her mother. The little girl had her arms all stretched anticipating the swap.

"No Mercy, I will get the food so you can feed her." Irene said.

"You want me to feed her?" Mercy questioned with a slightly higher pitch after a brief hesitation as she processed what Irene had just said. The public address systems had just come on and had made it difficult for Mercy to hear what Irene had just said.

With a smile exposing the gap between her teeth and the internal beauty of her soul, Irene handed a yogurt parfait cup and a plastic spoon to Mercy. Mercy looked straight and deep into Irene's face trying to decrypt her facial expression. A reflection of Irene's smiling face appearing on Mercy's cornea was the result of this close examination. Mercy's eyes shrunk and their commissures stretched as she reciprocated Irene's nonverbal communication with a beaming smile. The already awake and hungry toddler awoke even more at the sight of the delicacy coming her way.

Muungo had just finished a phone call and as he sat down, he let go, for a minute, a piece of his pain as he exhaled. The void created by the volatilized pain was followed by a smile-kidnapping image of Wilanne having fun with Mercy as the baby feasted on her yogurt—repeatedly dipping her fingers into and splashing the savoring dairy product all over her face and her bib. "*It is indeed true that nature has no love for vacuum,*" Muungo thought, as he smiled for the second time that day; "*after all it was not a bad idea taking Mercy with them.*"

The airport terminals were located on the upper floor, giving the anxious travelers a breathtaking view of the marshy-sandy landscape that surrounded the airport. The conifers, standing tall and proud, had at their feet a crowd of crawling stunted grass, fallen cones, and fallen leaves that veiled the dark muddy-sandy soil. Above the conifers, gliding in the direction indicated by the wind-displaced leaves, were blue and white clouds. The bright weather did not last for too long. At an almost blinding distance from the airport where dark stormy clouds. These clouds impregnated of water molecules gradually crept along the ether and invaded the flight space above the airport's tarmac. The sunrays coming into the second floor through the large transparent glass walls began losing in luminosity as the dark clouds flew over the Panama City ECP airport. The clouds came with a heavy but short-lived rain. The noise generated from the beating of the tarmac by the free-falling drops of water from the sky added to the chitchat of the passengers at the terminal and both entertained a belly-full Wilanne. The toddler's pupils changed sizes and bounced from event to event as she observed the businesses of the passengers restlessly navigating between terminals, restroom, and airport stores. Wilanne then suddenly noticed the drops of rain landing and then swiftly, but elegantly, rolling down the glass walls. Wilanne was captivated; a pure smile, one which kids alone have the secret to, lit her entire face as she used her fingers to trace in admiration the itinerary of the rain drops from the inside part of the glass wall.

Minutes later, after the rapid and bold rainfall had left temporary wet and dry spots on the airport tarmac, the air flight company staff began ushering passengers aboard their plane. The passengers rose from their seats, interrupted their improvised conversations of courtesy, and got off their mobile devices to gather their belongings and board the plane. Wilanne had fallen asleep and her father had taken her from Mercy, so that Mercy could wipe off some the yogurt that had spilled on her t-shirt.

Her head resting on her father's shoulder and her warm breath flowing along his neck, the little girl slept as they boarded the plane. Irene and Mercy came in minutes later and sat on the two seats in front of Muungo's. With all passengers on board the flight crew announced take off time and prompted passengers to respect safety instructions.

The vessel began rolling on the tarmac gathering momentum and generating more sound as the tires' treads made contact with the tarmac at a faster rate. The hissing sound of hydraulic pressure being transmitted in the mechanical structure of the flaps was accompanied by the images of conifers drifting pass the window as the engine sped up. Pointing its nose upward the plane began its ascension, the images viewed through the window went from inclined conifers to cloud, and finally the change in altitude created a sensation of stuffed eardrums. A sensation that woke up the toddler secured on her father. The vessel returned to is level horizontal position once it reached its cruising altitude and from then on it put cap on Atlanta, Georgia.

Muungo had covered the Panama City Atlanta flight many times and still he hated two things about this trip. The occasional long hovering of the aircraft over Hartsfield-Atlanta International-Airport while awaiting permission to land and the speeding up of the plane as it experienced greater gravity before touching down on the landing strip. But today, those two issues were of very little importance. *Throw a man in a gladiators' arena and a bug bite will be the least of his worries.*

The three-quarter of an hour flight was nothing compared to the five hours drive which Mercy covered every three months when she drove to visit her mother's and brother's resting places. On the most recent of those memorial trips she had experienced something unlike anything before.

It was on one hot late morning in the month of May and few folks had noticed a somewhat regular visitor at the graveyard. She had just said her prayers in her heart and dropped bouquets of flowers beside two tombstones. It was none other than Mercy Lewis. She had dropped fresh resplendent rainbow-colored flowers on the sand-dust dirt mix at the bases of the polished and chiseled blocks of grey marble—the tombstones on her brother's and mother's grave. The dried-off flowers of the last visit and her purse in one hand and a tissue in the other she turned her back to the tombs and headed for her car. Mercy walked on the gravel lining the pedestrian path between tombs, and a few petals of the dried-off flower fell to the ground as she walked on against a rebellious southwards breeze.

A black vehicle with tinted windows and windshield pulled over about 50 meters away from her, the driver hopped out and opened the door for the passenger. The passenger slowly and graciously stepped out of the car, his arms were wrapped around the largest circumference of a colorful wreath made of tulips and black roses. He marched, majestically, weighing every footstep before slowly landing it to the ground, generating long crushing sounds as the sole of his Italian classic leather white shoes pressed against the gravel on the ground.

48

The man carrying the wreath reached and passed Mercy on his way and headed straight to her brother's tomb. He squatted gently, laid the wreath, and whispered words to the edifice. He rose and walked back along the pedestrian path, analyzing and inspecting each step up and each step down. Mercy had glanced over her shoulder and saw the man drop the wreath, and she had instantaneously began walking faster. But her change in pace did not bother the man dressed in an immaculate white suit, a wide white bowel hat and a white scarf symmetrically hanging over his neck.

Mercy was a few meters from her vehicle when the black sedan that had pulled over and dropped off the wreath bearer, rolled closer to her car and parked in between Mercy and her vehicle. Mercy froze. She stopped walking meters away from the parked car and waited for a few seconds, but nobody stepped out of the black sedan. From behind her she could hear the composed weighed, measured, and counted steps of the wreath bearer growing louder and coming closer.

"Really impressive! If that's what you aimed for." Mercy mustered courage and turned around, and addressed the man walking in her direction, trying to see his eyes through his dark sunglasses.

"Sorry I didn't mean to have my boys show a lack respect to you Ma'am. I am so sorry! I needed to know from you what you would want me to do with the guys who killed your brother. I've got them in custody and your wishes are my orders." The man spoke in a soft but controlled and commanding voice, and his scarred lips held thin threads of saliva in between them as they parted when he counted his words.

Mercy's eyes went from the man's lips to the ground, tears rolling down her cheeks and her body trembling with emotion. A hand stretched out offering her a pack of tissue papers; she grabbed it, tore it with so much emotion that some of the tissues fluttered and landed on the ground. She lifted her head up and finally saw the guy's eyes. One of his eyes had clearly been injured in an accident, a scar on that eye testified to that.

"They did this to me when I worked for your brother, those bastards. Tell me how and I will do it without any question. I am not wearing a wire, but feel free to write on a paper or even on the dirt on the ground and I will read your orders."

Mercy was somewhere between her recollection of this encounter and her listening of the raspy and very masculine voice from her audio book when the flight attendant's voice announced their imminent landing at Hartsfield Atlanta International Airport. Appearing from underneath the nap of clouds, as the plane began its descent, were the skyscrapers of Atlanta basking under the hot southern sun, and the highway traffic resembling a march of worker ants towards a pack of sugar.

The plane's tires hit the landing strip and the squeaking of the brake pads resonated in the now noisy cabin. Muungo woke up from his daydream with his baby girl still fast asleep on his laps, a tired Irene woke from a short nap, and Mercy paused her audio book.

Atlanta, Georgia 2016

The Air France flight carrying Mercy, Muungo, and Muungo's family took off. The double engine vessel graciously raised her nose off the Hartsfield Atlanta International Airport's runway and headed away from Atlanta Georgia, Mercy's hometown. As the plane cruised through the cloud bubbles, the noisy take off and anxiety of the passenger continued to die down and by the time the lights went off most passenger were in the arms of Morpheus. Mercy and Muungo were amongst the few passengers who were still awake even though each of them could not boast of a great night's sleep during the previous night.

After this connecting flight drowned in the clouds which were veiling every structure from Atlanta City and Jackson

50

Hartsfield airport, Mercy felt quite queer; she had then just realized she was leaving home. In the past, no matter how far she had gone, the destination was always within the USA; but now, here she was, almost unexpectedly leaving Atlanta for Paris in France from where she was going to board a plane for Bell Town, Cameroon. From meal to meal, airport to airport, time zone to time zone, Mercy slowly got accustomed to the fact that she was going to be in a place where the only person she really knew was her friend Muungo, a place where her ancestors may have once walked.

Muungo knew it was not easy for Mercy, so time and time again he initiated some small talk with her to reassure her. Building short phrases with words that could reach and touch Mercy's troubled mind was his plan. But just like a river's water soaks into the guts of the earth when it flows along a dry path, Muungo slowly but surely ran out of inspiration and motivation. After multiple pauses, finding topics to fuel his small pep talk, he settled for a remix version of the story about his first months in the USA. With heart-reaping paragraphs omitted and scenes of bravery retold with high doses of emotion and optimism, the narrator told an abridged and family-friendly version of his story to Mercy. Despite his efforts of adapting the scenarios of the original version to the present circumstances, the narration had nothing new to Mercy. She could even help complete the parts where Muungo had experienced demoralizing events, those parts which Muungo was avoiding as he narrated his story for the nth time. Muungo did not have to play the emotional coach through his narration for too long, the monotonous sound of the plane as its wings sliced through the clouds and the silence of the other occupants of the vessels aided in knocking Mercy off to sleep more than once all through the long flight.

On one occasion when Mercy was in-between two naps Irene returned from the restroom with Wilanne and struck a conversation with Mercy. During the conversation, Irene asked

Mercy what she expected to see once in Africa. Mercy kept quiet for a moment, softly biting her lower lip.

"I expect to see trees, monkeys, lions, tigers, half naked women..." Mercy said smiling in response to the smile that was appearing on Irene's face.

Irene told Mercy that she too expected to meet a utopic society when she was moving to America. She was convinced that in America everyone lived in a mansion, without stress and no subtle racial segregation. But not long after she had landed, she noticed that the high-rise apartment complex in Maryland in which she lived with her aunt was full of tenants originating from Cameroon. From the lobby to their unit on the seventh floor, she would hear Cameroonians speaking several Cameroonian languages as well as Cameroonian Pidgin English. She also narrated the story of her visit to the Silver Spring Presbyterian Church. Irene said the house of worship covered in bricks had been nicknamed *Ntamulung*, by most Cameroonians. But, *Ntamulung* was the name of a Presbyterian church in the town of Abakwa in Cameroon. The huge number of Cameroonians within Silver Spring Presbyterian church congregation had not come unnoticed. From worship songs to instruments of praise, and church groups and members' outfits, the Cameroonian flavor was easily sensed in every Silver Spring Presbyterian church activity. It was this environment, less expected by Irene, that had helped her adapt to her life in America.

Irene could have continued saying more about her first experiences in America, after all Mercy had found those stories very hilarious. But when Irene began narrating the story about her first job as stock clerk at a wholesale store, she realized Mercy was dozing off. Irene stopped talking, put on her headphones, and began watching the movie "Aya de Youpougon" on her Entertainment touch screen on the plane. Mercy's head dropped to the side; her neck muscle tried to return the head back to a straight position but eventually the neck left the head tilting to the side—a posture imposed by the body in quest of some rest.

Chapter 3

Banks Of The River Wouri, Kamerun 2016

The aerial view of the city of Bell Town made the metropolis look like an ocean creature crawling out of the waters onto the sandy landscape. Beyond the historic colonial quarters, homes were spat across the sandy soil in no geometric form known to western architects; this chaos of habitat did not spare the airport and its surrounding areas. As the plane flew down at low altitude, getting ready to land on the battered tarmac referred to as the Bell Town International Airport's runway, when looking through the plane's windows one could catch glimpses of sheds hidden behind patches of green bushes. Even with her eyes focused on the images running past her window, Mercy noticed the agitation of the other passengers as they grew excited to have arrived home. This feeling of excitement Mercy did share or maybe she was just mistaking it with the thrill of finally being in Africa. Her excitement was not long lived as questions started darting across her mind in the form of neural signals traversing her brain's frontal lobe.

"How in the world could people rejoice so much to have landed on such an almost uninhabitable setting?" Mercy asked herself as the plane taxied around permitting her to realized that what she thought were sheds amongst bushes were in reality family homes surrounded by what seem to be small family farmlands. What was she going to see next? She wondered. Maybe a lion pouncing out of these farmlands or a royal welcome at the airport? Her excitement damped down a little bit as her breathing leapt to a faster rate, she was getting anxious. Added to her anxiety was the discomfort caused by the humid air outside the plane—a drastic change from the cool air in the plane. She softly gasped for fresh air during the early seconds of the walk into the unexpected humid air outside the vessel, and then pulling her collar and using her mouth as an additional pathway for air intake and outflow her respiratory system progressively adapted along the walk leading to a massive concrete structure housing the halls, services, and offices of the airport.

As she walked into the airport building, Mercy shifted her gear from anxiety to admiration. Captivating artistic paintings, culture-rich *lively* carvings and sculptures, and vibrantly colorful advertisement post signs lined up the concrete walls of the corridor after every few meters. The sounds of shoe heels and cases' rollers resonated on the carpet-deprived walkway. Mercy, and her friends walked alongside the other travelers in the long corridor which looked like a secret passage of an old castle. The *passage's* grey-colored unpainted walls in between the artistic decorations were visible to the predominantly one-way human traffic which seem not to be as impressed as Mercy. Meters away in front of Mercy, she saw the first group of the Bell Town International Airport Police staff. They were all sharply dressed in navy blue berets tilted to one side, sky blue short sleeved shirts, and straight navy-blue pants pressed to sharp edges. The three airport security personnel seem to be sharing jokes that made them all roar with laughter.

"Welcome to Cameroon dear sister; Welcome home!" Irene said to Mercy.

A phrase that took Mercy by surprise, then it dawned on her why she had gone through these different emotions: excitement, anxiety, admiration... Deep inside of her she had always longed to see Africa, she had built her own Africa in her mind. After about twenty minutes' walk, she had lived through a variety of emotions, but at the sound of Irene's phrase a warm feeling of joy spread out from her heart across her entire body. Her eyelids blinked rapidly, and tears rolled down her cheeks as she sobbed gently letting go of a genuine "thank you."

Even with all the emotions Mercy never stopped walking, just as she had never stop walking in her life even after the death of her mother and brother. She eventually slowed down at some point. The human traffic flow from the corridor forcefully slowed down as people reached the checkpoint of the Airport Police officers who had been laughing earlier from a distance away.

The atmosphere at the airport in Bell Town was somehow different from that in airports of western countries. At Bell Town International Airport there was this huge affluence of people who were neither travelers nor security or commercial personnel of the airport and its affiliated businesses. Like vultures in search of carcasses to devour, this category of people dove down on any person who seemed new to the airport and looked lost or confused. They offered a variety of services to their preys: renting out of phones for them to call their ride, cheap exchange rate of foreign currencies, hookups for easy and cheaper custom formalities, and many other services that one will not find in international airports in Europe and America. Muungo's demeanor did not give room for any solicitation on the part of these businessmen of another kind. Muungo never made any unnecessary eye contact and behaved as if he was a savant who knew all about the airport and the city. His face, veiled by a stern look, and his rapid carefree, bottom line impolite, gestures were a street code for "Do Not Disturb."

Once the travelers from Panama City had gone through the immigration formalities and informalities at the International Airport of Bell Town, and had been through the long wait for their luggage on one of the only two baggage carousels at the international Airport, they called their ride to let him know they were coming out. As they gathered around some of their bags, a young man with the looks of someone in his mid-thirties, with an old badge bearing the name "Sebastian" written in green ink and hanging obliquely across his chest pocket, offered them his luggage carrier services. Sebastian while conversing with his customers had succeeded in stacking their entire luggage on two trolley carts and had called on one of his colleagues to help him push the second trolley cart. Sebastian's grin survived through the squirm on his face, it expressed the extra effort he had to put on in pushing the trolley cart. Whenever this grin faded away, Sebastian, who seemed to know everybody, spoke enthusiastically to someone in Camfranglais—a Cameroonian linguistic cocktail fusing English, French, and local languages. It seemed as though despite his crippled arm a certain joie-de-vivre filled this man. He had single handedly picked the luggage off the baggage carousel and loaded them on trolley carts and had successfully pushed the carriage from the vicinity of the baggage carousel, located at the airport arrival space area, to the passenger pickup zone. Silently, Mercy observed Sebastian's maneuvers in a state of awe. Her eyeballs gorging out of her orbits in amazement to the physical aptitude of Sebastian were hidden behind her sunglasses. To everyone else Sebastian was just an ordinary guy earning a living, but to Mercy he was a source of inspiration and admiration.

Once the travelers had arrived at the pickup zone, Sebastian gestured with the elbow of his crippled arm to indicate to a red truck pulling over. He had noticed that the driver had been beckoning Muungo. Despite the sun glare on the windshield, Muungo was able to figure out that it was his paternal cousin, Tahfuh, who was on the steering wheel of the truck. Once the truck pulled over, and its back carriage propped opened, Muungo hurried towards the back to help Sebastian and his friend quickly load up the truck. The truck had to free the small pickup zone, which was scrambled for by many cars, as soon as possible. As soon as Muungo picked the first bag and swung it into the carriage, Tahfuh rebuked him. Tahfuh whispered to Muungo asking him to let Sebastian and his friend work for the money they were going to earn. Deaf to Tahfuh's grumbling, Muungo helped load up the truck and handed out a good remuneration to Sebastian and his friend. Tahfuh shook his head in disapproval; "the diaspora and her reckless spending habits," he thought to himself. Sebastian and his friend repeatedly expressed their gratitude towards Muungo's kind act. The jovial super excited luggage carriers each repeatedly clapped and clasped the palms of their hands for a few seconds after each clap. Nodding their heads and expressing their gratitude, with various local synonyms of "thank you," alongside the claps. Tahfuh, on his part, did not stop spitting out venomous words about luggage carriers and their nasty habit of demanding more money than they deserved.

"Welcome oh Madam!" Tahfuh greeted Mercy.

"Thank you, and I am just not a madam yet." Mercy replied looking up to Muungo to do the introductions.

"In that case I will have to marry you," Tahfuh joked, a sarcasm which Mercy did not comprehend.

"Tahfuh, here is my coworker and friend Mercy, and Mercy this is my brother Tahfuh, or cousin if you want me to be precise." Muungo hurriedly performed introductions realizing he had not done so earlier.

The driver in a little green Toyota Corolla behind Tahfuh's truck, slammed on his horn and angrily gestured from his seat, urging Tahfuh to move his vehicle. Muungo helped his crew get in the car while Tahfuh exchanged some rude words with the driver of the little car. Tahfuh hopped into his driver's seat, turned on the vehicle's ignition and drove off heading towards the airport's exit gate.

All this while, though drained dry by jet lag and inadequate sleep, Mercy kept combing the environment with her eyes-- looking all around her. Drowned in the car's warm atmosphere, filled with a mix of body odors, Mercy's attention floated alongside fine dust particles displaced off the dusty seat covers by passengers who scooched to create space for other passengers. At one moment, looking out through the window, Mercy stared in disbelief, her mouth slightly opened and her right hand placed on her left breast, at a flimsy motorbike carrying three adults and one child. Then a few minutes later, she was dumbfounded by the small size of the single lane roads and then the chaos at a traffic roundabout with malfunctioning lights. The avalanche of surprises did not stop until Muungo's wife interrupted the Brownian motion of Mercy's attention.

"I know it's a lot to process," Irene said as she swept across with her finger, panoramically pointing at the entire scenery, "eventually I will help you understand and enjoy this new life."

Mercy responded with a smile rapidly choked by the thought of the sad reason that had brought them to Cameroon.

*** Upper Nun, Kamerun 2016***

This was the sixth or seventh wailing and screaming combination that interrupted Mercy's afternoon nap. She had been hoping that a quick afternoon nap would help her somewhat recover from the jet lag. She felt aches caused by the jet lag and the rough road trip possessing every muscle fiber of and every joint of her body; this almost feverish feeling was accompanied by a strong, spell-like, desire to sleep. To make matters even worse, the repetitive wailing and screaming sent electrical impulses of very high intensity through her already tense auditory nerves making her entire being feel even more uncomfortable in its shell.

The first of these many sudden wailings had been the scariest; for the first time in her life Mercy experienced what Muungo called *tropical grief*. Muungo had told Mercy that in the cultures of most civilizations south of the Sahara the people associated a great deal of drama to the mourning of their lost ones. Usually, from the moment one received sad news announcing the death of a dear one right up to the moment when tangible proof of the sad news was available, people wailed, screamed, rolled and sat on the ground. This was all part of the grieving and the paying of tribute to the deceased. These emotional performances always reached their climax when the corpse was laid to rest.

This first wail had taken Mercy by surprise. The members of the team of travelers coming from Florida had just refreshed themselves and were grabbing a bite in the living room when suddenly the main door swung open faster than the blink of an eye. A woman, whose withered body structure and mostly baldhead signified she was advanced in age and certainly belonged to the menopausal and osteoporotic group of women, venerated by the tradition and blessed with longevity, dashed in and threw herself to the ground. Had it been she had not begun screaming before hitting the ground one would have thought that the fall was the reason behind the repeated deafening high-pitched screams. The situation had startled Mercy and Wilanne. The former jumped off her seat and dashed towards Muungo's seat and the later launched a loud and long cry. Luckily, for the frightened guests, Tahfuh hurriedly got off his seat, picked up and guided the woman to the outside quarters and asked that she be attended to. Mercy stood motionless her hand firmly gripping the ear of Muungo's chair, her toes curled up in her shoes, and her breath sounding loud and heavy-- the adrenalin in her bloodstream had triggered her flight response. Muungo apologized to Mercy and Irene calmed the baby. Then Muungo rose and locked the door after Tahfuh had walked back in. Subsequent wailings were annoying but not as surprising and as terrifying as this first one, and as such Mercy managed to force herself back to a nap after each emotional impulse. Then came this latest scene of African grieving hysteria which indeed woke her up.

Muungo's aunt, Tahfuh's mother, had just arrived at the Tahkuh family residence in the village of Mighang and had rekindled the wailing and screaming; it was from this lady and at this moment that a thunder-like sound awoke Mercy. The aunt, bearing the weight of her seventy years of existence on earth, ran at a speed convenient for her age. She ran, or may be walked rapidly, from the main entrance of the residence to the balcony. She threw herself to floor of the balcony, and with her feet and hands raised in the air and a voice under duress, due to repetitive cry sessions, she began crying out loud in the local language.

"Why not me? Why not me oh God? Take me and give me back my son!"

The other women in the yard rushed to her side and instead of helping her up they joined in the wailing and screaming. It was this choir of weepers that abruptly woke Mercy up.

Half awake, breathing heavily from exhaustion and the scare of the sudden choir of screams, Mercy sighed and lazily turned her face towards the bedside table and glanced at the glowing screen of her cell phone. She noticed that Brianna had tried to reach her via a smart phone application which made international phone calls possible whenever reliable internet service was available. Mercy reached for her phone, sat up in bed and tried to return Brianna's call multiple times but the weak internet signal yielded nothing except a great deal of white noise, combined with a delay in the transmission and eventually dropped calls. Awakened earlier than her desired time, Mercy placed her phone back on her bedside table after texting "goodbye" to Brianna. Then she got up from the bed and stretched herself; the muscle ache she had felt hours ago was subsiding. She stepped out of her bedroom and ran into Nsoh who was heading to the bedroom.

"Aunty, your food is on the table"; said Nsoh, an invitation to Mercy to come grab lunch.

Nsoh was the youngest of Mingo's daughters. She was 17 years old. Mercy had developed so much fondness towards the teenager, and similarly Nsoh was very fond of Mercy. They even shared the same room and the same bed, and if Mercy ever needed anything her first point of contact was the Benjamin of the Mingo girls. Despite Nsoh's very tight schedule she was always available for Mercy. The teenager's schedule consisted in getting up every morning ensuring that hot water was made available in the bathroom and on the dining table for Mercy's shower and breakfast respectively. In between check-ins with Mercy on regular bases, Nsoh cleaned the kitchen and made sure Wilanne, her little cousin from Panama City, was clean and fed. She was a hardworking adolescent and called every grown person either aunty or uncle depending on their gender. According to what Irene had told Mercy, at dinner on the night they had arrived Bell Town, Nsoh took so much after Mingo, her Dad. This very strong resemblance in character had made Irene burst into tears when she saw Nsoh for the first time since the death of Mingo. With very vivid but rare smiles Nsoh bravely lived through every day of this grief and separation from her father. It was this same attitude that Mercy had had when she lost her elder brother, and during the months after his disappearance. Mercy, years ago when she was grieving for her brother, had made used of so much counseling in order to deal with the grieving process. The grieving was made even more painful by the fact that her brother's mortal remains came in bits and pieces, at different times and at different addresses. It is because of this sad personal experience that Mercy kept wondering how Nsoh was going to cope with all this grief once the many mourners had gone and her father's remains had been laid to rest.

"Nsoh is a woman and she is going to deal with it bit by bit," said Mingo's wife as she addressed Mercy's concerns about her daughter Nsoh.

*** Bell Town, Kamerun 2016***

Before the day when Tahkuh's mother had engaged herself in a violent and acrobatic lamentation at the Tahkuh family residence, days after Mercy's arrival in Bell Town, Mercy was still feeling a little bit fatigued as her internal clock still had not synchronized with the Cameroonian time. But this feeling did not stop her and Nsoh from packing up a few things for the trip to Mighang. It was during this prepping for the road trip that Mercy and Nsoh began building their bond which only grew stronger when they got to Mighang.

Mighang was Mingo's hometown, where he was going to be laid to rest in their family cemetery. Mighang was about five hours from the metropolis of Bell Town, but with the poor

63

road conditions the trip could easily extend to nine or even ten hours. Cars taking that trip had to glide across the humid and hot Littoral plain, ascend the cold and foggy mountain ranges of the West and North West regions of Cameroon and finally dive down the Sabga cliff to end up in the Ndop plain. In order to deal with this change in topography and climate as one traveled across Cameroon—fondly called Africa in miniature—one had to dress accordingly. With Nsoh's help, Mercy had put on a gown over the tank top, pants, and pair of thick socks she had worn earlier. The gown was made of customized fabric on which was printed a specific design alongside Mingo's portrait; this design had been ordered for the occasion. Dressed in gowns, the two ladies had hopped into the car that took off for Mighang.

To Mercy this trip was physically challenging, a fortnight ago she had just gotten off the plane exhausted by the fifteen-hour trip and now she was embarking on another nine-hour ride. Yet, discovering Africa was such an enriching experience that she cared very little about the fatigue. She always had questions for the person next to her, and during these nine hours Nsoh was her source of answers. Every now and then Mercy asked a question and Nsoh answered her.

"What is that child doing?" Mercy asked frightened by the way a very young and skeletal boy, about six years old, made his way across the road in between moving cars.

There was a crosswalk which the boy was not using, instead he ran across the road forcing drivers to slam on their breaks or at times he had to stop abruptly if the driver did not slow down. With these risky runs and stops the boy had Mercy's heart rate racing and her hand gripping the door handle very firmly.

"I believe he is trying to sell his goods to the man in the car on the other side of the street" Nsoh replied, with a tone expressing her amazement at the shock sensed in Mercy's voice and question.

"He does not have to run to the man, he could get hit by the cars." Mercy replied slightly frowning in disgust at how careless the boy was being and how unconcerned Nsoh 's reply seemed.

"Aunty, he has been doing it for years." Said Mercy.

"But he must be younger than six!" Mercy retorted.

"...and if he does not get there first then he would lose the customer to one of those other kids" Nsoh replied as she pointed at other children who were taking the same risk.

Mercy saw a group of about 5 children running across the road. The boys were zigzagging in between moving vehicles and heading towards the same car as the lone boy. When the boys were out of sight Mercy focused on what was happening around her. That was when she noticed that Nsoh was using part of her gown to wipe off some tears on her face. Mercy fetched a tissue and handed it to Nsoh. After wiping her tears and blowing her nostrils, Nsoh's red eyes were turned towards Mercy as she expressed her gratitude for the tissue.

"It's okay dear, it is perfectly normal that you feel that way." Mercy said as she nodded in approval to the "thank you" from Nsoh.

Nsoh silently shaded tears at certain moments during the trip, and every time this happened, she tried to make sure Mercy did not notice it. Yet, with Mercy always having questions regarding the different things she encountered for the first time she always ended up looking at Nsoh when she needed an answer. So, on more than one occasion, when Mercy asked questions, she noticed tears in Nsoh's eyes. In reality, Mercy noticed more than just the tears, when she looked at Nsoh; she saw bullet holes, entry holes without exit holes. Holes which sorrow and grief had left on Nsoh's soul; she also saw the band aid of maturity which the poor girl used to hide the entry points of these bullet holes. Mercy hoped these bullets were not going to be lodged in the girl's soul forever.

There came a time when Nsoh was quivering and panting as she sobbed and, at the same time, tried very hard to hold back her tears. It was at this moment that Mercy pulled Nsoh's head next to her and placed the girl's head on her chest and then surprisingly she too began sobbing with an even greater intensity. Though their sobbing were out of phase, their stories about their grieves were very much in phase. But as they say *bonds built in sorrow live beyond tomorrows*; this moment not only made Nsoh feel she could be her true self when around Mercy, but it also made Mercy feel as part of the bigger family, not just an American tourist.

Soon after their moment of sorrow the two friends found themselves giggling. They had witnessed a very funny scene when the car in which they were pulled over by the road pavement. The scene was one in which an older hawker had tripped over his own merchandise during a quarrel with a younger hawker. It had all begun when the younger and agile merchant had convinced Tahfuh that the older guy's fruits were not fresh; he had compared the ages of the fruits to that of the older hawker.

"Boss! His fruits are older than him, so don't buy them!" The young man joked as he tried to draw Tahfuh's attention to his platter of fruits.

Tahfuh had found this joke so hilarious that he decided to buy from the younger man. With a smirk on his face this younger man added insults to the wound by offering to replace the older hawker's fruit inventory.

"Grandpa how about I replace your old tasteless fruits with my fresh juicy fruits? Hey Grandpa, I'm talking to you. Are your ears too old to hear when I talk?"

Slightly infuriated but mostly amused the older merchant sprang up to his feet faked a swing at his younger colleague. Sadly, things did not go as planned; the older hawker unfortunately tripped over the platter holding his fruits inventory and fell freely without much self-control.

The young hawker rushed towards his older colleague and helped him up. While they were picking up his fruits, Mercy pinched Nsoh and handed her a bank note.

66

"Give this to the old man, I feel bad for him he just lost all his inventory."

"Aunty, he is going to clean it and sell it to someone who did not see this happen; I can give him the money if we buy them for real." Nsoh said.

They offered to buy the older hawker's inventory and even though Tahfuh expressed his disaccord, Muungo hopped down the vehicle, stationed but vibrating on its humming engine, and went and bought all of the older hawker's fruits. After all they could be washed and peeled. He hopped back into car and passed the plastic bag full of fruits to Nsoh in the back seat. Wilanne who had awoken, began scrambling for bananas.

The truck's tires squeezed on the asphalt and propelled the vehicle forward. The journey continued just as life did with its joy and pain, ups and downs. Mercy had to deal with the little dose of dust that rose off the tarred road as the truck's tires' threads pressed down on the road. She was coughing and sneezing repeatedly, until Nsoh offered her a piece of cloth to use as a facemask. The omnipresent dust was still being dealt with when suddenly, without warning, the humid atmosphere gave place to the highland's cold air. Mercy felt better, she preferred dealing with the dust alone, instead of having the double whammy of humidity and the dust. In her mind, an exhausted Mercy pictured herself drinking good soup and going to bed as early as possible. She had had so much adaptation and learning to do these last hours. The most recent novelty to add to her life's experience was one that she never could imagine, not even in her wildest dreams.

Abakwa, Kamerun 2016

Their truck, part of a convoy-like arrangement which had left the city of Bell Town, had just cautiously ridden down the steep slope of a thin road bordered by deep valleys that ushered traffic into the historic town of Abakwa. The neighborhood harboring this slope was referred to as Up Station. As the vehicle banked on the inclined steep and winding slope of Up Station, the passengers caught glimpses of the town of Abakwa. Basking in the setting sun were tons of rusty and glittering roofs of small homes and grey slabs at the top of several high-rise buildings scattered over the uneven stretch of land that bore the town of Abakwa. Ordinarily Mercy would have grabbed her camera and taken snap shots of this view of the town of Abakwa but her mind was troubled by the discrimination she had experienced when their truck had begun its descent down the slope of Up Station.

Moments earlier before the descent down Up Station, the truck had travelled through the cold green highlands and finally reached the top of Up Station's slope. Like a bird perching on a branch for a panoramic view, the vehicle had stopped and perched above Abakwa. Tahfuh and his crew had to pull their vehicle over to the side of the road for what was considered a routine check conducted by the patrol police. The police officer, a man of small height and a protruding stomach that exerted a ridiculous pressure on the lower buttons of his short sleeve uniform, walked around the truck demanding to see everyone's identification.

"You and You come down! *Descendez s'il vous plaît*." He addressed Muungo and Mercy.

"These people are never tired of playing this broken record over and over again?" Tahfuh wondered aloud.

"Hey driver, you don't want to be on my bad side today, so shut up before I deal with you." The Police officer aggressively addressed Tahfuh.

Mercy looked in Muungo's direction; a nod of the head came from Muungo and so she did not hesitate to follow him. They both got out of the vehicle, stretched their painful joints, and walked towards the police officer.

"Do you have anything illegal in your bags, you these two American citizens?" He asked Mercy and Muungo as he walked away from them, heading towards a bench located under a makeshift tent on the side of the road.

"Boss we have nothing illegal; we are travelling to Mighang for a funeral." Muungo responded with a very calm and composed tone.

All this while Mercy had kept quiet just as Muungo had asked her to. She observed in absolute disgust the way in which the police officer was having a condescending attitude towards them.

"*Tu veux que je fouille les sacs là? Je parle en français parce qu'elle ne devrait pas comprendre ce que je dis.*" The officer spoke staring at Muungo's brown and weary eyes.

"Boss, I swear we have nothing illegal."

"*Tu crois que tu es très fort hein? Je te parle en français tu m'expose en parlant en anglais!* Okay! I am going to search every bag in the car, start taking the bags down and ask the other passengers to come out of the vehicle!" The Officer sounded irritated by Muungo's last response. His tone had gone up a notch and his eyebrows curled further inward. The officer reiterated his request in a tone that sounded aggressive and disrespectful. His feet got restless, showing signs of him wanting to head towards the truck in the next seconds. Muungo pulled a bank note from his chest pocket, squeezed it into his hand and approached the police officer pretending to offer him a handshake and handed him the bank note.

"*Ça c'est pas assez, tu viens de l'étranger avec ta femme Américaine, je te laisse passer et c'est tout ce que tu me donnes?*" The officer asked as he created diversion while slipping the bank note into his pocket.

"*Weh* my brother, we are going for a funeral; the funeral of Officer Mingo who died in Kolofata last month." Muungo tried to make small talk in order to dissipate the awkwardness that had invaded their space after the officer had collected the money from him.

"Oh yeah? You should have told me that long time. I knew him very well. So you are that his younger brother who lives in the US huh? " The Police officer responded while handing back to Muungo the two American Passports he had collected from Muungo and Mercy.

"*Merci Monsieur l'officier*!" Mercy thanked the officer with a clear sense of sarcasm, carefully applying her skills of a former French Literature Honors student. She made sure her pronunciations of the three words were audible and correct.

"*De rien.*" The Officer responded while turning his head towards his colleague, signaling him to open the control gate and let the truck driver through.

To Mercy, this was nothing shy of racial profiling, extortion, and police abuse of authority. Muungo knew what must have been going on in Mercy's head, and he also knew this was neither the time nor the place to teach her what it meant to be in a developing nation.

"T-I-A"; This is Africa (T.I.A), at least that is what he told himself. They both got into the vehicle and Tahfuh turned on the ignition and began cruising down the slope of Up Station.

The evening was announcing itself with streetlights coming on in the streets of Abakwa and homeowners turning on the lights on their front yards. Tahfuh made two stops: one to refill the truck's gas tank and allow the passengers to grab a bite, and one near some tall bushes so that everyone could go take a leak in the bushes before they hit the last part of their trip.

On the small winding road of the Sabga Mountain, travelled earlier by Tahfuh's truck, the cortege heading to Mingo's funeral, an array of vehicles which had formed itself at Abakwa's downtown quarters, dived downhill leaving Abakwa for Bamessing. The darkness, just like the sorrow of those accompanying the deceased to his final rest, grew deeper and thicker as the cortege drove into the Nun valley--the belly in which dwelled the history of the Ndop clans. Not everyone shared this sorrow, there were a few passengers in the cortege, like Ngeu Wowo, who were pleased because, finally, Mingo was dead.

Chapter 4

Upper Nun Valley, Kamerun 2016

BaNdop, the people of Nun Valley, clans of the Ndop peoples, had stayed faithful to the essential part of their culture as they migrated from present day Yemen to what is today referred to as Northwest Region of Cameroon. The BaNdop population had migrated from Yemen through ancient Egypt; from where centuries later they had continued on to Sudan via the lower part of River Nile. From the Sahel vegetation of Sudan, they ended up in Northern part of Cameroon in Ndobo. But, as the spread of Islam and later the hunt for slaves by Arab slave traders cascaded across the dunes and oasis of the Sahara Desert while heading towards the southern banks of Lake Lagdo, the custodians of the BaNdop culture fled southwards. The custodians ran down the slope of the highlands of Western Cameroon and swam across the River Nun and finally found refuge in the swampy plains seated at the base of the Nun Valley. This version of the story about the settlement of the people of the Nun Valley was different from those recounted by the griots of each of the 13 clans of BaNdop. The Mighang people, one of the 13 clans, believed that their earliest ancestors came from the swampy and dark sacred forest known as Pa'ah Nguong. Pa'ah Nguong was indeed sacred, just by the fact that it was a piece of equatorial forest vegetation surrounded by Guinea Savana vegetation. It was a patch of dense tropical forest majestically standing on thick trunks of tall and very old trees. With their great heights, the sacred trees seemed to gaze over the land and lake that formed the mainland and islands of Mighang. It was the inhabitants of these landscapes who incarnated the birth, marital, and funeral rites of the Mighang culture. Like that of Mighang, the narrative of the genesis of each clan was different from that of others even though all of 13 clans shared many

71

similarities whenever birth, marriage, sexuality, and death concepts and related rites were mentioned.

The cortège of vehicles and Tahfuh's truck, dusty and dirty, arrived the Tahkuh's family residence in Mighang after sunset. On the morning of the next day, after the corpse had arrived Mighang, Nsoh gave a synopsis of the story of the origin of the Mighang Kingdom to Mercy as they sat by the fireside and across from each other. The crackling sound of the dancing flames and the popping sound of juicy golden corn grains, arrayed on cobs roasted by the red-hot coal, provided the background symphony to the story. Her right cheek resting in her right palm, Mercy devoured the details, hyperbole, and beauty of the story; she was impressed by the fact that such a history, orally passed down from generation to generation over centuries, had developed wrinkles but not faded away. In Mercy's family, residing in the state of Georgia, and as in the homes of most other African American families, their history *began* somewhere in the 1600s when their ancestors reached the American shores after a perilous transatlantic trip. Passengers involuntarily and inhumanely transported from Bimbia, Bangou and other known and unknown slave markets. Even though DNA science and genealogy records helped track down and pinpoint the African American's region of origin and lineages, both tools never bore the twist and turns of stories of tribal and family legends. The stories from Nsoh and questions from Mercy never seemed to end, but once the meal was ready, they had to pause and postpone their conversation for another time.

Carrying a tray of food, Mercy followed Nsoh to the dining room, and then took a seat next to Muungo. On the table there was a variety of meals, but the host offered pasta and beef stew to Mercy. The host did not want to surprise the symbiotic bacteria that helped in their guest during her regular digestion of food by making her ingest their *strange* meals. But Mercy, stubborn Mercy, insisted on eating the local delicacies. She served herself a plate of *Njama-Njama* (sautéed huckleberry leaves), aromatized with lumps of *egussi* (ground squash seeds), and smoked *kèh-kung* (smoked Tilapia). She ate the vegetables alongside some corn *fufu* (corn flour dumplings cooked to a tender consistent mixture). Good old Mercy initially fumbled, she wondered whether she was going to use a spoon or her hands, like the locals did, in devouring the colorful combination presented to her. But seeing everyone else eating with their bare hands, Mercy decided to eat with her hands as well. Nsoh interrupted the degustation of her meal, and fetched water for Mercy to rinse her hands before dipping them into the plate. By watching the others empty their plates and fill up their stomach, Mercy easily and rapidly mastered the skills involved in eating *fufu* and *Njama-Njama*. Mercy did bring a little more than an empty stomach and big appetite to the table. She brought along boldness. She attempted to separate the fishbone from the fish fillet in her mouth just like all the others were doing with fascinating ease, but she failed. Everyone found that funny, especially because Irene had suggested beforehand that Mercy should not copy every detail of the Mighang eating styles. Mercy was not one to give up easily. She slowly but surely got a grasp of the fish-eating technique, and before anyone could notice she successfully sorted the fishbone from the fish fillet with much dexterity than she had at the start.

The appetizing meal eaten, the ladies retired to the kitchen where they continued with preparations for the next day. Once in the kitchen, Mercy was officially introduced to Tahfuh's mother, Mandieng Ngwatang, who was the oldest woman in the kitchen. Tahfuh's mother insisted on hugging Mercy. Despite her feeble body frame and her smile depleted by sorrow, she wrapped her warm arms around Mercy with the kind of love that only mothers could ever give. Her body looked feeble, but this was the same body she had thrown on the floor when she arrived at the family residence in tears right about breakfast time. After the hug, Mandieng initiated a conversation with Mercy, and Nsoh was their interpreter. The old tired mother was glad to know that a woman from the land of the white man had come to the funeral of her *son* -- nephew. She was so emotional that in between words of joy and sorrow she named Mercy Ndiandah.

Amongst the people of Mighang naming was not a casual thing, the name could be a prophecy, a cry of exasperation, a word of gratitude, and in Mercy's case a name of honor and adoption into the family. The name meant mother of the house; Mandieng said only the mother of the home will leave behind everything, money and comfort, to come bury her son. She asked Mercy to stretch out her right hand and open wide her palm, and as Nsoh translated this request she warned Mercy that the old lady was going to bless her by spitting in her palm and asked Mercy not be afraid or disgusted, at least not openly.

"Whatever the water washes away, the water brings back; whatever the ocean takes the rains from the sky and the returning waves of the ocean brings back." Were the few audible words of Mandieng's blessings.

With a hand stretched out and a palm open wide, Mercy allowed Mandieng to spit in her hands and profess blessings over her life.

Though sorrow hovered around every gathering and every activity, Mercy took pleasure in being amongst the women as they prepared dishes for the burial ceremony scheduled for the next day. Hours of work had run by and in between tasks. Nsoh and Mercy had parted from each other for quite a while. After hesitating for a moment, Mercy finally asked Irene where Nsoh was, Nsoh had almost unnoticeably stepped out of the kitchen after Mercy's conversation with Mandieng and still had not returned. Breathing loud, sweating profusely, and pounding heavily on cocoyam thrown in a wooden mortar by Mercy, Irene, who was slightly out of breath, responded saying:

"Nsoh has gone to another kitchen to help with the preparations."

Nsoh and her two elder sisters were spending the entire afternoon in another kitchen, a couple of houses down the street. The daughters of Mingo were preparing components for other meals; they were smoking meat and fish and picking and steaming vegetables. Half amazed and half shocked, Mercy still did not quite comprehend how a young girl could be doing so much work and had been maintained on a very busy schedule for almost a week now.

"Why don't we hire professionals to do all the preparations since there is so much to do," Mercy asked Irene.

"We are the professionals, there are none more professional than the women in the family and their friends," Irene spoke back after rapidly, swallowing a piece of smoked fish sandwiched in between two warm pieces of cocoyam.

"I feel as though Nsoh is made to grow faster than a girl of her age. She is not even 19 yet and she is in charge of large-scale cooking, cleaning and all other homemaker's tasks," Mercy drifted to a monologue as she masked her deception.

"Mercy, the cultures are quite different, you see." Irene proceeded after reading the deception on Mercy's face.

"Nsoh is not being overworked; she is being trained to be what we call here a woman of valor. You've got to understand that here, the saying *the way to a man's heart is through his stomach* is just part of the story *dearie.* "

Irene took upon herself to share with Mercy the Mighang culture from a Mighang woman's perspective. In between snap sounds, created as Irene broke freshly budded branches from the hard stalks of huckleberry plants, she explained to Mercy that, for as long as she could remember, the woman has had the place of the queen in a typical Mighang family. The woman has the privilege of making most of the decisions while the husband implements those decisions. The only condition to this division of role is that the woman's decision making must be done behind closed doors. The rationale behind this condition was based on a simple fact. Just as ruler needs his warriors well-armed, a woman needs her husband armed with his ego--big and unshaken in the eyes of the world. Thus, the woman keeps her authoritative apparel behind doors and uses it only when needed. When out on the streets the wife puts on her veil of a submissive and never-questioning housewife. Raising her head lightly to see if Mercy was paying attention, Irene noticed that her one-woman audience was giving all her attention and even more. Mercy had even stopped chopping the vegetables on the chopping board resting on her laps.

"The issue of the emasculation of the man is not something we appreciate in the African culture." Irene continued.

At the mention of this topic, Mercy got even more captivated. Unconsciously, Mercy placed down her knife on the chopping board, folded her arms as she paid exclusive attention to Irene. Like a frog blending in a green environment waiting to snatch a stray fly, Mercy listened to Irene's analysis waiting to counteract it.

"It is not the major reason, but the scars of *emasculation* have dwelled so much in the spirit of some African-American women up till the point where their men feel as if marriage is nothing but a way of trading their birthrights." Irene continued.

Irene explained that like in most parts of the world the girl was prepared, *domesticated and trained,* for the marriage arena while the boy was not. Yet, the only way to take advantage of this unfair condition was for the well-educated woman to attract more than one suitor and to be the one to choose which of them she would take as husband. The best way for a woman to sway a man, many men, and most of all keep him and his male compass needle from darting from one skirt to another, was to be indispensable to his wellbeing. Being indispensable consisted in being able to win over the heart of the man's mother, controlling and managing the household in such a way that would make any man proud.

Mercy had been listening to all what Irene had been saying. She replied with a sense of seriousness as if she felt singled out by the claims of *emasculation* which Irene had subtly made.

According to Mercy there was not an issue of emasculation, if the black men had decided to be neither husbands nor fathers it was more of a personal decision.

"Once upon a time despite all odds stacked against them most black men were family leaders, but today very few men fight back the storms. *Emasculating women* is the weakest storm in the ocean of the black men's lives. Drugs, black on black crime, baby daddy pride, and overly dependent brother attitude are the greater plagues facing the black man. "

Mercy paused for a moment catching her breath after uninterruptedly spitting out her version of the *truth*.

"But let me say this, by grooming a girl for a successful marriage and home you are not solving the problem. Until blacks around the world and society at large groom both boys and girls to become men and women respectively, we will spend our time indexing less scary demons such as emasculation, baby daddy pride, welfare dependent independent women, drug-business-enslaved free black men, and unfaithful homebound loving husbands. This piece of advice is relevant to all other races."

Mercy elaborated on her opinion, before she picked up her knife and resumed with the chopping of vegetables, as if she had just ended her plea and said, "your honor, with this I rest my case." Irene was impressed at the mass of knowledge and weight of wisdom which Mercy had. She now began to understand why Muungo always cited Mercy as someone he would like Irene to spend more time around. Both friends continued their activities, trading anecdotes and theories every now and then.

As the activity in the hive kept the sorrow on the back row, family and friends slowly regrouped at the Mingo's residence in the village. This time around, the wailing and agitation that characterized the presence of most mourners did not affect Mercy as it was the case earlier, she must have become used to it. She had been assigned to a very particular task by Muungo when he had shown up around 1:40 p.m. Mercy was tasked with fixing and sealing sardine sandwiches and then making lunch packs. She worked under a tent set up for feeding the population after the burial. Easily noticed because of her white shirt that mapped out her very firm and perky breast, Mercy was seen instructing, and demonstrating, to a handful of girls how to set and seal the airtight refreshment packs. Simultaneously, a set of young men had made it a duty to try to gain Mercy's attention. These young men walked and paused around the tent under which Mercy and the girls were. They were roaming for no specific reason. All the while they were heard attempting to mimic the American accent. Mercy had not noticed them; not until Nsoh's elder sister approached her giggling. According to Nsoh's sister, Eve, these young men were fans of the Hip-hop and the supposedly *gansta* culture of America. Many other boys of the same age groups as these young men copied the slants, the fashion, and at times they even embraced the negative stereotypes associated with the Hip-Hop culture. But at this particular moment they were only trying to draw Mercy's attention and why not woe her off to a date.

It was after talking with Eve that the bulb lit in Mercy's mind. She was more amused than flattered by the *kids'* enthusiasm. Mercy was so amused by them that while she made the last few refreshment packs, she began thinking about the influence that the media had had on her own perception of Africa. In her busy silence, she also examined the impact the same media had had on the perception of America by Africans. So many times, in the past she had had conversations with Muungo revolving around the role which the media played in the portrayal of Africans and African Americans. They had agreed on the inaccuracy of the images painted by the media.

The first image she had ever seen of Africa was a picture of a child soldier stooping a few meters from the edge of a pit and pointing an assault weapon at three kids who were digging gold in a muddy and slippery pit. This image was glued to a white cardboard brandished by a protester. The protester and her acolytes were participating in a human rights protest. They chanted their grievances on a street across from a jewelry shop in downtown Atlanta. The little child that Mercy was back then had stopped for a while, at loss for words as she stared at the image. She had stood there long enough for the lollipop in her mouth to melt completely, and then she had pulled out the candy's stick. After rolling her tongue against the roof of her mouth roof she had tapped the lady brandishing the child soldier's signpost. Then she had asked the elderly white lady holding the sign board what that image represented. With a voice barely making it amidst the loud protest chants, the lady had explained to her:

"You see my dear, in Africa children like you do not go to school, do not have either thanksgiving or other holidays because they are involved in forced labor. These children have had their family killed by bad guys and they are transformed into diamond miners or child soldiers. While they suffer all sorts of atrocities the jewelry store makes billions of dollars from the diamonds dug out by the kids."

The old woman paused for a moment to see if the then little Mercy was going to say something else. Instead of a horrified facial expression, Mercy's face lit up with curiosity.

"How do you know that?" Mercy asked, a little too late as the woman had resumed shouting at the top of her voice with the other protesters who chanted, and repeatedly stabbed the air as they raised and lowered their signposts.

This brief explanation only served at reinforcing a certain image about Africa in Mercy's mind. After all her classmate, and son of her 5th grade English teacher, had told her that Africa was full of savages and wildlife. He also claimed to have once heard another one of their classmates, who was of African origin, speaking the *savage* language to his grandmother at the mall. Children are known for their gullible and courageous personalities, and so Mercy had believed a great deal of what this boy had said.

Fast forward to many years later, here was Mercy experiencing another world order, another Africa different from the Africa she had heard about, seen, and read about. Just like Mercy, one day these young men who were trying to be too American may be fortunate enough to realize that the image they have of America is out of focus, virtual, and imaginary. They will come to realize that their Africa was misconstrued as a Jungle, a war front where no human rights existed, and that America was not a Hip-Hop scene ruled by a hip-hop culture and *gansta* lifestyle, and certainly not the most beautiful place on earth --It was just another beautiful place on earth.

Mercy's mind returned to the present and as she placed the last refreshment packs on the trays waiting for the girls to come and help her, she noticed that the attention of the boys, that was once exclusively directed toward her, was currently drawn to a particular direction. She peeked in that direction and that is when she caught sight of someone walking towards her. It was a young man dark in complexion, straddling on a pair of convex legs, and interestingly enough, he was wearing an Atlanta Falcon jersey. May be the jersey was what had caught Mercy's attention, but it certainly was what had kept her attention on him. A half-torn tag hanging off the bottom right of the jersey did not steal any glamor off the jersey's authenticity. Mercy was a diehard football fan and an unconditional Atlanta Falcons fan, and when it came to apparels of her favorite team, she knew the real deal when she saw one. The young man walking in her direction was well groomed. Eyes blinking at various speed, lips bitten over and over, nose pinched on multiple occasions…what an obvious struggle he endured trying to find the perfect facial expression that could mask his combined shyness and seriousness. The combination of emotions was quite overwhelming that it stole away the brightness of his neat cut. He bit and twisted his lower lip multiple times until he found himself at an audible distance from Mercy.

"Hello, how are you? My name is Blaise and what is yours?" He uttered in quick succession as if he had rehearsed it a thousand times in front of his mirror. Because he certainly had used a mirror, based on how well groomed he was: neatly kempt eyebrows, tiny glossed lips, short neat hair and a smooth face covered with facial hair aligned downwards like unending sheets of water racing down from the top of a waterfall.

"Hi Blaise, nice to meet you, my name is Mercy."

Mercy responded with a chuckle, waiting to hear what he had to tell her. Her chuckle was actually a midway point between the desire to ease the tension on the boy's face and her laugh at the comic side of the palpable tension.

"Do you have a moment? I will like to talk with you for a quick second." Blaise inquired. Swiftly taking his hands out of his pocket in attempt to quell any thought of arrogance. His unveiled hands revealed his long slender fingers and their delicately manicured fingernails. His left wrist wore an Apple Watch with the protective plastic still in place though trapping a few air bubbles on the watch's screen.

At the sound of this request, Mercy's face turned to one of surprise; her eyebrows drew closer to one another and her eyes sort of widened up as she hesitantly responded by "suuuuureeeee."

Blaise cleared his throat and then began addressing Mercy with much more control than he had had at the moment of introducing himself. The cloud of nervousness over his head seemed to have drifted away giving his smooth face the chance to reflex light rays and reveal his cuteness. His facial expression brightened as the flame of confidence blossomed from within.

"I heard from people that you were from the U.S. and I also heard that you had come alongside the Tahkuh family for the funeral of their brother and father. I don't want to sound like I don't care but what I am about to tell you is of the utmost importance. Do you mind if we stood somewhere that can ensure nobody else but you hears what I have to say?" Blaise ended his words with a lower pitched voice, and fidgeting fingers mingling amongst themselves indicating that his nervousness had resurged once more.

Mercy pointed to three seats located at a quiet place in the yard under a shade created by the big long branches of a mango tree that bore tons of leaves and unripe fruits. The two walked towards the tree, their footsteps squash the dry leaves covering the base of the tree. Just before they reached the seats Blaise began speaking while Mercy listened with much attention to something, a deep secret, which she never could have expected would be object of their conversation.

Finally, the day of the burial ceremony came. On this day, the decor put in place all around the Tahkuh's Family residence was very colorful; the color combination, purple, white, and black, was simultaneously heavy to the soul and elegant to the eye. The largest tent was dressed in purple and white drapes hanging off its metallic skeletal structure. In it the coffin was place at the center with four candle carriers next to each corner of the coffin. The polished shiny dark brown wooden coffin was surrounded by wreaths with messages expressing sympathy and love. Located at the main entrance of the tent and in front of the coffin was a wooden picture frame leaning on a deformed wreath made of red, pink, white and black roses. The golden-brown wooden picture frame containing a portrait of Mingo was not easily missed. In this portrait, Mingo was smartly dressed in his dress uniform; almost unnoticeable at first sight, Mingo's lips on the picture were slightly shifted to left of the vertical symmetry of his face. This gave a kind of appealing smile to the image on the portrait. But Mingo's *smile* on that portrait was the only smile under the cool shade of the tent. People marched in and out of the tent leaning over the coffin and taking a peek at the embalmed remains of the war hero. On either side of his coffin there was a sentinel guarding the coffin: standing at attention with a weapon in hand. Still on either side of the coffin, but a few meters behind the sentinel, there were arrays of white and blue chairs and bamboo stools reserved for the coworkers and relatives of the deceased. The rigid spatial orientation of the decoration and accommodation made the palpable sorrow omnipresent.

This sorrow hovering over every eulogy and testimony became more and more unbearable for family and friends who could not hold back their tears. It was only later that day after the Reverend Pastor of the local church had ushered words of consolation and hope that everyone else seemed to see the silver lining beneath the dark cloud. Mingo was dead but he had died doing what he loved--protecting his country and all those he loved. A representative of the military decorated the coffin with a posthumous medal and then the military procession began. The coffin was carried to the burial site by six military personnel in dress uniform and wearing stern looks on their tired faces. Once the coffin, previously draped with the national flag, had been uncovered, lowered and positioned six feet into the ground, Mingo's cap and the neatly folded flag were handed over to his widow. Crushed by tears and pain she was unable to get up and receive the memorabilia and so one of the soldiers, holding back his tears, carried them over to the widow and kneeling on one knee in the brown dust he handed the flag and the cap over to his colleague's wife. The military's mission was accomplished, and the men of valor melted into the civilian crowd after wishing farewell to their brother in arms. The Pastor said one last prayer and dropped some dirt on the coffin. The funeral wailing resumed once more as the family members walked to the grave and dropped handfuls of dirt and stalks of roses on the coffin.

Professional grave fillers, who previously had served as gravediggers, patiently waited for the family and friends to say their adieux, then they came up to the grave with their shovels and began filling up the grave. With dirges sang in deep voices and measured by the tempo of foot stomps, the grave fillers danced on the mounds of dirt on the grave. As they danced, they added more and more dirt. Their foot stomps help pressed down the dirt and level up the gravesite. Once the grave fillers had finished their job and had been invited to share a special meal, in which boiled maize and peanuts were mandatory, a group of princes slowly gathered around the grave. Tahfuh rushed to the gravesite where he joined Muungo who had begun chatting with the princes. As part of the tradition the princes began simulating some sort of bargain with Muungo over the remains of his brother--a symbolic price had to be paid for the corpse to be buried away from the royal cemetery.

Mingo was not a prince as such but his ancestor Tahkuh, because of his legendary loyalty and bravery, had been granted the same rights as a born prince of the Kingdom of Mighang. This privilege, manifested by a secret sacred ceremony of induction into royal knighthood, had been performed on Tahkuh centuries ago and the benefits were passed on from generation to generation. In this time and era, Mingo was the heir to that knighthood. Now with Mingo dead the title had to pass to Muungo because his late brother did not have a male child. Neither Nsoh nor her sisters could inherit the title because it was only reserved for a male descendant according to the laws of the Kingdom of Mighang.

So, as part of the simulated negotiation, an improvised trade drama took place over the grave. After a brief moment of whispers accompanied by hand gestures and facial expressions in reaction to price offers and rejections, an agreement was reached between the two parties. A couple of coins were drop on the compressed mound of ground beneath which Mingo rested alone. The princes picked up the coins. Hugs concluded the simulated trade and gave place to a celebratory dance.

Voices and their echoes resonated above the noisy atmosphere as a vibrant celebratory dance sanctioned the successful bargain. As part of the dance, the princes and first-generation descendants of princes formed a queue headed by the oldest prince. They executed delicate and engaging dance moves while heading towards Pa'ah Nguong--the sacred forest. The humming sound of those who did not know the wordings of the song was drowned by the instrumental resonance, and both sounds gradually distanced themselves from the burial site as the performers headed for the forest. It was uncommon for a woman to be too close to the queue of princes during this rhythmic procession into the sacred forest, but because Mercy was a stranger and because Muungo had put in a special request, the oldest prince accorded her this unique privilege. She was granted permission to follow the princes' right up to their entrance into the sacred forest. Her camcorder in hand, Mercy walked next to Muungo, who was midway in the queue, while filming every detail of the ceremony. Following her moves with their gazes, some villagers began murmuring out their discontentment regarding a woman accompanying the princes into the sacred forest. This popular reaction came at a perfect time for Prince Ngeu Wowo. In the blink of an eye, Prince Ngeu Wowo began making his way up the queue of princes, pushing out of his way the other princes while he sprung forward stride after stride.

Immortalized moments of the setting sun's golden red rays, the rising brown clouds of dust, and the resonating chants and captivating dance moves all cramped on the pixels of the images created by the lens of the camcorder. Sliding her finger over the zoom control button of the camcorder the lady behind the camera magnified the image appearing on the camcorder's display screen, it was the image of the oldest prince. He was topless and this appearance exposed his chest covered with black and grey curly chest hair. Below his torso, slightly above the waistline, he wore a traditional attire, a piece of cotton fabric cloth with Africa symbols woven in red and yellow threads and spread all over the primary navy-blue fabric.

This piece of cloth is worn in a unique way, and it is held in place by a belt. The belt, made of cow skin is worn around the waist, it holds the front part of the cloth covering the frontal side of the abdomen slightly above the waist level. Then the loose end of the cloth is passed underneath the pelvic area in between the legs where it is purposefully made saggy. From underneath the pelvic area, this loose end is passed over the dorsal side of the abdomen and is also held in place by the belt. Both ends of the cloth are kept sufficiently long so that they have flaps hanging off the belt. These flaps cover the anterior and posterior part of the thighs and drop down to the level of the knees and calves in the front and back respectively.

The tense muscular tissues underneath the dark brown hairy skin of the oldest prince's arms, covered in camwood, stuck out and expressed the effort he put in keeping the princes' banner up in the air and in an oblique position. The banner was made of a long bamboo pole of helical morphology carrying amulets at the end pointing up to the sky. These amulets were tied with the help of fresh roots of a particular plant. The leader of the princes' group swung his hips from side to side as he danced his way towards the sacred forest. With every sideways swing of his hips, he stabbed the air with the end of the bamboo bearing the amulet and sang a few words of the procession song. The princes behind him responded to his words as they too danced and marched towards the forest. The prince dancing directly behind the bearer of the banner carried in his hand a gourd loosely wrapped in a net. The net comprised of strings woven together and running through dried seeds of canarium fruits. And as the gourd bearer sang, he held the gourd's neck with his right hand and pounded the gourd on the palm of his left hand. These rhythmic collisions between his left palm, the gourd, and the many dried canarium fruit seeds created a clacking sound. The ears of the population savored the musical aroma made from the fusion of the clacking sound, the tweeting of the evening birds, the singing of the princes, the tooting of a horn blown by the last person in the queue, and the echoes of all these sounds. These echoes were generated when transverse sound waves originating from every sound source bounced off the trunks of the tall, old, and big trees. These tree trunks reflecting were covered in thick green moss, symbiotic organism that had accumulated on tree back over the many centuries spent in the heart of the forest. Mercy, unintentionally, nodded her head and clicked her tongue to the enchanting cadence as she filmed the scene.

Carried away by her admiration for the dance choreography and the harmonious singing, Mercy slightly went pass the forest's limit beyond which only princes and village elders were allowed. A loud collective inhale of surprise was heard from those who had been watching Mercy's interaction with the princes' procession. This limit was marked by a flowerless shrub, with dry scaly bark covering its short stem and stunted branches. The shrub grew alone and isolated from all the other plants of the forest environment. The plant was located at the center of a circular patch of land bearing no vegetation, it is believed that the shrub was responsible for this strangely barren parchment of land.

"Sorry! but you cannot go pass this shrub!" Muungo warned Mercy as he raised the amplitude of his voice trying to speak above the loud song sung by the princes while continuing his march with them.

Instantaneously, Prince Wowo grabbed Mercy by the hand and pulled her away from the limit.

"Be careful with how you mix tradition and modernism," Wowo rebuked Mercy and Muungo with these words and a severe look.

Mercy looked around to see who it was pulling her by the arm, and the frown on her face got more significant when she realized it was a stranger. She shook the stranger's hand off her arm at the same exact moment when Muungo pushed the stranger's hand off her and said something to the angry stranger in the local language.

Mercy remembered the instructions the oldest prince had given them when they had asked for permission to film the procession. After rapidly calming herself down Mercy nodded at Muungo who had already moved on with the group beyond the limit, then she immediately turned around and walked in the direction opposite to the procession. As she turned around and avoided bumping into one of the princes who was staggering and dancing, clearly under influence of alcohol, one of her legs rubbed against the flowerless shrub causing her to lose her balance. Mercy quickly regained her balance. She now stood less than a meter away from the shrub and continued recording the procession despite what she seemed to have noticed. She had noticed that many eyes had focused on her and many fingers were pointing in her direction; certainly, in relation to the mistake she had just committed by walking past the shrub of the sacred forest.

By sunset, word on the street was a reflection of a unanimous thought: everyone said the burial ceremony, scheduled on the day before the life celebration and masquerades' dances, had gone very well. To most people the most powerful moment of the burial day belonged to Solange, the oldest of Mingo's three daughters; with a vocal timbre like her father's, she had pronounced a very touching eulogy. Words that described admiration, words from which sprouted good memories, and words from which the cold tentacles of sorrow stretched out gripping the hearts of all those attending the burial all came from Solange. They were many other powerful moments during the burial ceremony, yet the meaning of a burial ceremony gone well was very subjective.

To some folks, it was the quality and quantity of food and drinks served to them that made the burial ceremony a good one. After Mingo had been laid to rest, a variety of delicious healthy and colorful local dishes were served to the guests. These tasty dishes were accompanied by beverages such as freshly tapped palm wine, homemade liquor produced from overly ripe banana fruits and edible sugar canes, and popular beers and sweet drinks from the breweries around the country.

To others, a burial ceremony gone well meant it was characterized by unperturbed adherence to the established program. Well, to Mercy the burial having gone well was defined by the fact that she had experienced, through the burial ceremony, a celebration of the dead as she had never read before from any book or watched in any documentary.

On the morning of the next day after the burial and hours before the entire village had awaken to savor the anticipated beauty of the events marking the celebration of Mingo's life, through a culturally and artistically rich ceremony called *cry die*, Mercy's sleep was interrupted at its lightest phase. She moved around on her bed and for a short instance wondered where her neighbor with the noisy truck was, only to realize she was in another part of the world. Mercy's sleepy eyes gazed at a shy beam of very faint early morning sun rays of the dawn. The rays cruised through a crack on the windowpane and crashed against the cream white wall of her room, leaving the room partially dark. Lying next to Mercy on the bed, an exhausted Nsoh was fast asleep with most of the covers pulled over her body. Mercy sat up on the bed, and her change in posture modified their weight distribution on the mattress. Some of the bed's springs reacted to this change in mass distribution by producing a long, faint, squeaky sound as they went from being compressed to expanding to their original state. Nsoh rolled away from Mercy and the irritating faint squeaky sound. Nsoh ended up pulling even more of the covers with her and creating more of the squeaky sound. As the covers slipped off from Mercy's feet, she noticed some sort of skin rash—red and mildly swollen spots on the skin. The rash appeared in patches, very much like flowers blooming at different angles on a tree. Indeed, they were like flowers, because each time Mercy tenderly rubbed a rash-infected spot with her soft fingers it immediately began to itch and if she dared to vigorously scratch it then the ill propagated some more—another patch of rash will appear in the vicinity of the original rash being scratched. The beams of sun rays coming into the room had still not revealed a complete sunrise, but the rashes on Mercy's foot had covered most of the skin over her tibia. Terrified by the idea that this could be one of those deadly African infections, Mercy hurriedly hopped out of bed, grabbed her phone, took a picture of her tibia, and ran out of the room looking for Irene. Wrinkles of confusion and fear spread across her forehead, and with a stuttering speech she explained what she had just experienced to Irene. Irene, who had been feeding Wilanne, passed the baby to Muungo and took a look at the rash, but she could not make much out of it.

"It is not that much! I thought you said it had almost entirely covered the skin over your right tibia?" Irene asked Mercy in a tone impregnated with curiosity while involuntarily biting the left corner of her lower lip.

"Hmmm! What can I tell you? It seems to be going away because I told you about it or may be because the sun has risen above the horizon," Mercy responded in a carefree tone that actually masked her lack of an explanation.

The rash had indeed gradually faded away after the sun had completely risen, but Mercy and Irene's concern did not fade away. Irene went back and forth between the yard where the funeral ceremony was to take place and the room occupied by Mercy. During that period Mercy spent her time searching online for information about the rash. Mercy finally took a break off attempting to disinter an explanation to her early morning rash when the first masquerader invaded the yard.

The arrival of the first masquerader was preceded by acoustic waves emanating from the rattling of nutshells wrapped around the ankles of the masquerader's feet. The rattling on each ankle was produced when the nutshells crashed against one another. The masquerader wore a full-face mask. The mask had two parts: a first part made up of a white piece of thick mesh cloth, gone brown over time, knotted at one end, and worn from the top of the head to the neck; then a second part consisting of an old black wooden masked firmly resting on top of the head and covering the knotted top of the mesh cloth. This dress-up created the illusion that the wooden mask was the masquerader's head while the white piece of mesh cloth was a cover to his apparently particularly very long neck. Multiple interwoven and intertwined strings carrying nutshells were wrapped around the ankles of the masquerader. Every foot stomp from the masquerader caused dust to rise from the ground into the air and produced vibrations. These vibrations travelled from the sole of the masquerader's barefoot to the nutshells strapped around his ankle thereby causing the rattling sound. The instrumentalist walking behind the masquerader screamed incantations to the gods of the land and commands to the masquerader, and at the same time he executed percussion by rhythmically banging on a gong.

In response to the musical incantations and tribal rhythm coming from the gong the masquerader stomped his feet amidst many acrobatic dance moves. The masquerader was so swift in his dance moves that his gown, made of sackcloth and bearing tons of bird feathers, lagged in movement behind his supple body moves. It was so captivating; and with every abrupt stop of the masquerader in his dance moves, the lagging movement of his gown looked like a slow motion and special effect scene of a motion picture on a high-definition screen.

At the sounds of the gong, incantations, and nutshells' rattling, neighbors and friends gathered in the yard of Mingo's village residence. This spontaneous gathering of people in the yard and the gong's rhythmic sounds caught the attention of Mercy. In a series of quick actions, Mercy pulled out her camcorder, and from her bedroom window, she captured and immortalized these moments; special moments where she witnessed a unique transformation of sorrow into joy—the celebration of the life of a dead person.

The crowd swelled as the dance of the masqueraders intensified. In slow majestic and commanding steps, the first masquerader walked towards his audience bearing a spear in hand and aiming it at his audience. He got closer and closer and closer. Then in the blink of an eye, he darted in the audience's direction, creating panic amongst the population. The screams of women and the uncontrolled adrenaline-provoked flight responses in the crowd blazed up as the people ran in all directions pushing and even falling over one another.

Indifferent to the chaos inflicted on his audience, the masquerader turned around and repeated the same terrifying moves on another section of his audience. It appeared the people enjoyed this rush of adrenalin, after every scare they were attracted back to their original position by an unexplainable force. The gong player did not stand too far behind his dancer; covered in black glittering soot-like ointment, the gong player continued his entertainment while being almost invisible to the eyes of the audience whose attention was given completely to the masquerader.

A few more moments of scare and screams caused the by solitary masquerader went by. Then a group of four masquerades, with mesh clothes masking their faces but no wooden masks on, rushed on to the stage, lined up, bowed down to, and then squatted, face-down, in front of the one who had been there first. Entering the stage with them was a group of other musicians, xylophonists, and drummers. The tempo of xylophone, drums, and the gong accompanied the lead masquerader as he repeatedly switched feet and hopped around on one foot. As part of the group's introductory choreography, after each dozen hops, the lead masquerader suspended his foot a few centimeters above the back of one of the masqueraders squatting in front of him. At the end of the lead masquerader's troop inspection, the xylophonists and drummers changed tempos and launched a loud and dance-provoking rhythm. The dry and sharp musicals notes cut through the soul of the squatting masqueraders, and like one man they all spontaneously rose to their feet, joined their captain, and executed a close to perfect choreography. The music and dance festival were heading to its climax, spectators' mouths were wide open in amazement exposing their buccal content to flies and dust particles, when suddenly the lead masquerader broke out of the group routine and planted his spear in front of the xylophonists. The leader lifted his hands and placed them on his mask, a queue for the xylophonists and drummers to play another musical piece. This change in cadence was to accompany the solo act of the lead masquerader while the other masqueraders squatted and marked time to the rhythm. Once again, the agile leader steered the general euphoria to a point closest to that of joyous explosion, and then, with a hop, he landed on one foot next to his spear and the orchestra paused one more time. He grabbed the spear, lifted it, and the xylophonist introduced a soft rhythm to which the other masqueraders continued marking time and moving their bodies from side to side while still squatting. The lead masquerader hopped, one more time, and planted his spear in front of one of the squatting masqueraders. This other masquerader, with the spear planted in his front, rose and performed a solo act accompanied by the orchestra. This solo act entertained the crowd until it was interrupted by the lead masquerader who picked the next performer, out of his group of squatting masqueraders, for a new solo act. Each masquerader took his turn and inflamed the joy of the population basking in the morning sun that was growing in intensity. All this while, Mercy was filming and enjoying the show from her bedroom window.

The moving, growing, and glowing sun crawled from the east to the west and the crowd kept increasing. The makeshift tents began to fill up as spectators brought their refreshments and shared with friends. The show only got better, and Muungo knew that, sooner or later Mercy was going to find it difficult to capture memories from her bedroom window. Following Muungo's request, Eve, rushed up stairs and walked through the half-opened door of the room in which Mercy was. She convinced Mercy to join the rest of the family, seated under the biggest tent, in appreciating the celebration of her father's life. Once outside the house the two ladies squeezed their way through the already dense crowd, and found comfortable seats, reserved for them by Nsoh, under the tent. Masqueraders and dance groups took turns to perform at the center of the yard and Mercy captured every gesture from the spectators and the actors while biting and chewing on roasted plantains and baked African plum fruits. No one, not even Mercy, thought about the cause or contamination risk of the skin rash that Mercy had developed earlier that morning.

The beautiful, colorful, and rhythmic display of the death celebration took place the day after Mingo had been laid to rest. Irene, Nsoh, Nsoh's siblings, and Muungo had been watching the show from their seats located at one corner of a tent reserved for family members. Prior to heeding to Muungo's invitation and settling on one of the bamboo stools in the family tent, Mercy had been discovering, admiring and recording the ceremony with her camcorder from her bedroom window. Unafraid of the invasive dust, she had cracked open the bedroom window because she feared that the once transparent windowpane, now timidly opaque thanks to the brownish color of dust and rust, would affect the quality of her recorded images. Mercy knew that the closer the better the immortalization of the scenes, but she had chosen to stay indoors and record from her room for a rather undesired reason. She fixated on the fact that she had developed a weird type of skin rash earlier that morning, and because of this strange rash she had thought of isolating herself or staying in quarantine. She made this somewhat extreme decision simply because she was neither sure if she was a potential vector of some contagious pathogen nor of how rapidly it would propagate over her skin. While all alone in the bedroom, the rash had made her recall Brianna's warning; "You know almost every deadly disease originates from Africa... so do not take any infection or weird feeling for granted." Mercy heard Brianna's voice in the back of her head. But in this case Mercy was not able to locate the ground zero of her skin rash, the only thing she knew was that it had happened somewhere between the night of the day of the burial and the early morning hours of the day of the *cry die*. Now that she was closer to the actions of the day, she got carried away and forgot about her resolution, and for a long moment everything concerning the strange morning rash was out of her mind. Every single one of her six plus one senses was tuned to the festivities. Of the multitude of performances that she visually bit with passion, three performances blazed her. The most loved of the three acts, the one considered the headline act, was the dance of the princesses. The least loved of the three acts was the performance of the princes, and the second most loved of the performance trio was the masquerades' final show.

Moments before the princes took to the stage for the second opening act, and the third best act in Mercy's books, one last group of masqueraders delivered the performance of a lifetime. This time their orchestra consisted of a gong banger, drummers, xylophone players and a piper. Just like before, the dancing was done by a group of masqueraders led by one of them who was a particularly agile and talented dancer. This masquerader was the captain of the group, the design of his ivory mask and his gown made of colorful plumages from a variety of big majestic birds made him stand out amongst the other masqueraders who had simple gowns made of smoothen pieces of nutshells. The masqueraders carried in their hands locally manufactured fly whisks, made of a colorful carved wooden handle and horse tail hair. Smooth pieces of nutshells were strung around the ankles of the masqueraders who performed a well synchronized, unfamiliar, but captivating choreography.

As part of the action-filled choreography, they tossed and exchanged their fly whisks in the air with breathtaking precision and dexterity; they defied gravity and human contortionist abilities, and the way the sounds made by the nutshells on their ankles and gowns fitted in the music was a pleasant-sounding harmony. The masqueraders bewitched their audience with non-scary and all-pleasing dance styles. Smiles and applauses from the audience joined the orchestra in animating the show. The ambiance generated by this performance was so powerful and electrifying that even the jittering of the leaves in the wind seemed to match the tempo of the music and dance. The captain incarnated precision at its best. Everyone in the audience found it difficult to tell if it was the lead masquerader's dance speed and the gestures of his fly whisk that determined the tune from the orchestra, or it was the other way around. It was on this high note that the set of masqueraders left the stage to the princes equipped with their machetes and guns. The masqueraders left their awestruck audience humming the rhythm of their instrumentals and whisperingly decrying the end of such a memorable performance.

Next, a group of males of all ages from the royal families of different generations got on stage, a stage still shaking from the intense performance of the masqueraders. Amongst the princes were some dressed in same style as was the oldest prince on the day before, others kept their casual pants and shirts on, princes with official traditional titles wore *Toghu*--the traditional outfit, and the wealthy members of the fraternity wore *gandura*-a long loose broad gown, with or without sleeves, and the matching hats. It is in these mixes of attires that the princes made their entrance to the stage. In their hands, slightly raised above their heads, they held and brandished machetes. The machetes' blades were almost rectangular in shape, except for their concave lengths. A few of those dressed in *Toghu* and *gandura* had guns and blank ammunitions; these few were usually the richer princes.

Accompanied by self-sung songs, these princes danced with a measured sense of royal arrogance; with every step, they each lightly lifted one foot off and then dropped it back to the ground after gently moving the foot sideways and forward in the air. One young prince was standing next to a trio of drummers who were beating vigorously on their animal skin drums, and he was in charge of intoning the songs while the other chorused. Then came the moment when the young man's intonation and the drum beating reached the climax and all the males got very erratic with their dance moves. At this moment, in alternating groups of two, most men raised and collided their machetes in the air, while the other princes in groups of three or four picked up their rifles and ran towards a safe zone and in an orderly manner fired consecutive shots into the air. By these actions each group was saluting the memory of the deceased, -the memory of a warrior.

The smell of gunpowder diffused in the air as the smoke puffed out of rifle barrels. It floated then merged with dust particles displaced from the dry ground by the foot stomps of the dancing princes. This was a display of bravery and bravado, some of the princes had actually been to battle while others were merely parading for the show. The crowd, on its feet and surrounding the performers, cheered and screamed at the top of their voices in admiration to the display. One particular prince dressed in a brand new *Toghu*, known to be living in Germany, was the center of attraction. He executed exquisite and well-mastered dance moves. His body's twisting and arms' dexterity stole the high pitch hollering from the young ladies and jealous stare from the ladies' boyfriends. This prince was none other than the younger brother of Prince Ngeu Wowo. Because of his wonderful dancing ability some jealous men impatiently waited for the princes to vacate the ceremony stage.

"Mingo was not even a prince as such," one unhappy and jealous young man voiced out.

"The next time you say something so ill placed I will strike you with my broom stick, and you will find out the name of he who placed water inside the coconut shell." An angry village elder retorted with his eyes scanning through the crowd to find which of these poorly educated young men did not know the bond between the Tahkuh and the royal family of Mighang.

A few meters away from the elder, the disrespect towards the Tahkuh was also endorsed by some princes, Ngeu Wowo being one of them. He showed his disrespect by using his political fame and power to play the first role at Mingo's funeral. Wowo, who had not been dancing, rose from his seat and marched towards the princes' dance group and asked them to wrap up their presentation.

"He may have been an important man in this community but do not forget he was not a prince. Do not give the king's dog the best part of the meal while princes starve." He told the princes.

Ngeu Wowo's influence was anchored on money and mystical powers. With his tough mean words, the princes knew it was time to leave the stage. The second most beautiful dance act, per Mercy, was over.

Mercy had barely recovered from the banging of metals and the explosion of gunpowder produced by the princes and the breathtaking choreography of the masqueraders when the princesses of all generations took to the stage. With less violent musical patterns, the ladies danced in, holding branches and handkerchiefs, and waving them from side to side. Amongst these women all dressed in African wrapper were Nsoh, her siblings and mother, and Irene who all executed the dance moves without any difficulty. At a moment in time Muungo offered to do the filming for Mercy so that she too could join the crowd of princesses. In the blink of an eye, the super excited Mercy had caught up with the dance group and began attempting to mimic their dance moves. A few missed steps and loss of tempo were noticed, after which Mercy mastered the dance. A small girl hesitantly and shyly walked towards Mercy and handed her a branch. Mercy smiled back and without any questioning or hesitation she too started waving the branch sideways like everyone and danced along with the other women. During a short musical pause Nsoh, rushed over to Mercy and took off one of the two wrappers she was wearing and wore it on Mercy. So, when the singing and dancing resumed Mercy was not easily distinguishable amongst the group of princesses.

Prince Ngeu Wowo had been watching what he considered a sacrilege. He had just returned from a moment of refreshment when he noticed Mercy dancing with the princesses. Burning of anger, the infuriated prince asked the oldest prince and his younger brother to follow him to his residence. Three silhouettes were seen vanishing behind the crowd and the packed vehicles, before the end of the celebration, at a time when the crowd was too excited with the second and final performance of the masquerades.

The euphoria characterized by cheering and screaming faded as the drummers and princesses progressively wrapped up their presentations and gave way to the last group of masquerades who made their final and grandiose entrance on the stage. Mouths wide opened and eyeballs popping out in astonishment and admiration the population welcomed the masqueraders and their performance.

This second set of masqueraders of the royal court, after the first that preceded the princes, had also come all the way from the palace to the burial ground. Different masks, different apparels, different choreographies, and different ambiances succeeded one after another as the masqueraders ran onto and out of the open space that served as a stage. There was one particularly science-defying incident which occurred when a pair of masquerades carrying a long wooden pole on their right shoulders ran to the stage at full speed and barefooted. The spectators scrambled as they rushed backwards, toeing an imaginary line and avoiding being in the way of the masqueraders exhibiting their god-like powers.

Very few people missed what happened next, and those who missed it must have been those who had fallen to the ground when the spooked crowd had pushed backward. Preceding a thick cloud of red dust one of the masqueraders swung his right foot and kicked into the air a plastic drum container, with a capacity of 50 liters, filled to the brim with fresh palm wine. The container flew into the air, the eyes of the crowd rose, and its voice resounded in awe as the drum's content gushed out while it spun in the air. The amplitude of the sound waves of the wow of astonishment had barely damped down when suddenly the masquerader leading the pole-bearing pair slipped and crashed into a pile of firewood stacked against the wall of a building. The spirit's incarnate never let go of his pole during his dangerous fall. He had barely hit the ground when he sprung to his feet and resumed his mad race in spite of the fact that the fall had left him with a bleeding cut on the right elbow. Such display of supernatural powers was what made the presence of masqueraders the *plat de resistance* of the funerals of titleholders amongst the BaNdop people. Once the masquerades last show was over, the crowd of spectators began shrinking like a highly radioactive element whose constituents were diffused in different directions.

Not only did the dust settle but the very high joyous emotions of the day gradually sunk back in the pool of sorrow. As some of the spectators helped to dismantle and pack the tents, they each had a heart-touching story to tell about Mingo's life. The most charismatic spectators made their entire story heard, while the others nodded and sneaked in comments as a way of corroborating the stories being told.

In one corner of the kitchen, not too far from the slowly emptied stage, Mercy was breaking the ice with some princesses who had gotten curious and approached her after her dance performance with the group of princesses. It was at this moment that Irene, with Mercy's permission, mentioned something concerning the rash which Mercy had dealt with earlier that day. One of the princesses, a sister to the enthroned king, seemed to know one or two things about that particular type of rash. She asked Mercy and Irene to call her and stop by the palace the next day if Mercy experienced the same condition the next morning. As the conversation continued, Mercy temporarily zoned out, fidgeting on her smart device and posting pictures of herself and *her Africa* online. There were these two pictures: one where she was being helped by an older princess in adjusting her wrapper, the piece of cloth tied around her waist, that had gotten loose while she was dancing, and the other picture of her receiving a branch from a very young princess. She stared at them with some sort of attachment before posting them with the caption: "A day in the life of a Mighang Princess." To Mercy, though the pictures did not have the glitter often associated with royalty, it reflected a rich tradition and cultural identity. Far from the purple capes, red carpets, and heavy armors that accompany western royalty, this African culture expressed royalty as a duty whose pride resided in the fact of being a custodian of a culture. A culture often condemned and fought against by western civilization.

The night spread out on a moonless and starless sky. The last drunks of the village searched their ways home as they stumbled in the dark. Stray dogs were heard crushing bones and growling at each other around the pile of trash next to the trash pits. Mercy had sleep spurts, maybe it was the sound of a rodent gnawing on the bags of peanut in the storeroom that awoke her over and over, but her conversation with Blaise, the young man she had met the first day of the funeral, did not help her find sleep. Blaise was not just one of the many boys who dreamt of America. He was, per his words, the son of Muungo, the son he took care of but never spoke of. Muungo did not want Irene to know that Blaise was his son, a son he had with Irene's closest friend when they all were in high school. Muungo was dating Irene and had a one-night fling with her friend. All that belonged to the past. What Mercy did not get was why Muungo had given her the impression he had just recently met Irene, that he had met her after his quest for Brianna had ended fruitless. Muungo was her friend! But, did she know him that well? Now that the funeral was over, was she going to sit down with Muungo and talk about this Blaise issue or not? She questioned herself.

An uneven dusty path, squeezed on both sides by stretches of half-withered Bahamas grass, connected the main road to the front yard of the palace. Barely visible broomstick traces on the ground curling away from the once immaculate facade of the palace remained behind as proof of the sweeping of the palace's front yard that had been completed the evening before. These unperturbed broomstick traces were partially covered by uncrushed fallen dry leaves; this meant that Muungo, Mercy, and Irene were among the first visitors to the royal courts of Mighang. Waiting for them at the entrance of the corridor leading to the first quarters of the palace was the elder sister to the king. The previous evening, she had told them to call her and come to the palace if by any chance the rash resurged on Mercy's skin. So, early that morning as a very feeble sun, choked by an early morning fog, announced the seventh day of the week, the rash resurged on Mercy's skin, on the same spot as the previous morning. It was unnecessary to go fetch Irene, for Irene herself had awoken early to check on Mercy. It may have seemed bizarre that an undiagnosed pathogen was not taken to a medical center for examination. But to Irene and Muungo who knew Shengweh, not just as a princess and sister to the king but as a world-renowned dermatologist, bringing Mercy to her was the smartest thing to do. Shengweh rose from her seat made of bamboo and led her guests into her mother's living room.

"The queen mother travelled to Mendenkye, her motherland, to look after her aunt, so please be lenient with me hosting you in my mother's living room. I haven't built a nest for myself yet"; Shengweh said as she smiled in an attempt at creating a more convivial atmosphere.

Shengweh's guests sat next to her on wooden stools arranged in a horseshoe spatial organization. Mercy immediately noticed the carvings on the sides of the wooden stools. The wooden structural supports connecting the seat of each stool to its base were covered with carvings in the form of human beings. Shengweh noticed the curiosity in Mercy's eyes. Mercy's gaze travelled from the stools to the masks and to the leopard skin. The masks and leopard skin were hanging on a wall tainted black by centuries of soot deposits. The room in which they were had been built during the reign of King Youngnjo'oh the architecture and the size of the openings bore witness to the age of the room. The unique architecture and decor captured Mercy's attention for a moment until Shengweh called out her name. The dermatologist asked Mercy to follow her into another room connected to the living room. That other room was as old as the living room but had undoubtedly undergone significant transformation. On the top shelf of a cupboard in the room was a TV with the mute symbol visible on the screen; the mute symbol explained why no sound came out of the speakers placed on the middle shelf. Stretching out her hand the doctor gestured to Mercy to sit on the bed as she pulled the curtain over the open door in order to create some privacy.

"Mercy, may I take a look at the rash ...the sun will soon be master of the sky." Shengweh requested, as she pulled out a pair of latex gloves from a box and delicately wore them on her hands.

Pulling her sweatpants up to the level of her knee Mercy revealed the rash on her tibia and the dermatologist drew closer to examine her. Shengweh patted the infected area to assess the tenderness and asked a few questions to her patient during the examination. With Mercy's permission Shengweh rapidly and tenderly robbed the rash infested area and observed it for a moment; new patches of rash grew in the vicinity of the original patches. A troubled look invaded Mercy's face but Shengweh nodded and reassured her that the situation was under control. The examination did not last for too long, it was over even before the morning fog had begun disappearing. Shengweh got up and walked towards one of the walls of the small, renovated bedroom. She took a cylindrical rod, the length of her arm, off a hook on the wall and then returned to her seat next to Mercy.

"I am pretty sure of what this rash is; it is as unique as a DNA can be. Permit me use some alternate medicine, okay?"

Shengweh explained to Mercy who slowly nodded as she convinced herself that everything was going to be fine.

Shengweh gestured to Mercy to pull up her sweatpants one more time. As soon as the rashes were visible Shengweh requested for Mercy's undivided attention.

"I need you to be attentive and watch this... You will understand why I said it is as unique as a DNA." Shengweh continued.

With a one-way swing of the cylindrical rod over the rash, as if it was some magic wand, Shengweh made the rash disappear.

"What the f...!" Mercy screamed. "Is this some kind of African Voodoo or what?" Mercy asked as she began moving away from the dermatologist.

"Relax, relax, relax; this is absolutely not what you think, and I will explain to you what it is you have and why it appears right before dawn and fades away once the sun rises above the horizon"

The high-pitched voice of astonishment that had initially come from Mercy, when the cylindrical rod had made her rash disappear, had drawn Muungo and Irene's attention. The couple looked at each other to validate what their next move will be. Either they walked into the room next door or remained in the living room and simply asked if all was fine. They chose the latter option, and it did take a couple of seconds before a response from Mercy came out through the door and the two got an answer.

"No ...No you don't need to worry; I just got spooked out by alternate medicine."

Mercy answered in a voice whose amplitude gradually died down. The answer did not reassure Irene, but she could see from Muungo's calm that panicking was not part of acceptable behavior. Back in the small room, where a wooden mask on the wall seemed to be an all-attentive spectator, Mercy was listening to Shengweh's explanation. According to Shengweh, the rash was caused by the leaves of a unique type of plant that grew at the entrance of the sacred forest and inside the secret quarters of the royal palace. For generations, this plant is known to produce that rash as an allergic reaction for certain people. Over the centuries, the Mighang people named that plant *Muminaong*—child of the sun. Just as children run all over the place when their parents are absent, so too does the plant-induced rash evolve. This rash will spread all over the infected skin in the absence of the sun. Legend says that the allergic reaction was once known to be unique to certain children of royal lineage, this was back in the days when the kings of Mighang married many wives with only one of them crowned as the favorite and mother of the heir. It was during this era, when gods ruled men, that the idiom *the king is missing* was used for the first time to suggest that a king had given up the ghost.

"It's a long story; but to cut the long story short, botanist have found out that this plant grows nowhere else on earth except here at the palace and the sacred forest." Shengweh summarized her exposé to avoid being a boring nerd.

Mercy asked if she should expect the rash to reappear anytime soon. She was told not to worry about the rash as long as she did not come in direct contact with the sacred plant. The patient walked out of the improvised examination room and gave a brief recital of what had transpired in the small bedroom to Irene and Muungo. The recital was one that had Irene and Muungo listening with significant attention, wondering how Mercy felt after this experience. After all, it was Mercy's first experience of African alternate medicine and God knows those things, even though they have deep scientific foundations, sometimes lack logic in the laymen's eyes. After completing missing parts of Mercy's recital, the dermatologist decided to walk her three guests up to the main road. Even though Mercy was curious to know more about the legend of the sacred plant, she was even more curious to find out if the rash will reappear the next morning. Whatever the outcome of this fascinating alternate medicine session, Mercy had just survived another story about Africa. She could not wait to get home and tell people her story.

"On another note; Muungo is anything the matter between you and Prince Wowo?" Shengweh asked.

"Hmm hmm." Muungo responded shaking his head from side to side. "Why? Did you hear about something I need to know?" he inquired. "Not officially, but I know he was here last night to inquire from the King to whom Mingo's title will be given to, now that Mingo is dead with no son to his name." Shengweh responded.

Then came a silence concerning that particular topic, but it was not a silence due to lack of words and ideas, it was a silence due to excess of words and ideas about what may have been going on behind closed doors in the palace.

"I see dark clouds in the sky." Shengweh continued, referring to the potential tension between Muungo and Wowo.

"May they bring quiet rains and not thunderstorms." Muungo looked at Shengweh and added "then it will create abundance instead of ravage."

"Walk with me for a moment." Shengweh suggested to Muungo; and both slowed down their pace, thereby falling behind Irene and Mercy.

Before heading out for an early breakfast, the last meal before they hit the road, Mercy took a quick look at her tibia. The rash had indeed gone for good. With a smile and sense of profound relief, Mercy touched the place where the rash had been. Her less imposing touch was a sign of doubt as to whether the rash was going to reappear once she touched its previous niche. Then came her sigh of almost absolute relief that the pathogen was gone to return no more. She had taken pictures of the rash-infected spot before and after her treatment, so she did have tangible proof of her story of African science, witchcraft, or whatever people called it. With a victorious smile on her face and a growling empty stomach, Mercy headed to the living room for breakfast. There, she saw some of the young boys whom she had seen on the day of the burial—the wannabe American rappers. They were busy helping move the luggage into Tahfuh's pickup. One of the boys had put on a black tee shirt with an almost faded print reading *black panthers*. This scene triggered something in Mercy's mind; how could she leave the Mighang Kingdom without getting a souvenir just like she would do on trips to Malibu, Philadelphia or Washington DC.

"Nsoh, do you know of any store where I could buy some souvenirs of my stay in Mighang?" Mercy asked.

"Well, we could stop by the Mighang Handicraft Center by the village market before taking the road to Ongola City especially since Daddy Muungo said we will be taking the back road through Bamoun Sultanate to get to Ongola City. Nsoh responded in between two bites of her piece of bread.

The itinerary of the travelers was modified so they could go buy some souvenirs for Mercy. The pickup drove off panting along the small dusty and bumpy road leading to the village market. The village market was still at the same place as it had been during Tahkuh's era. On the sides of the road were smaller paths leading to clusters of buildings; every now and then one could see smoke rising from the roof of one of the buildings—probably the kitchen. On more than one occasion the car slowed down as Muungo and Tahfuh waved their hands in the air and expressed verbal salutations to either a passerby or someone standing by the road and basking themselves in the morning sun. Most traffic signs were invisible because tall grasses and leaves from low hanging branches of trees had covered them, and so Tahfuh could barely read the recommended speed limit of 35 km/h. Yet, the driver maintained an average speed of 30 km/h during the ride to the market. This relatively lower speed gave Mercy the chance to see another face of Mighang for one last time. She thoughtfully observed a handful of cyclists pedaling their way with jugs safely secured on their bicycle carriages. Most bicycles were heading in the same direction as Tahfuh's pickup, while a few cyclists rode in the opposite direction. The jugs strapped on the bicycle carriages reminded Mercy of the burial ceremony.

During the burial festivities these same kinds of jugs were delivered with great amounts of locally made palm oil and freshly harvested palm wine. By the time these jugs were picked up they had been emptied of their content by those attending the burial. Today, the story was slightly different, full jugs headed towards the village market while the empty ones swung loosely and banged off the metal frames of the carriages of bicycles leaving the market. As the saying goes, the empty vessels literally made the loudest noise. On board the truck was a *half-empty vessel*, silent and filling itself with memories and sceneries of Mighang: the people, the green of the Grassfield, the brown color of the road and the mud bricks of the homes. In Mercy's eyes this decor was an absolute harmonious ecologic painting, one in which she felt so very much at home. She was still admiring the vegetation and civilization when the truck drove into the famous marketplace.

Carefully placing one step after another Tahfuh and his crew of exhausted passengers climbed up the dilapidated steps of an old brick building. On the building's wall part of the cement plaster had fallen off revealing mud bricks, which visibly were gradually being eroded by rain. Tahfuh and his passengers grunted in exhaustion as they made it to the building's veranda. Once on the veranda, they made their way into the house by navigating through rows of traditional apparels hung on drying lines running across the veranda. Past the rows of apparels, they entered the souvenir shop.

The decor in the souvenir shop was organized chaos; it did not follow any sort of standards. Nails were planted, here and there, and pierced deep into the brick walls. The nails either supported some suspended items or served as knot-points for ropes running from one wall to another and carrying some other commercialized items. In addition, there were no extra seats, no price tags, no fitting room or wall mirror, no trashcan, and no cash register. Instead, there were a few shelves on the back wall filled with statues, masks, and other traditional and cultural objects. Despite this chaos, the dusty and poorly displayed artifacts did not lose any of their elegance. Wooden staffs adorned with delicate carvings crowded one of the back corners of the room. On the adjacent back corner, masks and statuettes appeared alive, hungry, and as tired as their owner, Nchofong, who sat and feasted amongst them. Apart from one drum which served as a dining table to Nchofong, other drums of various sizes were tied up in batches and kept on the front corners of the room. Traditional apparels, not hung on the drying line outside or ropes inside, were spread open on some of the batches of drums. It was one of these traditional apparels lying on drums that caught Mercy's attention.

A greeting followed by a discussion in *Chirambo*, the language spoken in the Kingdom of Mighang, was initiated between Tahfuh, Muungo and Nchofong. The shop owner, like most villagers, had heard of Muungo's friend who had come all the way from the USA for Mingo's funeral. News about strangers never lingered too long when travelling from one end of the kingdom to another. Nchofong got off his seat, rinsed his hands in a bowl of water, and left his unfinished breakfast unattended and uncovered. With a broad smile revealing pieces of vegetables stuck in-between his teeth, Nchofong walked towards Mercy as he dabbed his wet hands off his slacks in an attempt to get them dry. At a step or so close to Mercy he then stretched out his hand for a handshake.

"You are a guest to my brother and therefore you are my guest, I will give you a good souvenir." Nchofong spoke as he gently shook Mercy's hand.

"You've got so many beautiful things, but I really like this apparel." Mercy replied, pointing at the apparel with her left hand while subtly wiping her right palm off her jeans pants. She had felt the moist palm of Nchofong's hand, and she did not really trust the procedure by which Nchofong had cleaned his hands before greeting her.

"That one was hand-woven and decorated with *ngrafi* embroidery by my sister. She made it all alone... from scratch." Nchofong said, "And she is the King's favorite wife." He added with pride as he began a marketing policy to win over his new client.

It was important for a piece of art to have a unique story. A story filled with strong vivid memories. The lady who, by Nchofong's claims, had handcrafted the piece of art was indeed a queen but not a sister to Nchofong. *Anaa* Fohnpah was a naturally gorgeous woman in her early twenties, and her pregnancy made her beauty glow even brighter. *Anaa* Fohnpah was standing across the street from the souvenir shop trying on a pair of flip-flops. On her right ankle a bracelet made of cowries sparkled as she raised her right foot to try on the flip-flop.

"Did she make those ankle bracelets too? Do you carry them? I love them!" Mercy hopped to another topic.

Nchofong felt stuck in his marketing snare. Nchofong stuttered as he explained to his customer that he did not carry those rare artifacts. He further explained that the beautiful ankle bracelet made of cowries was reserved for queens. A female person, no matter the age, wearing an ankle bracelet made of cowries was an *Anaa*--a queen. Queen Fohnpah's wedding band found its beauty in the contrast that existed between the white cowries and brown coffee color of her melanin-filled skin. It was this contrast and beauty that captivated most of Mercy's attention. Redirecting the conversation back to the traditional apparel that interested his client, Nchofong negotiated a lucrative deal with Tahfuh--Mercy's negotiator. At the end of the bargain, the buyer walked out of the store with more than just the traditional attire. In her shopping bag, she had a traditional wear, a handbag made from palm tree fiber, and a small calabash. All these items had been purchased at the original price of the chosen traditional attire. As the shopper and her friends galloped happily towards their car a young man approached them.

The young man had just climbed down a bike and hurried towards Muungo. He spoke to Muungo inaudibly and his right hand swung in every direction while his left hand held a helical-shaped horn. His hand gestures suggested that he was quite serious about whatever he was saying. The smile on Muungo's face vanished, his lips folded inwards and his eyes looked to the ground. With disappointed looks on his face, Muungo kept listening while sporadically contributing to the conversation. Tahfuh felt obligated to sound the car horn to remind Muungo that they were working on a very tight schedule. But Muungo did not react to the honk. So, Tahfuh stepped out of the car and joined the two men in their discussion. The young man delivered the King's message to Muungo and did not wait for an answer. The King had arrived in town that morning and had dispatched a messenger to Mingo's residence and another one to the village market. The messengers were tasked to personally inform Muungo that the King will like to meet with his American friend for about 30 minutes.

Prostrating and clapping both hands like everyone else, Mercy greeted the King of the Mighang people. She had been told it was against the tradition for anyone to shake the hand of the King, look directly into the King's eyes, or have their behind directly facing the King. Few people had had the privilege of shaking the King's hand, and each time this privilege was awarded to someone the handshake was initiated by the King himself. After clapping and bowing to the King, Mercy moved to the side freeing up the space directly in front of the King. As she moved, she thought she had caught a glimpse of him stretching out his hand towards her. When she raised her head, she indeed saw a muscular hairy arm protruding from the right sleeve of the royal *Toguh* made of fine sparkling navy-blue fibers and decorated with beautiful exotic colorful embroideries. Bracelets made of Ivory, bronze and gold perched on the King's arm close to his wrist. Mercy offered her hand in response to the King's stretched hand. Her small soft hand melted into the soft and yet imposing grip from the King's hand. As he shook her hand the bracelets gently clattered against each other, and Mercy could feel the pulse of the handshake as her breast gently bounced inside her bra.

"I do apologize for interrupting your trip Ms. Lewis." The King began speaking, breaking the silence that had followed the verbal greetings from his guests.

"Your Majesty, I am honored to be in your, and as a matter of fact I will like, if Your Majesty pleases, to take some pictures to immortalize this moment." Mercy delightfully responded and added her request.

Her words most definitely bore the sense of her feeling honored to meet an African King. The King did not respond directly to the request concerning pictures. Instead, he dove straight to the heart of the subject. He told Mercy that while he was in the town of Abakwa, a couple of days ago, he had premonitory dreams. His dreams warned him of somebody making use of certain powers found in his royal court without his permission. And when he arrived last night his sister, the dermatologist, recounted to him details of Mercy's last visit to the Palace. He continued to explain that nothing had been done that warranted them to be scared or worried about him summoning them to the palace. Instead, he would like, with Mercy's collaboration, to confirm her allergy to the plant that had allegedly caused the skin rash. Consequently, he would like to see how the cylindrical rod made the rash disappear.

By the time the King was done speaking, Mercy was in all of her states. First of all, it was not normal that the dermatologist had spoken of her condition to the so-called King without her consent. And now she was going to be used as a guinea pig for some unfounded African voodoo. Why was she not surprised by this kind of mentality from an African King? After all was it not these same African Kings who sold their subjects into slavery. Just as Mercy was about to give the King a piece of her mind, Muungo began speaking. Muungo had known Mercy for years and could tell that cracking her knuckles over and over meant she was upset. He also knew most of all the kind of the things that could upset Mercy.

112

Treating her as an object and invading her privacy were two things that evidently brought Mercy the fierce out of her shell. Muungo knew that in Mercy's book these two principles had been violated by the King. So, he had to intervene before Mercy went ghetto on this *ancestor of Kunta Kinte*. Muungo had to rapidly reconcile two distinct cultures from the same race or else this female African American Engineer would mutate into an Atlanta hood rat—as Mercy herself liked to put it.

"*Mbèh!* May I speak on behalf of Ms. Lewis?" Muungo began.

With Muungo seizing Mercy's right to response, she immediately recalled what Muungo had told her on their way to the palace. He had told Mercy that he will be the one to make sure that she was respected and that any possibility of misunderstanding during her meeting with the King be avoided. Taking over from Mercy, Muungo explained to his King, in *Chirambo*, that it was somehow against the rule in Mercy's homeland to do such a thing. Muungo reassured the King that if given a few minutes alone with Mercy he could make her understand the King's request. The King took a short moment to assess Muungo's plea while starring straight at him; uneasy because of the stare and in accordance with the tradition Muungo kept his eyes to the ground awaiting an answer from the King. At the end of his brainstorming, and without responding directly to Muungo, the King reformulated his proposition to Mercy but this time with much consideration.

"My subject has brought to my attention that things are done differently in Obama's land; Once again I am sorry to have rubbed you on the wrong side. "The King said.

His total disregard to Muungo's plea was a clear sign that Muungo had crossed the limit between him and the King. Muungo gradually guided himself back to his seat, while the King addressed Ms. Lewis.

It is quite difficult for me to explain the whole situation to you Ms. Lewis. But I will nonetheless give you the main idea and the final decision will be yours. A long time ago after the Kingdom of Mighang had come into existence, rumors, rolling down the slope of the green stuffed highlands of the Grassfield like loose rocks after an earthquake, made mention of the presence of a white man and his troops. The white man's troops were at war with the Bafut people, another kingdom of the Grassfield. The white man had come from the faraway land of Germany. Dr. Eugene Zingraff was his name. Hearing about his visit to the Babungo Kingdom, the then Mighang King was worried about a German invasion of his kingdom. In preparation for war and invasion, His Majesty the King of Mighang rallied his allies, the King of Ngohmbi and the King of Mendenkye. He suggested that they each send a wife and five of their children, especially the princes who were potential heirs to the throne, to a haven. The King of Mighang detailed his plan to his peers encouraging them to pick amongst their many wives the ones who were sisters or close relatives to his beloved wife, so that they all could go seek refuge in the same kingdom. This kingdom where they had to seek refuge was located North of the River Nun and basked in the mesh of the tributaries of the River Benue. It was home to a savanna vegetation perched on a fertile and well irrigated plateau, and by virtue of its altitude and the warfare culture of its inhabitants, it was an ideal fortress where the queens and children would be safe. After a prolonged discussion the kings sealed a blood pact and promised to look after each other's descendants and keep their royal lineages alive. This alliance between the kings and their kingdoms was made even stronger because, as I told you earlier, their wives were sisters-- daughters from the same Royal family from Bankim in the Adamawa plateau. Of the three half-sisters the queen of Mighang was the oldest.

The queens, some of the princes, and their servants disguised themselves as Fulani men and women travelling up north to the Adamawa Plateau—the land of Bankim. Alongside their luggage, servants, guards, and children, the queens travelled through a longer but less travelled route that went through the Bamoun Sultanate and North of it to the land of Bankim. The Bankims are relatives to the *BaNdop* and were certainly not going to deny asylum to their daughters and their households.

Unfortunately, for the three Kings, Dr. Zingraff had troops monitoring the route between the Bamoun Sultanate and the Adamawa Plateau--two areas where he was very unpopular. His soldiers attacked the queens' caravan. A bloody and rowdy battle followed, but the people of the Mighang Kingdom were no match to the guns of the German troops. The queen of Mighang, in order to save the pride of her king and husband, who had devised the escape plan, called for peace and accepted to be held captive while the other queens returned to their kingdoms. In addition to being held captive, the queen from the Mighang Kingdom offered ivory to her captors in order to buy the freedom of the children. This ivory was originally intended to be a token of appreciation to the queens' family in the Adamawa plateau. But when confronted by Zingraff's troops, the queens had claimed to be ivory dealers. The queen of Mighang, thanks to her fluency in Fulani, was able to make her captors believe that she was only just a traveler from the Adamawa Plateau and not the wife of a King. Her captors were convinced that she was merely returning home to her family, and after keeping the spoils for themselves they decided not to honor their deal. They decided to send the queen and her son to the German plantations, despite the deal of liberating children. These German plantations were found at the coast, a short distance from Bimbia, the same place where slave ships departed for the Americas.

Upon the return of the queens of Ngohmbi and Mendenkye to their kingdoms in *BaNdop*, the king of Mighang learned of the misfortune that had befallen his kingdom. He grieved for his beloved wife and son who had been captured by the German troops. Every day that went by his pain grew bigger, dug deeper, and weighed heavier for he had not only lost the most beloved of his queens and his beloved son, but also his friend and advisor who had led the expedition and had been made captive by Zintgraff's men. That friend of his was the ancestor of your friend Muungo.

The King paused for a moment, giving time to Mercy to finally gain her breath, she had dived so deep into the story that she seemed to have stopped breathing. Her head turned to the side, and she looked at Muungo imagining what his ancestor would have looked like.

"Your Majesty if I may ask, how does that story relate to me?" Her voice sounded calm, but it was made crooked by a shy raspy tone due to her prolonged silence. One could feel in her voice that the storm of anger had died down. She cleared her throat in order to get rid of the raspy tone; while she closed her eyes and pressed her lips sealed so as to control a yawn. The King continued the story.

The King's grief and loneliness was so profound that he decided to temporarily abdicate the throne. All through the king's absence, his twin brother was the regent king. The later took overpower and ruled over the kingdom. The transition was not too complicated for the people of Mighang, considering that in our culture special roles, privileges, and names are prescribed to twins. You see at the heart of our culture twins, albinos, and children born in feet-first position are considered special gifts from the gods and their parents count themselves blessed. Thus, Mighang considered herself blessed for having twin as a King.

On the unforgettable cold, dark, windy, and silent night of the abdication rites, the king and his twin brother were presented before the members of the sacred society, the King's councilors, and the war Generals of the kingdom. The deepest secrets of the kingdom were passed to the king's brother, the most sacred gashes were made on hidden parts of his body, and the king-to-be swore on his life and that of his descendants to rule in accordance to the traditions and to return power to the king upon his return or hand over kingship to the king's descendants if ever they requested that it be done. Towards the end of the rites, the natural leader was asked to leave the room before mystical powers were transferred over to his temporal replacement; tradition forbade and still forbids that two kings meant for the same throne be in the enthronement room at the same time else their totems will affront one another until one of the totems and his owner die. Following this warning, the natural King talked with his twin brother for a brief moment and after confiding in his Generals, the abdicating King carried his grief and loneliness in his luggage, headed out, and went in search of his wife, son, and friend.

Lo and behold the King never returned. It is believed that the King died while in search for his family and friend. On that day when it was confirmed that the King was not coming back, the sacred, encrypted, and dreaded expression *"the king has gone missing"* was whispered in every household and every gathering while the loud melancholic voice of the town crier propagated the sad news. That sad news meant that the hand-woven royal tunic and the colorful royal hat adorned by bright multicolored feathers of majestic birds had been found somewhere perched on the King's spear, while the King himself, immortal amongst the mortal, had vanished into thin air. This is what it means to all the *BaNdop* clans when they say their King is dead.

Legend has it that because of her beautiful fine silhouette, her thick silky black hair and her sparkling dark complexion, the queen of Mighang was not used as plantation worker when her captors handed her over to the slave trader. An owner of a slave ship bought her and her son. The ship owner tried in vain to win her affection and make of her his concubine. Alas, the grieving and lonely woman died on the way to the Americas. Some say she died same day at the same time as her husband, because their union had been predicted by the gods. Her son may have made it to the Americas or stayed at the plantation, much is not known of what became of him after his mother's death.

It is said that till this day, while in the afterlife, the King still goes in search for this queen and his son. He is capable of doing this thanks to a well-known Baya'a alchemist, Nanguele Dumo, whom he had met on his way to Bimbia. The Alchemist's descendant, the Alchemist Tetou Awouba, talks of a story in their family history in which his ancestor had given the King, and a few other people of integrity who had been separated from their family by the gruesome sin of slave trade, the possibility of reincarnating themselves into hurricanes at their time of death. This permitted the King and his friends to destroy many of the slave ships and to even attack, till this day, some of the land that welcomed the slaves. These attacks are in retaliation to the forceful separation of the people from their loved ones.

Now back to our story. Thirteen moons after the departure of the King of Mighang in search of his family, the chief priest of *Pa'ah Nguon* announced to the people that he had received a vision. In his vision, he was told that the king and the queen were no more. He nonetheless reassured the people that the prince had survived. The *Quifohn (Ngumba)*, met in the sacred hut of the palace and agreed that the younger brother of the dead King, the regent King, had to stay in power until the crown prince returns alive. In order to be sure that a usurper did not claim the throne, the council decided to consult the gods of the land. They were told that the late queen and her son always had an allergy to a plant that grew only in one of two places, the entrance of the sacred forest, *Pa'ah Nguon*, and next to the sacred hut in the palace. The younger half-sisters of the late queen confirmed the words of the chief priest. After which the chief priest said these word "many moons and season will come, the River Nun will shrink and expand, and then one day the rightful heir will blossom like a flower in season. He will rise at dawn and bow to the scepter of his father."

The King adjusted the sleeves of his traditional regalia and softly moistened his dry lips with his fairly wet tongue. It is forbidden for a King to dine or drink in the presence of mere mortals. So, though the King was thirsty he insisted on finishing his narration. Facing Mercy's direction, he could sense that she was struggling to make the link between her experience and the story; he let her raise her head toward the ceiling and focus for a while in her analysis then he said:

"You came to this land, you had an allergic reaction to the plant, and the allergy was healed thanks to the scepter of the rightful King."

He paused for a moment, as if to let his conclusion penetrate Mercy's cloudy and foggy mind.

"You can either accept to try the experiment or not to; the choice is yours. But please feel free to take some pictures and do take your time to think over what you just heard." The King concluded.

Silence ruled over the setting where the King had received his guests. The distant voices of children playing in the courtyard, the annoying cry of a baby, and the recurrent braying and spurting of a buck in heat were the only sounds that threatened the silence. The King rose from his throne with the aid of his staff. As he rose, everyone else rose as a sign of allegiance to the throne. Mercy was still daydreaming when she felt Muungo gently hold her by the arm and make her stand up as the King rose from his seat. The King retired to his Chambers for about ten minutes. When he returned, with wet lips and a half smile on his face making him look refreshed and unstressed, he took a number of pictures with his guests— especially Mercy. Once again, he retired to his chambers. But this time before retiring the King asked the messenger who had met Muungo at the market to take the guests on a tour of the Royal Courts while he entertained a private discussion with Muungo.

The guests walked around taking pictures and asking questions about the things they saw and the places they were forbidden to visit. All through the photo shoot Mercy's mind, and probably that of all the other guests, was ruminating the

119

story she had just heard from the King. At the end of their tour, Mercy asked the messenger if she could meet with the King one more time. The messenger spoke with one of the King's guards and then he told Mercy the King was not going to be available for the next two to three weeks. He told her that the King had concluded his discussion with Muungo and had immediately left. He had gone on a trip while they were visiting the palace and he did not wish that his destination be revealed, or his personal number be called. The special guest did not insist, they waved goodbye to a crowd of curious children that had been following her the during the tour. They stomped their feet on the first step to shake the dust off their feet. They climbed up the steps, mounts of cements with minute fissures due to changing temperatures and reached the veranda where Muungo stood ready to explode.

Muungo's chest was raised up and his nostrils wide open, his eyebrows curled inward and downward with the weight of his frustration. That look was one which Mercy and Irene instantaneously recognized and did not like.

"Darling what is the matter?" Irene asked.

"Nothing. Nothing. Nothing" Muungo replied. But the fact that he repeated the word three times was proof that there was an underlying problem.

"You are such a traitor! I can't even believe you stoop that low?" He continued, but this time he was addressing Tahfuh who had frozen after ascending the steps with the ladies.

"What did you expect me to do? You were not here, and Mingo had no male child." Tahfuh replied. His tone grew louder towards the end of his sentence as he mustered courage or what seemed to be courage.

"Couldn't we talk about this as brothers? Oh, not at all! It was easier to work with Wowo and connive against your own blood." Muungo yelled.

For a moment Tahfuh tried to explain himself but it only pushed Muungo to raise his voice and raise his temper even higher.

"Keep this in mind: 'if there is no enemy within then the enemy outside can do us no harm'; remember that." Muungo said.

The two cousins argued, and their voices grew louder and louder. The ladies tried to calm Muungo, but their soft female voices were drowned in the loud deep male voices of the cousins. A distance away, at the end of the path leading from the main road to the palace, Prince Wowo, his younger brother, the oldest prince, and some village elders were seen walking towards the Muungo. The group of men walking towards the palace had kept quiet but had made sure that the special traditional regalia held tight in Prince Ngeu Wowo's hand, which was only worn by people of late Mingo's rank, could be seen swinging over Wowo's left hand.

"Who do you think you are?" Muungo asked as he turned in the direction of Prince Wowo and his gang.

"I am what you are not and will never be!" Wowo retorted. Wowo and his gang climbed up the steps and came to a face-to-face confrontation with Muungo.

"That's what we will see!' Muungo moved swiftly between Wowo's group and his cousin Tahfuh. With an angry swift swing of the hand, Muungo knocked the traditional regalia off Wowo's hand and to the ground. One of Wowo's group members screamed out "Sacrilege!" The unexpected, unimaginable, and unavoidable had happened.

Photons plunging in the pond's clear water revealed the interlocked flat stones, once dirty-grey but now green-layered and brown-layered, which were harmoniously stacked next to each other at the bottom and sides of the circular pond. The pond was lodged between two giants roots of an oak tree. These two roots shot out of the stem, diverged away from one another over a distance of about two meters only to converge and crisscross further in front. These two roots created a circular bowl-shaped space delimiting the expansion of the pond. Buried under the mass of clear water and hidden in between the stones were two or three water inlets, in the form of cold-water geysers, from which water enter the pond in a pulsatile manner. For each geyser the pressure of the outgoing water pushed against the water mass above it, and by so doing created a short-lived pulsating bump on the water surface. The intermittent bubbling was located directly above the submerged geysers. It was this incoming water which replenished the pond. It was this pulsating nature that made people believe in the legend of *Anaa* Mighang.

Legend says *Anaa* Mighang was the first mother of the tribe, tired of not seeing death had asked to be buried alive underneath the stones lining the bottom of the pond. She was transformed into the cold-water geysers that never went dry because she had asked the gods to transform her immortality into an ever-flowing spring. Some people even go as far as claiming that this sacrifice explains the healing power of the water from the pond and the abundance of maritime life in the water bodies all over the kingdom.

The overflowing water from the everlasting pond produced a splashing sound as it crawled over the stones and roots that formed the rims of the bowl-shaped pond. Fresh and withered petals, sepals, and leaves, and bits of sticks floated on the water course created by the spilled-over water produced from the overflowing pond. These debris navigated away from the pond carried by an endless troop of excess water molecules that paved their way, diligently eroding the dirt from the pond to the nearby thick and dark raffia bushes where the water disappeared under the decaying leaves and bamboo.

The flat stones in the pond were covered with slimy brown and green algae, and green spongy moss. The moss crept out of the pond and spread onto the bark covering the oak tree's roots and stem. The green algae were not the only green magic found in the mythical pond, there were fallen green leaves floating in the water. These green leaves falling from the oak tree were the tree's resources most used by the villagers. Originally, these leaves and broken branches, bullied by the disarrayed air current, powerlessly took a dive from the oak tree's network of thick branches and landed in the pond. Once in the pond, the fallen particles generated shock waves whose reflected ripples, traversing the water, tossed the leaves up and down. It was common for mothers to come and collect these leaves to use them with water from the pond in bathing their newborns on the day of the naming ceremony. The leaves were believed to have therapeutic virtues that protected the newborns from ailments caused by the sins of their parents.

The shock waves traversing the water were even greater when generated by villagers plunging their calabashes into the pond when in need of the sparkling and curative cold water from the pond. It was because of this beautiful, natural, and mystical setting that children spent most of their time at the pond when commissioned to fetched water or leaves. The sounds of children's voices, their clapping, their drumming of their empty vessels, and their dancing for their friends and the leaves and sticks racing out of the pond, combined with the water's splashing and birds tweeting to produce a unique melody. A melody and scenery that captured Mercy's attention when she went alongside Nsoh to fetch water from the pond.

Nsoh had just generated an avalanche of ripples as she scooped water from the pond with her bucket. Lifting the water-filled bucket in the air, Nsoh grunted gently as she attempted to place the bucket on Mercy's head. She hoped Mercy would be able to carry her bucket of water like every village girl who fetched water from the pond—walking straight and tall with a bucket of water balanced on her head. Unfortunately, the *katta*, circular-shaped bundle of dry and soft leaves and grass serving as head cushion, danced all over the place on Mercy's head as she struggled to adjust her posture for Nsoh to successfully place the bucket. One little girl who was squatting by the pond playing with her distorted reflection on the water caught sight of Nsoh's multiple tries at placing the bucket on Mercy's head. The girl could not comprehend why a grown woman could not carry a bucket on her head, especially when she and other kids were experts at the task. The little girl interrupted her fun time and immediately drew the attention of the other children around her towards Mercy and Nsoh.

Finally, Nsoh placed the bucket on Mercy's head after an intense struggle. Nsoh's tired arms immediately dropped to her sides and her biceps and triceps took some time off to recuperate from the bucket-loading experiment and the nerve-wrecking gaze of the children. Less than three seconds later, Mercy's bucket slipped from side to side on her *katta*, while drops of water spilled out of the bucket over and over again and at a faster rate each time. It was a clue for Nsoh to rush to her rescue.

Time stood still for a couple of seconds, no other sound but the sound of Nsoh and Mercy's shifting footsteps was heard. Everyone at the pond was waiting to see if Mercy was going to be able to regain her balance with the bucket on her head. The struggle to keep the bucket balanced grew intense. Nsoh's hands began quivering with warm drops of sweat rolling from the arm, pass the elbow, to the biceps. Nsoh rested her biceps and triceps for a short moment and then returned to lifting and holding the bucket above Mercy's head, while Mercy tried to gather her momentum and gain stability. Despite her quivering, sweaty, and tired arms, Nsoh once again gently lowered and placed the bucket on the head of a Mercy who was now squatting.

The little girl and a few other kids giggled as Mercy struggled to balance the bucket of water while rising from her squatting position and attempting to stand up straight. Mercy fumbled with her load: one leg placed here then moved over there, and then one hand holding the bucket's rim at the spot where Nsoh had asked her to hold, and then that same hand hopping to another spot on the rim of the bucket. Mercy tried to gain and maintain her equilibrium and to balance the bucket on her head. But her staggering created a swirling pattern in the water in the receptacle. The water swirled faster and bashed harder against the sides of the bucket. This aquatic chaos repeatedly took Mercy off balance and in turn increased the swirling of the water as Mercy tried to find a stable posture. One excess step and the bucket came crashing to the ground. The kids burst into a cascade of rowdy mocking laughs. The mockery ended up abruptly when Nsoh threw an angry look at the kids with her two tiny eyes glittering on a frown-filled face.

The two ladies walked home with just one bucket of water. Nsoh cheered Mercy up with stories of how she too fumbled with utensils common to village lifestyle every time she visited the village. Captured by the narration of a story about how Nsoh had once poorly wrapped fresh corn paste in banana leaves causing the *kighang*, the corn pudding, to spill out of its wrapping during the cooking process, Mercy slowly found the fun in her failed water fetching adventure. This fun relaxed the tension in the atmosphere and prompted Mercy to also tell her own jokes about her failed cooking sessions with her mother.

Mercy recalled one thanksgiving when she was given the unique task of preparing the collard green. The bunch of green leaves laid on her mother's kitchen counter, and the teenager whom she was back then spent more time shuffling the music in her handheld device instead of accomplishing her task. When push came to shove and all the food was ready except for the traditional thanksgiving vegetable, Mercy's mother began shouting out the teenager's name, scolding her for lazing around instead of helping out with preparing the family meal.

The infuriated teenager had rushed into the kitchen picked up a knife and hurriedly and carelessly began slicing through the flaccid leaves. In her teenager rage, the force and emotion exerted on the knife caused the knife to cut rapidly and easily through the leaves. One cut through the leaves, then another, then another and then in the blink of an eye the knife cut into her index finger. Few microseconds went by as the yellowish fatty tissue of the cut-open index finger progressively went red with blood racing through the capillaries. Then came the voluminous flow of blood as it gushed out of the finger, dropped on the table and then the vegetables.

That thanksgiving kicked off with that cut, an unfortunate event that rallied the entire family around Mercy. Mercy quickly connected this memorable blunder to the present event; the death of Mingo had allowed her to have a new family around her. Sometimes it takes a slip for one to land on a gold mine, at times the trip of a fall helps us go pass the finish line in time. This meeting with her new family was going to end soon, but it had come with its own drama, its own family drama.

The trip back to Bell Town had been rescheduled and Mercy had chosen to stay busy in order to keep her mind from thinking about all what she had heard and seen at the King's Palace. In order to stay busy, she had decided to go fetch water and then cook with Nsoh. Looking down at the piece of broken bucket in her hand, she doubted if it had been a great idea. Because once the jokes had died down her mind returned to all the drama she had lived in the last few days: her possible genetic connection to people of Mighang, her refusal to take the sacred shrub's genetic exam, and the 7 days' ultimatum given to Muungo to forever leave his homeland due to the altercation between him and the village elders.

Mercy noisily exhaled moments after she and Nsoh had begun walking up the path leading away from the pond. That noisy exhale was the sound of the exasperation created by the questions without answers and the worries wrestling in Mercy's mind. Like a Frisbee disc, she tossed the piece of broken bucket into the bushes ahead of them. The gesture caught Nsoh's attention, and her eyeballs swung to her right taking a quick glance at Mercy. At that specific moment Nsoh's eyes made contact with Mercy's and she could not pretend she had not glanced at Mercy.

"Do you know Blaise?" Mercy asked in a low tone as if she feared that the breeze blowing past them was going to carry the question to an undesired destination.

Nsoh stayed silent for a moment, leaving room only for the noise of their sluggish footsteps and their loud heavy breath as they walked up a slope. Finally, she answered somewhere in between two loud breaths.

"Aunty that is not a question which I should answer."

"Why?" Mercy asked right back before Nsoh's next exhale was over. "Why can't you answer?" She doubled her question with a barely perceptible sound of frustration. "You do know your Uncle is hiding the truth from some people? Right?"

"Aunty, Daddy Muungo is the one who can give you an answer; please I am just trying to deal with my own uncertain future right now." Nsoh replied. The last part of her answer bore so much weight, that it seemed Nsoh felt a little better after admitting she had a bigger fish to fry.

Mercy looked at the girl and realized that Nsoh was indeed dealing with something worse than what Mercy was trying to drag her into. She too had sensed the relief that had sprouted in Nsoh's voice after those last words. Nsoh's strides grew stronger and her footsteps firmer; a warrior marching onward and ready to deal with her fate.

"The King is giving away my father's inheritance and wants me to get married to a Prince if I wish to keep any of the inheritance. All this drama because my father had no male child, and my uncle cannot fully play the role of a King's advisor while living abroad especially because some people believe he is trying to use his acquired western mentality to destabilize the cultural niche of our people. So, they have exiled my uncle from the village." Nsoh choked towards the end of her sentence, the emotion in her words had invaded her voice, and the strong hand of powerlessness squeezed her throat tight.

The relief she had exhibited moments ago was gone in a flash. Her feet hit the ground with more force than before, she snorted and spat into the bushes as her eyes grew watery and red.

Mercy paused at the sound of this other revelation, while Nsoh continued walking away, stomping one foot after another as a way of expressing her frustration.

"What has your mother said about this? For God's sake isn't she the widow in this case and has absolute say over how things should go?" Mercy inquired, while shaking her head in disbelief and dropping a smaller piece of the broken bucket which she had held in her hand all this while.

Mercy resumed her walk, hastening her footsteps to catch up with Nsoh's answer. Expressed in a universal language, Mercy clearly read the answer to her question off Nsoh's face. Nsoh's lips were folded inwards and, just like the rest of her body, it trembled with anger. Her mother had not done anything to oppose the King's decision; not that she could do anything even if she wanted to. As a matter of fact, her mother had already met the prince in question and had been repeatedly urging Nsoh to meet with him since the first few days following Mingo's funeral.

The two had carried their silence and frustrations to the top of the hilly road from where they took a glimpse of the sun setting behind the savannah. The faint yellow-red rays of the setting sun were uncomfortable to their eyes and so they dropped their heads down, kept their eyes directed towards the red dusty ground beneath their feet, and continued their walk home. Every now and then they looked up for a quick capture of the road ahead of them and once again the glare from the setting sun forced them to rapidly look away. In between the distant setting sun and the two ladies at the top of the slope, one could have an aerial view of the Mingo-Tahkuh family residence.

Crisscrossing arrays of buildings covered in aluminum coated panels; brand new panels covered newer buildings while old rusted panels, weighed down by logs of wood and other heavy debris, rested on the roofs of older buildings. The geometrical orientation of the building blocks interrupted the stretch of shrubs and grasses covering the Mingo-Tahkuh family estate--this old and vast estate which the *Ngumba* had now decided to take away from Mingo and his family. At the heart of the cluster of buildings was a vast courtyard lined by a layer of red ground hardened by the many steps that had trampled over it for many generations. This courtyard was also the place where the tents had been set up for the funeral. This aerial view of the courtyard from the top of the hill, more precisely at the exact spot where Nsoh and Mercy were, was charming and bewitching. Above the battered red ground of the courtyard, the leaves on the branches waved with the wind, and the smoke from the kitchens sneaked as it rose to the sky. It was at the top of this hill that many generations ago, Tahkuh had looked back at his home for the last time before heading to the last mission assigned to him by the king. From the top of the hill, Nsoh's and Mercy hastened their steps as the vertical component of gravitational pull acted on their steps and hastened them down the slope. All the while resisting the pull due the gravity, the ladies noticed a group of people walking from the main road into the courtyard of the family residence.

"Looks like we have visitors." Mercy noted audibly.

"They are certainly coming to express their condolences to Mama; we better hurry so we can attend to our guests." Nsoh responded as she allowed herself to be pulled by gravity and walked a little faster down the slope while masterfully gripping the rims of the bucket of water resting on her head. Mercy followed right away her eyes glued to the magic with which Nsoh used to keep water in her bucket while hurrying down the slope. Deep in her mind Nsoh had a sudden dark thought: "Nothing could guarantee that these *visitors* were not coming to expel Muungo and his family out of the kingdom before the deadline."

A silver-colored Sports Utility Vehicle (SUV) was parked next to the stony east wall of late Mingo's house and opposite to the withering shrubs that stood in-between the northern bushes and the grid of houses. Village kids gathered all around the vehicle to admire its fine contours, imposing size, and technological aura. The back-passenger window had been lowered all the way down, so the kids devoured, with their restless eyes, the black and shiny leather seats and the fluorescent dash populated by the touchscreen interfaces of the vehicle control system. In contrast to Tahfuh's pickup truck, this SUV was bigger and larger, probably engineered by Americans. The dusty untarred roads had laid a layer of dust on the lower part of the SUV's chassis. But this did nothing but gave the car the appearance of the mechanical beast used on the Safari road trips seen on TV commercials.

"Cho! Cho! Cho! Cho! Cho! Yi ni moto preshident!" (This is the President's car!); one of the kids exclaimed in *Chrambo* as he stared at the car with is mouth agape in astonishment, unaware of the laughter which his inaccurate conclusion had created. A swarm of kids, then another swarm, and another swarm of kids ran toward the electromechanical beauty, contemplating every detail of its imposing artistic, mechanical, and technological beauty: its silver color, its finely defined curved and big rig tires, and self-adjusting sunroof.

Across from Mingo's house, in a poor lit room, that was used as an outdoor bathroom and had an atmosphere filled by the stench of damp earth, there was another kid. This kid's fate was being decided in the living room. Her name: Nsoh; her crime: being fatherless and not being born a male child.

Minutes earlier, Nsoh and Mercy had arrived home and had noticed the gathering of kids around the Car. Mercy had walked straight to her room to get her belongings and then go take her shower. Nsoh, had begun walking towards her father's house as well when a queen stepped out of one of the other houses and called her to the side.

"Nsoh, come here you cannot go there my daughter," the queen said.

Immediately Nsoh's imagination guided her to what could possibly be happening. The prince, her supposedly husband-to-be, had come to meet her family. He had come alongside some members of his family to officially asked Nsoh's hand in marriage.

Nsoh froze at the request of the queen. Her heavy bucket of water resting on her head, she felt conquered by all sorts of sensations; she felt as throwing up, peeing on herself, bursting into laughter, tearing down into tears, or just vanishing from the earth's surface. She turned around with the bucket of water and walked into that exterior room of the old building, that room which was now used as an external bathroom. Nsoh slowly put her bucket down on the damp red floor and sat on a wooden stool located at the center of the room. Though the atmosphere in the room was filled with the smell of the wet dirt that made the floor, Nsoh's olfactory sub-system did not detect the smell. The legs of the wooden stool left pressure marks on the damp ground beneath them and revealed various positions where the stool had been placed earlier. In the same way, Nsoh's father's death was digging deeper and deeper into her heart revealing the true faces of many; had he been alive most of the conflicts and confusion would not have happened.

Suddenly, celebratory yodeling and thunders of applause emanating from the living room of late Mingo's house reached Nsoh in the bathroom. The sounds invaded the calm of the bathroom and even shook its old feeble frame. It took Nsoh by surprise. she had expected that whatever celebration was taking place, the celebrants would have waited for her father's guts to be spilled in his grave before they all go into party mode.

In the living room, after a celebratory yodeling came what sounded like a speech. Nsoh's ear lobes stretched wider and her head turned sideways as she adjusted her posture to listen to what was being said in the living room. From the first decibels she immediately recognized the voice, it was her uncle Muungo who was speaking.

"The sage among our people say that one must cut down a tree in order to make a drum. We did not cut down the biggest tree of this family, instead it was thrown down by strong winds. Nonetheless we are not going to let it rot away, with the help of an extra pair of hands we will sculpt the most beautiful drum and make vibrations go from the banks of the Nun to those of Benue!"

Once more screams of celebration rose and this time, they overshadowed Muungo's voice. Nsoh rose from her stool, walked out of the bathroom and through the withering shrubs, and headed towards the dense bushes surrounding the building. The cracking sound of the dry leaves and branches crushed underneath her feet were lost in the loud shouts and claps that came from the living room. Nsoh walked through the bushes, crossing the family burial ground and the place where the path that connected Mabangoh's hut to Tahkuh's hut had once run. The century old grass that had covered this path were split apart by Nsoh as she furiously walked away from the family residence. Blades of spear grass cut through her skin, thorns from wild plants clung to her feet and clothes. Yet, Nsoh kept on walking away having as her only companion the sound of her heavy breath from exhaustion and the tickle of the sweat drops that ran down on her back.

"Can I come in?" Irene's shaky voice came after a few knocks on the door of the room assigned to Mercy and Nsoh.

"Sure Irene, come in." Mercy replied as she recognized Irene's voice and lifted her eyes off the screen of her cellphone which she had been holding in one hand.

Like a drum roll, the squeaky sound from the poorly lubricated door hinges preceded the white face, bulging red eyes, and trembling limbs of Irene. She walked straight towards Mercy and sat next to her.

"Do you happen to know where Nsoh has gone to?" She asked Mercy.

"No! Why? Is she missing?" Mercy questioned as the fear of a missing Nsoh pulled her voice one pitch higher.

"I think so, we have been looking for her and calling her cell phone for almost one hour now; we have been screaming her name and still no response." Irene announced to Mercy, randomly pausing in her articulation of words without any respect for punctuation as she tried to subdue sobs that were fighting their way out of her fear-constricted airways.

About an hour ago, after Muungo and the family had decided to introduce Nsoh to her fiancé, they had, in accordance with tradition, dispatched some ladies who were wives and mothers to go bring Nsoh. Irene and Nsoh's mother had both risen from their seats to go look for the future bride. Both ladies' behinds swung in simple harmonic motion as they walked, with refined feminine delicacy, crossing the living room space and heading outside.

"Nsoh! Nsoh oh!" The ladies began calling.

No answer came their way. The young darkness had driven away the many admirers of the SUV, thus there was nobody to go looking for Nsoh other than the two ladies. They visited every building that made up the family residence and all the buildings of their surrounding neighbors' homes looking from Nsoh, but they could not even detect the trace of her body odor.

"I saw her walking in that direction about 50 minutes ago"; the queen who had asked Nsoh not to go into the living room reported to Irene. This queen, who was the future groom's mother, had also walked out of the living room and joined the two ladies in their quest because she had sensed that something strange was going on.

"My daughters go look for her, I will stall my family for a while... I think she might have gone into hiding somewhere not too far from the house." The queen told the two mothers and then turned around and headed back for the living room.

It was not unusual for young future brides to go into hiding prior to their official engagement, especially when their future partners had been chosen by someone else. Even the girls caught by the special unit of *tchinda*, royal guards, trained at scouting and catching wives for the King usually ran off for a few days after they had been picked as wives for the King. It usually took the young girls a time of tears and fear before they were either forced or convinced into accepting their new lives as wives of the King. In her days as a young girl, the reigning queen and mother of the future groom had run off for almost a week before her parents convinced her to go live with her King and husband. Here she was 27 years later, mother of the heir to the throne. "We are nothing but young beings in a very old world," she thought as she appeared in the living room confronting hungry eyes and thirsty ears waiting for information to devour.

"Our daughter has gone to fetch water, and then clean herself, so let us patiently wait for her" The queen announced as she went back and occupied her place in the living room.

A hand scraped the bottom of a bowl as it cleared the last grains of salted boiled peanuts which the Tahkuh family had offered to their illustrious guests. The conversation between the two families had slowly died down; it had gone from loud jokes and uncontrolled laughter to whispers and avoidance of eye contact. The last most important statement, before the sweet conversation had turned to sour whispers, had been made by the queen when she had announced that Nsoh was getting ready and will be joining them in a short while. This proclamation was already about forty-five minutes old, but the wait had seemed to be 2 hours long. Even Muungo was becoming nervous about the whole situation, because his wife and sister-in-law had not yet returned with any updates on Nsoh's whereabouts.

Muungo slowly rose from his chair, the squeaky sound from the joints of the chair's wooden frame tore through the almost silent atmosphere in the living room and attracted the attention of all the people in the room. With a deer-in-the-headlight look, Muungo froze and gazed all around the room. His eyes made contact with other eyes whose eyeballs were bulging out

134

of the eye sockets—expressing their curiosity at the abnormally prolonged wait for the future bride.

Muungo's eyes and lips shrunk, and his nostrils widened, he put on his serious face and walked out of the living room. No one was bold enough to interrupt his silent threat or intercept his rebellious walk. One of the elderly men from the future groom's family shook his head from side to side in disapproval and muttered the words.

"America, America."

He cursed that nation of freedom that gave younger men, like Muungo, the guts to ignore village elders like himself. According to the tradition, Muungo would have risen and politely asked for permission from the elderly men before walking out on them.

Outside and unaware of the old man's feelings, Muungo's head pivoted about his neck as his now widened eyes scanned the courtyard in an attempt to detect silhouettes in the darkness; a darkness whose thickness was perturbed by the light rays that escaped through the cracks on the wooden windows and doors of the buildings making up the family residence.

"Where has she gone to?" Muungo asked the three silhouettes which were approaching him.

"She is not around; she probably has run away." Nsoh's mother retorted before sniffing and speaking in between sobs:

"Mingo you have finished me! You have made me a widow and now my daughter is gone. You never told me about this kind of tradition and forced marriage for anyone of your beloved daughters. Is this the Medical School you promised she was going to attend; Mingo you have broken my heart oh!"

"Please; this neither the time nor the place." Muungo whispered with force, and instantaneously looked over his shoulder worried whether the people in the living room had heard either the cry or the whisper.

"Wow … Oh my God! I never expected this from you Muungo." Mercy said in a disappointing tone that ended with a loud sigh. She had walked out of her room with Irene and joined the search party soon after she was told that Nsoh may have run away.

"Imagine someone did this to your daughter Wilanne; how would you feel about it? She stressed on every syllable as she addressed Muungo.

Avoiding even the slightest and fastest eye contact with Mercy and ignoring her criticism, Muungo lowered his head, licked his lower lip, then turned around and walked back towards the living room. The guests were on their feet when he entered, they certainly had sensed that their presence had triggered undesired tension.

An old man from the future groom's family spoke to Muungo as soon as his eyes, ill-equipped with a vision depleted by the effect of *afofo*--a locally brewed liquor, blurrily identified Muungo.

"My son, our people say that the fight between the hunter and the game is not of any concern to the one eating the game once it's been cooked. You invited us to eat, but the game had not yet been caught. Let us not fill our stomachs with *fufu* in the absence of the soup. We will go fetch the palm wine while you catch the game and prepare the soup."

An affirmative chorus of "uh huh" came from the groom's family as approval to these words of wisdom from the oldest man in the future groom's inner circle.

"Can a mockingbird refuse to echo a great melody?" Muungo asked and the people responded once again in chorus "uh uh."

"Our father has spoken, and our ears have heard. If a grasscutter escapes from your trap, do not worry for it has gone to fatten itself for the next catch. My son here, our queen, my father and you my family will be called upon once we have everything set." Muungo completed his short speech. It was the future groom, his mother and the old man that he had addressed as son, mother, and father respectively.

136

The silver-colored SUV drove off into the night, its red taillight lighting up with every tap of the brake pedal by the driver whenever he slowed down and avoided the potholes and other very rough road topography on the driveway. The expected groom to be and his family left the Tahkuh's family residence with mixed feelings. Mixed feelings were also shared in the Mingo-Tahkuh family residence.

"Muungo, I'll like to talk to you." Mercy proposed.

"Can we do this later; I need to make sure we find Nsoh as soon as possible"

"No, we cannot do this later, except you want to find Nsoh and make her run for good this time." Mercy responded.

"Do you know where she is?" Muungo asked.

"Maybe I do, maybe I do not; but I know what is bothering her."

"This is neither the time nor the place Mercy; Believe me there is more to this which you do not understand." Muungo said in a voice forcefully mastered to mask his anger.

"Oh really? I won't understand? A teenage girl forcefully sent to marriage? A teenage boy forsaken by his father?" Mercy responded as she forcefully chuckled and faked a short laugh.

"What teenage boy are you talking about?" Muungo asked in a calm, deep, stern and firm voice. Leaning his head sideways as if it was weighed by his curiosity.

"Blaise your son, that's the boy I'm talking about!" Mercy answered as she looked straight into Muungo's brown eyes. Her stare was powerful and close enough for her to notice the sudden pupil constriction and blood rush into the capillaries of Muungo's eyes.

"I wish you could stay here for my wedding," a bright smile from Nsoh added so much emotion to her tender words.

"I wish I could, but most importantly I hope you are happy and are not being forced into getting married," Mercy responded.

The two friends remained silent in their bedroom. The rustling of tree leaves outside could be heard. The sudden cough from Wilanne in the room adjacent to Nsoh's joined the sound of the leaves.

"Are you sleeping?" Nsoh asked after clearing her throat.

"No. Are you?" Mercy questioned back.

"No!" Nsoh replied as she chuckled at the absurdity of the question from Mercy.

Mercy too joined in the laugh. Moments later Nsoh tried to calm the laugh by shushing Mercy.

"Shush we are going to wake everybody up, Aunty Mercy."

"Shush!" Mercy replied, only for both to start laughing again.

"Oh my God, today was an unforgettable day; I am going to miss you so dearly." Mercy muttered as she helplessly transitioned from laughter to tears. The sound of her clearing her runny nostrils, caused by her torrent of tears, added to her sobs.

This was not the first time Mercy had shed tears on that day. Earlier that day as she listened to Nsoh's narration of her attempted escape she could not help but let tears roll down her blush-full cheeks.

The darkness of the night on which Nsoh had run away was slow at moving out of the way of the sun. Gathered in the living room, everyone had improvised a sleeping spot waiting for the early hours of dawn to become part of a search party and go look for Nsoh in the fields and hills around the village.

Dawn had barely introduced herself, the faintly visible half crescent-shaped moon still lingered in the sky and dewdrops rolled down the leaves of plants. The early villagers sang at the top of their voices as they headed for the fields to tend to their crops, and to the water bodies to catch some fish. In the Tahkuh family most adult family members as well as Irene, Mercy and Nsoh's mother had formed a horseshoe in the middle of the courtyard. They listened to instructions from Muungo on how to go about searching for Nsoh.

With his left palm covering a big yawn produced as a result of a sleepless night Muungo momentarily paused his briefing. The fumes of warm air leaving his mouth were proof of the low morning temperatures that had everyone dressed in thick clothing.

"We will head in that direction, towards the rice fields. The women! You will take the roads while the men will take the shortcuts in the fields. Ask every person you meet on your way if they have seen Nsoh. We will reconvene at the borderline between Ngohmbi and Mighang. Take water, food, pocket change, charged phones, flashlights, and comfortable shoes."

Like a castle of cards, the horseshoe formation crumbled as everyone grabbed at least one last item which they had forgotten to take before the briefing. Then the group of men began walking off through the small curvy path that pierced through the mix of fresh and dry bushes located at the back of the family residence. The women went through the wide main entrance of the residence, ascended a gentle slope, slightly banked to the left and leading onto the main road. Once they reached the main road, they began climbing the hill leading to the village pond and to Ngohmbi as well. Seen from the family residence, the search parties shrunk in size as the ladies covered longer distances while walking the dusty and red stony road going from Mighang to Ngohmbi and the men snaked through the savanna vegetation between the kingdoms.

Far off, there were uncountable palm trees, as many as the hair of a head, which populated the southern borders of the Ngohmbi Kingdom, especially at the imaginary Ngohmbi-Mighang boundary line. This boundary line was imaginary because the blood relationship that linked the people of Mighang to the people of Ngohmbi forbade the existence of any physical separation between the descendants of the two brothers. To the men on the search party the sizes of the distant palm trees that made up the tree-curtain on the boundary line was going to be a metric scale used to estimate their distance from the borderline. Presently, with the moon finally gone from where the men stood the closest palm trees were almost in the size of *Mih-gih* (sardines).

After about an hour through the bushes and dusty dry land, the men reached the rice farms. Almost an hour of search and still they were a long distance away from Ngohmbi, not because Ngohmbi was far from Mighang but because they were carefully examining every trail, interrogating all passerby, combing through every blade of grass, and looking behind every ear of rice.

The green and greenish-golden yellow ears of rice covered hundreds of acres of swampy land and announced the field of palm trees that constituted the natural boundary between the villages of Mighang and Ngohmbi. At this point, the palm trees had the size of mature *kèh-kung* (Tilapia fish) in the eyes of the men. It was not uncommon for the people of Mighang to use the sizes of mature aquatic creatures as a scale of measurement, simply because fishing was an essential part of their daily lives. Even in the swampy rice farmland, the people had developed very advanced ways of fishing through the swamp.

The men plunged their feet into the mushy swampy soil without even noticing the morning mosquitoes that buzzed and bit. The men's eyes examined every moving ear of rice, every posted scarecrow, and every leaf and fruit of the tomato plant, as they walked through the fields and carefully avoided trampling on the rice farmers' products. Occasionally, they heard delirious shouts that overshadowed the tweeting of birds and the croaking of toads. The sound waves from these shouts were almost immediately followed and prolonged by their reflections. The shouts and their echoes were the sounds of the voices of the rice field guardians and the reflection of these voices off the cluster of palm trees in the rice field perimeter. The most recent echoes eventually damped off slowly into the wet vegetation, and the steps of men pressuring the mushy soil were once again heard as they walked and combed every piece of vegetation.

Less than ten minutes through the mushy landscape, just as they reached the part of the swamp with no rescue banks and nothing but entrapping mud, the cloud of silence hovering over the men's search party was broken by the voice of its obvious leader.

"If she took this path she would not have gone too far." The search party leader, Mbantahpah, a renowned and revered tracker, hunter, and fisherman declared after the moments of silence during which the men had walked by plunging and pulling their legs through the thick black sticky clay of the swamps.

"The sun just rose and even a mad man or mad woman will not dare cross this part of the rice fields at night."

The hunter squatted for a moment beckoning his dog as he whistled; then he folded four of his fingers and isolated the index finger of his right hand and then used it to examine the footprint in the soft black clay of the swamp. After examining the prints, he addressed the men in his search party.

"I have been carefully examining the mud and clay beneath our feet, and based upon the freshness, depth, and localization of prints I can conclude that rice farmers are the only people to have left these prints. We are going to put more speed to our process and once we reach the palm trees in Ngohmbi, we will walk in the opposite direction to the ladies."

All the men of the search party agreed to this suggestion, at least they could not question the hunter's and village expert tracker's tracking ability. He was known all over Mighang for being good at his job. So too were his father, grandfather, great-grandfather and all his ancestors before him. Their skills had served their people for many generations, and even in that day and time when community hunting and tribal wars were not as frequent as before, the secret of this science was reserved to the Mbantahpah family and was passed from one male to another.

Finally, the men had reached Ngohmbi just in time to see the sun free itself from the grasp of the mist crowding the top of the mountain. The members of the search party took off their warm wears, as their body began to feel the heat of the sun, and immediately made a u-turn. This time they took the main road, walked in the direction opposite to that of the ladies, and headed back to Mighang. After about an hour of walking on the red dusty path, the men met up with the ladies and the two search parties merged into one. With more resources to spare, the joint-search party combed the road and small bushes previously scanned by the ladies. The men were way more zealous, while the women, who were revisiting places where they had been moments earlier, searched their hearts for comfort more than the searched for Nsoh in the surroundings.

Nsoh's mother, exhausted but still alert as a result of the ongoing situation, silently walked close to Mbantahpah; she whispered prayers expressing her hope that the experienced tracker would find a trail to help locate her daughter. Mercy, though exhausted too, walked beside Muungo alongside a cold silent atmosphere that had befriended both since the previous night. They both had been very cold towards each other after their heated exchange about Nsoh's runaway, Muungo's position with respect to Nsoh's marriage, and Blaise the known stranger. Muungo, Mercy, and their silence walked at the tail end of the search party, trailing the group, as they combed the area already visited earlier that morning by the women. Mungo had tried to avoid Mercy by altering his pace and position in the search party, but with each trial Mercy sneaked and ended up next to him.

"Ahem!" Mercy pretended to clear her throat when she actually was trying to draw Muungo's attention. She wiped her face with a handkerchief and let her palm glide down from her forehead to her lips that she gently pulled forward in the cusp of her hand. Her arms slowly drop down to her side and she began speaking.

"I know I crossed the boundary yesterday and I am sorry, that was a very poor display of my gratitude towards your hospitality. I was trying to be a good friend, but I was actually being a nosy and pompous friend. I am sorry."

Muungo heard the words and felt the breeze of a genuine apology that carried the words as it caressed his stern face. But he kept his composure and his silence. A couple more steps; he left shoe prints on the dusty floor as the search party walked with shorter steps. Mercy waited for an answer from Muungo in vain. Disappointed, she once again wiped her face with her palm and began speeding up--exiting Muungo's private space and trying to catch up with the rest of the group. That was when Muungo responded to her in what was a voice somewhere between an audible chat and a whisper.

"Blaise is not my son, but I cannot tell him that, and I will not tell him that. I rather have him hate me than have him destroy his family. As for Nsoh this marriage is what her father talked about for the last couple of weeks before he died. This crown prince had met Nsoh's father and her father was impressed by the prince. Before his fateful exit on the battlefield, Mingo had been looking forward to having a chance to introduce the boy to his daughter. Mingo somehow knew, thanks to one of his many premonitory dreams, that he did not have many days left. Nsoh's father also said that this young man was not only fit to be the son he never had but is destined for greatness." Muungo ended his words with a short pause in his footsteps, during which he stared down at the ground and his rigid broad shoulder rose and fell down as he exhaled-- feeling a great relief to have said all those things.

His interlocutor paused as well and was staring at him with her mouth agape and her eyes wide open in surprise. She had barely closed her open mouth when Mbantahpah and his dog dashed down a thin path covered with yellowish-green withering Bahamas grass. The path branched off the main road and dwindled its way amongst trees, it led to a small well at the heart of a field. The well was covered with a piece of aluminum sheet of metal which in turn was held in place by logs of wood pressing it down. The very dry and dusty ground all around the well meant that nobody had drawn water from it in the last hour.

"She was here earlier this morning." Mbantahpah announced.

Every eye in the search party focused on Mbantahpah, astonished at how he could make such an assertion. But the old man looked up in the sky, his head tilted backward revealed the wrinkled skin of his neck sparsely covered by curled grey hair. He sniffed the air for a moment and then said: "she was heading in the direction of Mighang. She must have gone home" he concluded.

Later that day, right before noon and its scorching heat generated by the red-hot tropical sun stationed at the zenith of a naked blue sky, the search party returned to Mighang and found Nsoh at the family residence. Surrounded by curious ears, brightened eyes, and peaceful hearts, Nsoh recounted the headlines of the story of the night before. It was only later, when she was with her mother and sisters, uncle and family, Mbantahpah, and Mercy that Nsoh went into the details of her story. Nsoh claimed to have had a revelation and thanks to it she had found out a lot of secret and sacred things about her family and her father. Those things were the main reason why she returned home. Gathered around her, everyone listened attentively to what Nsoh had to say.

On the night of her running away from home, Nsoh had ignored the chirping of crickets, the croaking of the toads, and the hooting of the owls. She had paved her escape route through the shortcuts of the village, paths known only to a few. It was along this path that she had stumbled upon a woman named Mahbangoh.

Nsoh had just taken a scarcely travelled, grass-covered, path leading to outskirts of the village when she noticed the silhouette of a woman squatting down next to two bundles of dry branches. Nsoh kept walking and had slightly gone past this woman when she heard the woman say in a fragile and very tired voice.

"Please my daughter I beg of you, I am travelling to the outskirts of the village and I will appreciate if you could help me cover any distance with this second bundle of branches, no matter how short the distance is."

For a moment, Nsoh thought of turning down the offer, but then she quickly realized that by helping this woman she could be having a travel companion for a reasonable amount of time. Nsoh turned around, bent over, and then she lifted one of the bundles of branches and placed it on her head. In between grunts of effort, she assured the woman that she was going to carry the branches right up to the woman's home. Moments later the two silhouettes walked off with bundles of branches on their heads. As they walked side by side they began conversing and gradually a cloud of familiarity and friendship built over them.

It was not too long into their discussion and their walk that this woman began telling Nsoh things about Nsoh which nobody, other than Nsoh herself, knew. Guided by some sort of friendly spirit, that progressively but imperceptibly took control over her will the more she spoke with Mahbangoh, Nsoh followed the woman through the thick darkness right up to a tent built in the middle of peanut fields outside the village. The tent stood on four Y-shaped branches planted upright deep into the ground with their Y-shaped ends relatively high above the ground. The Y-shaped branch tops were oriented in pairs mirror-image to one and other and supporting a horizontal branch in their forks. The supported horizontal branches supported other crisscrossed branches carrying dry banana plant leaves and palm fronds. These leaves served as the roof of the tent, protecting its occupant from the burning sun and drizzles. This kind of tent, far from being absolutely waterproof and big, usually served as kitchen space, dining space, and rest areas for laborers who worked in the fields under the scorching sun and heavy rainfall.

Nsoh and Mahbangoh sat facing each other, at opposite ends of the flames of a fire they had lit in the tent. The fire burnt as they journeyed deeper into the winding path of their conversation. The ice-cold wind of the night rushed pass the trees into the tent and forced the flames to lean on one side. The drifting flames obstructed Nsoh's vision, making it impossible for Nsoh to clearly see the face of her interlocutor—not that it mattered to Nsoh who by the way was under the influence of the friendly spirit. Then from the fire came a pop sound as air trapped in a moist log of wood escaped. A series of less loud pop sounds and cracklings of the flames followed. The old woman tossed some of the branches they had brought with them into the flame. The flame shrunk as it tried to emblaze the newly added branches and resist the drift caused by the ice-cold wind.

Then suddenly the flames grew bigger and wilder with the number of sparkles flying into the air increasing exponentially. In a normal situation Nsoh would have risen and run away, but this time the adrenaline in her paralyzed her limbs and made the heart underneath her breasts race faster and beat stronger, almost breaking pass her sternum. The expanded flames slowly lost their golden yellow color and then became transparent. Behold, dancing within the flames, was a vivid image of Nsoh's father. From the transparent flames, Nsoh's father began talking to her about her family history, her destiny, and what she had to do considering that he was no more. The exchange lasted the time of an atemporal trance.

After Nsoh had spoken to her father through the flames, the big flames suddenly died down to feeble small flames dancing in the wind and the woman who had sat across from her was gone. So too was the spirit that had invaded Nsoh all this while. Strangely, not so shaken by the recent happening, Nsoh added more branches to the fire and while it rekindled progressively, warming up its surrounding, the young girl fed off some roasted sweet potatoes and meat which the woman had left lying on some banana leaves by the fireside. After her meal, Nsoh still was unable to explain what had just happened to her, so she lay down in the pile of dry grass covering part of the tent's floor. As she stared into the starless sky, she fell asleep. She slept all through the night.

During the early foggy morning hours, as the first songs of the birds overwhelmed the chirping of the night crickets, Nsoh rose from her sleeping spot. Still thinking about her spiritual experience of the night before, Nsoh walked up to a well not far from the tent. She picked up some fruits from the trees next to well and drank some water from the well. With a full stomach and armed with the conviction that she had just had a revelation, Nsoh headed home retracing her steps through the shortcuts she had used the night before.

Nsoh had just finished recounting her experience from the previous night to her select audience, when Mbantahpah sudden exclaimed:

"My people, can a goat give birth to a Lion?" He was so spontaneous and loud that everyone was startled. But that did not stop him from walking up to Nsoh who was sitting on a bamboo stool in the center of the living room. Mbantahpah held up Nsoh's right arm and pulled it towards himself. Nsoh opened wide her palm in response to this gesture. The old man loudly professed blessing on the young girl while intermittently spitting very little quantities of spittle on her open palm.

"When you walk and stumble on a rock, the rock will break, and your toe will stay strong. You will never go hungry, and if you inadvertently ingest a poisonous substance, it will transform itself into food. Your hands shall sow and harvest what your mouth shall eat." Mbantahpah then dropped Nsoh's hand and walked to the main door of the house and addressed the ancestors.

"Here is our daughter, our mother to be. Her womb will be like the fields and her children as many as the pieces of a kola fruit. The stump of her umbilical cord shall bear green large bunches of plantain fruits and shall bud-off many plantain suckers. Her father was a good seed sown to you ground, may

147

you give us much of his kind in return." Mbantahpah concluded with these words by pouring libation, fresh palm wine, at the doorstep.

With every call for divine blessing Nsoh's mother bowed down and yodeled louder with her right palm on her right cheek.

Sitting, her arms folded across her chest and weary of the days walk, Mercy was silently watching the entire show. Too tired to record the event, she just digested it through her tired eyes. The completely confused Mercy turned and looked in Irene's direction. The look coming from her shrunken eyes, and her slightly raised eyebrows expressed her curiosity towards what was happening. But Irene was too busy joining the other women in the yodeling that it was only at the end of the celebration that she provided an answer to satisfy Mercy's curiosity.

Mercy could feel her cellphone vibrate in her pocket, she dipped her hand in her pocket and pulled out her phone. As soon as she saw the caller's identification, she hurriedly got up and walked out of the living room. It was Blaise who was calling her. She had promised to meet with him later that day, and to talk about several important things. One of the most important things was to help him find out the reason why Blaise's *father* did not care about him. As Mercy took advantage of the euphoria in the living room to sneak outside into the courtyard, gradually deprived of its diurnal clarity, she pondered on what her answers to the boy's questions would be. There was a truth that was needed but was not to be shared.

"Hey Blaise! How are you?" Mercy began the conversation.

Mercy was on the phone talking to Blaise, repeating her phrases or asking him to repeat his own phrases each time they had difficulties hearing each other because of their very distinct accents. Then all of a sudden, she heard what seemed to be a collective grumbling and a multitude of footsteps hastily crushing dead leaves. Both sounds grew louder and when she looked in the direction of the sounds, she recognized a face, it was the face of the man who had rough handled her during the funeral--it was Prince Ngeu Wowo.

Ngeu Wowo's race ended at the doorsteps of late Mingo's home, he stretched his hand toward one of the men who had been walking with him. He received a wooden gourd from that man and smashed it on the doorsteps of late Mingo's residence, the same house where Muungo now resided. The broken gourd revealed a snail shell, a black feather and a bone all tied up together using a piece of red cloth. At that moment the town crier who was part of the uninvited party began to hit his gong and his sharp voice resounded as he made his pronouncement:

"The big nines of the kingdom, the founders of our people do not tolerate any form of insubordination. The shadow shall not run faster than the object, a tooth that bites the breast that feeds it can't go unpunished. Tahkuh Muungo shall leave this village before sunrise tomorrow, and never shall he return to this land."

The town crier had barely finished his speech, his loud voice scaring away a cluster of chicken that had been picking through a heap of dirt nearby, when Munngo came out of the house and stopped at the main door speechless as if stricken by a sudden and all-powerful spell of incapacity. All around the Tahkuh family estate, brave women rushed out of their homes, the less brave looked through the windows of their homes and began wailing. Some of the women threw themselves to the ground crying and pounding on the dirt. As for the men they pretended to keep their composure and yet they gathered in small groups staring at and murmuring about the drama in astonishment and disbelief. No one was bold enough to confront the bearers of the injunction, for it is consider a grave crime to challenge an injunction anywhere else than the traditional court presided by the King or the highest ranked village elder.

The town crier regained his breath after which he moistened his dry lips with his tongue, placed his gong in a bag he carried all this while and followed the group of men who had just turn around and left the Tahkuh family estate. Muungo's internal strength resurged, and he regain control of his motor skills, he lifted his once heavy legs and walked back into the house where he had been sharing dinner with Mbantahpah before the interruption. Not noticing Mbantahpah's eyes locked on him, Muungo sat down, pushed his plate to the side—he had lost his appetite. Next, he buried his face in his hands and shook his head from side to side in shock and disbelief.

"My son, hurry and go to the palace and inquire from the King the reason for this notice of exile," Mbantahpah suggested as he interrupted his eating for a few minutes.

"*Tah*, the King is not in the village, that is reason why we have not yet sealed Nsoh's engagement ceremony; and with this exile notice I am beginning to doubt if anyone from the Tahkuh family can marry someone from the Royal family."

"Thinking about a poison has never served as the antidote to the poison." Mbantahpah interjected.

"*Tah* I know that, and you are right on that topic. But to me this exile does not have any significance, at least not right now. But given that I am the head of the Tahkuh family the children and wife of Mingo are directly affected by this."

Mercy walked towards the steps, and before she could reach the amulet that had come out of the broken gourd, Irene, from a window of the building, shouted to her.

"Mercy don't step on or over that bundle and the pieces of the broken gourd; instead, use the backdoor of the building." Irene knew it was forbidden by the tradition for anyone to step over or remove an injunction meant for someone else.

Mercy did not get what Irene had said, so she looked up at the window and gestured asking Irene to repeat herself while she continued walking towards the steps. An agitated Irene gestured to Mercy to get away from the amulet and even shouted louder but Mercy still did not understand her. Bending forward, Mercy picked up the amulet and began climbing the steps. The heart of every person who saw that scene skipped at least two heartbeats. Mercy had just committed an abomination by picking up the injunction of exile that was destined for Muungo.

A virus of fear spread and fed on every person in the vicinity of the Tahkuh Family estate. This was too much, even for Mbantahpah. Mbantahpah, had finally lost his appetite, so he tried to galvanize his mood by smoking a pipe. From his bag, he pulled out a wooden pipe and a sachet containing supposedly dry tobacco. Pinching the tobacco with the thumb and index finger of his right hand, he crushed the tobacco bolus into fine powder that landed into his pipe's chamber. He lit the tobacco in his pipe, puffed a couple of times but derived no utils from the consumption. He puffed over and over and still did not find the smoke appetizing. Holding his pipe by the stem, he tapped and emptied the chamber over an empty old ashtray lying on the table. "What are you going to do?" He asked Muungo.

"I do not know! I sure do not know. What is the protocol to follow when something like what just happened with Mercy occurs?"

"She needs to be cleansed by a village priest." Mbantahpah responded while putting his pipe and tobacco sachet back in his bag.

"If I have to leave before dawn, I cannot leave her behind, and neither can I let her go with the risk of some curse or anything of the sort." Muungo turned and looked at Mercy who had come in and sat on a chair in the living room. The all so important cleansing was the last thing she expected. As she prepared for her return to America, she did not want to be involved with any more of this African voodoo related issues, especially after the story the King of Mighang had told her concerning her supposedly mysterious disease.

"I'm sure I will be fine. Let's get the hell out of this forsaken Bermuda Triangle before another voodoo spell comes our

151

way." She told Muungo who had been facing her direction for a while now, probably strategizing on their next move or may be regretting to have brought her along on the trip.

"She is a foreigner, so technically none of this should affect her, isn't it?" Muungo asked Mbantahpah.

"Your brother Tahfuh is better placed to answer such a question. I heard he is getting ready to be crowned as a member of the *Ngumba*. This means he is knowledgeable about the ins and outs of such injunctions."

"Hmm!" Muungo exclaimed as he struggled with the desire to spit on the ground in disgust. "You mean he is getting ready to inherit Mingo's title …. that piece of shit traitor that he is."

"Son the night is rapidly advancing, the spirits of the dark are getting excited, you should consider leaving the village before the rooster crows at 3:00 a.m. Go to Ngombhi's Palace and ask to meet *Anaa* Nantono, I am sure she can help you."

"Who is she and why will she help me?" Muungo asked and paid an even more intense attention to Mbantahpah by pulling his chair closer to Mbantahpah's.

"It is a very long story; if you meet her, she can tell you the story. All I know is my grandfather told me that she and her entire lineage are highly respected in Mighang. Every King of Mighang always gets a wife from that family. If not of the oldest Bantu tradition that obliges Kings to be warriors, takers of lives, while the same tradition forbids women, givers and preservers of life, to be warriors, then *Anaa* Nantono's family could very well have been the paramount royal family."

Mbantahpah paused for a moment as if he was listening to someone else or if he was busy tracking an element. Then he vigorously shook his head from side to side before whispering something in the most ancient words of *Chrambo*, the language spoken by the citizens of Mighang. His words loosely translated to: "He who does not bury a corpse and he who disinters a corpse better be insensitive to the nauseous stench of the corpse."

"What are you trying to say *Tah*?" Muungo asked.

"I am not going to repeat myself; pack your things and leave. I smell unpleasant burns in the air. Go and meet *Anaa* Nantono and if nothing good comes out of it then try to meet with the King of Ngohmbi." As he said these words, Mbantahpah sent his hand in to the side pocket of his *dashiki* and brought out a piece of a tree bark. He tossed it into his mouth, vehemently chewed it and spat the pasty product of his mastication into his palm. He rubbed his hands together, uniformly spreading the paste over his palms. Then without asking for permission, he applied the paste on Muungo's forehead and on his Achilles tendons. It was at this precise time that Irene and Wilanne came out, without their travel companions but accompanied by a handful of women who helped carry the travelers' luggage.

"Let us go. Let's leave. Immediately!" Irene ordered.

"Nsoh bring your sisters and mother, lets us go." Muungo relayed as he obeyed Irene's order.

"But we have no vehicle" Nsoh's mother interjected coming in through the back entrance to the building and appearing with her clothes partially covered in dust after haven thrown herself to the ground with the other women at the proclamation of the exile orders.

"Musa, one of the drivers who often travels this road, lives 5 minutes from here. Go see him; he will take you to town." Mbantahpah suggested. "They have begun the fire to come burn down Muungo's home. I can smell the ingredients from here. You should leave if you wish to see this home unscathed."

Musa's stench of fermented corn beer had not subsided, he had spent the whole trip talking about the bad road conditions, the negative influence of financial power in the mechanics of the Mighang Kingdom, promiscuity among youths, and complaisance of the intellectual elite of Mighang. The choice of sitting next to the driver had been some sort of martyrdom for Muungo. So, Muungo kept quiet and did nothing but turned and tilted his head incessantly in order to avoid the air current that carried the alcoholic breath from Musa's mouth to Muungo's nose. Musa had just begun talking about Prince Ngeu Wowo who had blatantly bought his way into the sacred circle of the big nine, when Irene interrupted him from the back of the bus. She had leaned forward from her seat, cusped her right hand on the right side of her lips and shouted above the roaring and sputtering sound of the engine, asking if Musa was familiar with *Anaa* Nantono's residence.

"Yes, I do," he responded shouting back, "she is the aunt to the cousin of my second wife's uncle. I even met her last week at…"

Musa had begun one of his very long talks and Irene rapidly countered:

"We know all that Musa, please just take us to her place, we need to see her immediately."

She made eye contact with Muungo and could tell from the frown on his face, which also produced wrinkles on his forehead, that he did not approve of the idea of telling a drunkard where they were planning to go once they arrive Ngohmbi, especially since Muungo had just been exiled from amongst his kinsmen.

The drunk driver shut up for five seconds and once again began talking about the wedding of the queen mother's son to a girl from Bell Town. He continued his noisy driving until he stirred his old blue van onto a driveway. The driveway led to a brick house hidden behind rows and columns of tall and well-trimmed majestic palm trees, each tree crowned with green long wide palm fronts. The brick house had a wide facade which bore an even distribution of window frames, and a light bulb positioned at the level of the facade's vertical median. The light bulb hung from the ceiling and feebly shone the main entrance to the house of *Anaa* Nantono. Though faint, the light bulb's rays revealed the big and thick wood used on the doorframe. On these very old wooden frames, chisels and other tools had been used to carve exquisite figures and ancient symbols that proclaimed the power, strength, and longevity of the bond between the Ngohmbi, Mighang, and Mendenkye Kingdoms.

Built in isolation from the other huts and buildings of the Ngohmbi palace, the four walls of handmade sunbaked bricks that formed *Anaa* Nantono's house were connected at the four corners by quasi-rectangular pillars. Connecting a pair of orthogonal walls, each pillar rose from the foundation buried under the dirt to the thatched roof of the house. Characterized by uneven sides and rough edges, the pillars were visibly different from each other. Yet, somewhere along the height of each of the four pillars, there was a spherical hump carefully painted with fresh white paint. The fresh coat of paint was laid over an existing coat of white paint gone brown. Each pillar hump was wrapped by a string made of cowries. Musa's old blue van drove close to the house and its left headlight came so close to one of the pillars that Irene scolded Musa : "Watch where you go! How long before you become sober?" Musa immediately slammed his foot on the breaks. The sudden jerky sensation and Irene's shout awoke Mercy, Nsoh and all the others who had dozed off.

The reluctant sliding door of the blue van finally opened after much use of force by Muungo and Musa. All this while, an old woman stood inside the house staring at the van and its passengers through the door of the main entrance. On the outside of the house, next to the open door, stood three adolescents--a boy and two girls. They too watched the ongoing struggle between Musa, Muungo, and the van's door. Jiggle, pull, wiggle, push, and then the van's door opened, and the passengers began climbing down from the vehicle. The two girls and the boy moved out of the way of the old lady who came outside and let the feeble light rays from the bulb over her head transform her blurry silhouette into an image of a magnificent black woman—*Anaa* Nantono.

Emerging from the dark interior of the house to the poorly lit front door of the house, *Anaa* Nantono whispered to the children around her and immediately they rushed to help the passengers off load their luggage from the vehicle. She was a tall long-legged woman, with a skin covered in different shades of glowing dark brown. She also bore silky long black and grey hair and cherished a sporadic smile that revealed the pink gums and the middle-gap in her blinding white symmetric dentition.

"What took you so long? I had been expecting you for so, so, long now." She asked, her eyes directed to a group of three: Mercy, Nsoh, and Muungo.

The last image the guest had had of their host was her bare back as she turned and walked back into her house—her shoulders were exposed and every part beneath the shoulders was covered by a large piece of cloth tied around her torso and her bust and running all the way down from her armpits to her ankles. The three adolescents who had come out with her were of great assistance to their many guests. They took their time as they transported the guests' luggage, showed their guests to their bedrooms, prepared warm baths for each of the guests and offered them a sumptuous dinner. The dinner menu was made of *Kati-kati, Njama-Njama, fufu,* and *Mboh. Mboh* is a delicious pudding made of peanut paste, smoked fish, and dried meat; the combination is wrapped in plantain leaves and blended into a quasi-homogeneous bread texture via an endothermic process of steam cooking. *Kati-kati* is made of smoked chicken, seasoned with hot pepper, ground garlic, curry, and ginger, with the chicken all sautéed to perfection in palm oil.

After the guests had finished feasting on their dinner, the chewing of bones and cleansing of teeth with the tongue almost over, the adolescents, who did not utter many words, served them fresh palm wine. The beverage was so fresh that it still had foam flowing slowly out through the opened top of the gourd. The fresh palm wine served; the teenagers told the guests that their host had asked to meet them first thing in the morning. The guests were lost in the enigma—the great reception and the executive-like meeting appointment from their host. Nevertheless, they choose not to find their way out of the beautiful enigma. Nsoh quickly noticed this popular indifference to the unjustified nice treatment administered to them, so after perfectly timing and picking an instant of general silence and light munching, she tried to resurrect the discussions on the injunction incident. But in between sips of sweet fresh palm wine, Muungo commanded that nobody should worry about the injunction and the exile. Grabbing the gourd of palm wine and pouring out its last drops into his cup, Muungo promised to find out some more about why Mbantahpah suggested, in the very first place, that they come seek a solution from *Anaa* Nantono. Irene's sudden look and prolonged stare in Muungo's direction meant she was not okay with this decision pregnant with suspense, especially because she was concerned about what could happen to Mercy who had naively moved the injunction, the amulet, left behind by Ngeu Wowo. Without letting himself make any eye contact with Irene, because he already guessed Irene's state of mind, Muungo chose to keep drinking and to linger behind.

He decided to stay a little bit longer at the dining table after everyone had gotten up from their seats and gone to their rooms. He lingered behind looking up at the ceiling made of interwoven bamboo slits; on another realm he was gazing at the heavens coming crashing down on the legacy his ancestors had built. Save by the bell! While he was somewhere in his state of deep trance, his cell phone began vibrating in his pocket. The vibration startled him, and he jumped up from his seat, and when he looked at his phone, he saw the least expected name from his phone contact list on the caller ID. The least desired name appeared on the lit up screen of his phone; Tahfuh was calling him.

More surprised than shocked by the phone call, Muungo slowly sat down in his seat at the dining table. He would not want Irene to notice that Tahfuh was calling in addition to her already wondering why her husband had not insisted on knowing more about their visit to *Anaa* Nantono. He held his phone, already set to silence mode, and waited for another incoming call or a voicemail notification. Behold, Tahfuh did not let Muungo down; Muungo received an avalanche of incoming calls that ended with a text message. The text message read.

"I wish you'd had picked up the phone, but more than anything I wish in days to come you'll understand why I did what I did. The members of the *Ngumba* need you to hand over the bag, which was in Mingo's room, his *Ngumba* bag. They will do ANYTHING to have that bag, so please before matters escalate any further send them the bag. Stay safe brother."

Upon reading about the bag Muungo's heart sank in his belly. He realized it was either Nsoh or Irene who would have dared to take the bag. If it all depended on him alone, he would have left the bag, but that ship had already sailed away. "I have to deal with the present scenario," he thought to himself as he buried his face in his palms supported by his elbows resting on the dining table. A couple of seconds later, he lifted his face out of his palms, he willingly supported the weight of his crown of trouble. Muungo closed his eyes so tightly that he felt the pressure of his eyeballs against his eyelids. Eyes closed he remembered how his late grandfather, late father, and late brother venerated that *Ngumba* bag. It was a bag made of tanned leopard skin, with dozens of amulets sewed along the bag's strap.

Each amulet was unique and was a tangible proof of the owner's greatness, immortality, and rank in the society. The first of the amulets was a small sack, one made of tanned leopard skin too; it contained relics of all previous owners of the *Ngumba* bag. Following Mingo's death Tahfuh had made arrangements to collect some relics, Mingo's fingernails and hair, for the amulet. Prior to concluding this arrangement, Tahfuh had informed Muungo about the budding plan, and had assured him that these relics will be handed over to him. Sure enough, Tahfuh never kept his promise. The second amulet was fluffy and colorful; it was made of a stack of feathers whose hollow shafts were bundled up together. Overtime the afterfeather of most of the plumes had fallen off leaving behind a crumbled rainbow-like mix-match of colors from the feathers' barbs. Each feather was a symbol of either an acquired societal title or a military rank earned by the warrior during war expeditions. There was a third amulet sack presumably made of human skin. It contained hard items which felt and sounded like marble when rubbed against each other. Muungo could have been wrong but if his memory served him right, the third bag contained the human teeth. The teeth of enemies killed in times of war by the different owners of the bag during their tenure. Most warriors usually decapitated their dead opponents and uprooted a tooth from the opponent's mouth. The victor also cut off and used the scalp of the opponent's head as skin to craft a new teeth-sack for their increased collection of teeth, and then he gave the remainder of the decapitated head to the King. There were many more amulets on the bag's strap but the nature, content, and power of the other talisman on the bag were only revealed to those who became members of the *Ngumba*. A position certainly coveted by Tahfuh and others.

Muungo stopped querying his mind about the bag, and then pondered on whether he should respond to the text message. He went to the text message application of his phone, opened the message editor and began typing up a response. After Tahfuh's text message and Mungo's unsent text, there wasn't any more incoming phone call from Tahfuh. So Muungo got up from his seat paced around the dining table for a while as he revisited, in his thoughts, several events that had happened since the death of his brother. Though he was not the oldest, Mingo was the highest in rank among the members of the *Ngumba*, and as such by virtue of the powers that were his, Mingo had made the decision not to be buried indoors, not to have camwood paste rubbed on his corpse, not to have his relics added to the amulet, and not to have a bamboo fitted from the top of his grave to his mouth. These choices were bold moves never heard of, moves which most conservative traditionalist members of the *Ngumba* did not approve of and the few who did not openly oppose them pretended to be neutral. Yet going against the highest ranked member of the most sacred secret society of the kingdom was also something the other members of the *Ngumba* could not even imagine because the tradition did not permit them to do so. Until this very moment, Muungo had not seen in these decisions of the deceased the fact that it was an affront to conservative traditionalists who often utilized the status quo anchored on tradition to exploit the citizens of the kingdom.

Stepping back and looking from a purely traditional perspective, Muungo began to better understand Ngeu Wowo's and Tahfuh's recent moves. Ngeu Wowo, as Musa had said, had bought his way up the ranks and certainly coveted the highest rank in the *Ngumba* circle. Tahfuh on the other hand saw in Mingo's death and Muungo's absence an opportunity to turn his life around by gaining fame and respect within the kingdom and even the nation. Tahfuh was clearly not going to let the little Nsoh seize this opportunity from him by means of some arranged marriage. Muungo turned around nodding his head in approval to the fact that he was now putting the pieces of the puzzle together. As he turned his back to the dining table, he caught sight of a bag on the brick wall. He rapidly turned his head back in the direction of the bag and noticed that the bag was almost identical to Mingo's *Ngumba* bag but had even more amulets and feathers that than of Mingo. "Who really was *Anaa* Nantono?" he wondered.

"**Come** in, seat down. Make yourselves comfortable" *Anaa* Nantono invited her guests into a small dark room in the house. A small fire and light rays that squeezed through a small window, located directly opposite to the door, lit the room. Across from the door and close to the window was a wooden stool resting on leopard skin. Behind the stool were various gourds, clay pots, sacks, drums, and other wooden utensils

160

hanging off the wall. Two beds, made of bamboo and carrying mattresses made of bags stuffed with straw, were placed one each on either side of the door. It was on these beds that the guests, who were dressed for the occasion, were asked to seat.

Prior to coming into the room, the guests had been dressed in pieces of cloths cut from ancient hand-woven fabric; the rectangular shaped pieces of clothes were wrapped around the guests. For the women the cloth was tied above their breasts and over their shoulder blades, it went one and a half turns around their torso, and it ran all the way down from their armpit to their knees. For the only man of the group the cloth was tied around his waist and covered the lower body from the waist to the knee. Some uncovered parts of the body were not left untouched, instead camwood paste was rubbed over their feet, arms, a dot of the paste was put on the forehead, between the eyebrows, of each guest admitted into the small room. In addition to dressing up and make up, each guest had a small sack of kola nuts in their left hand and a leaf-full branch of the peace plant in their right hand. Right up until that moment, Tahkuh and his family were still unaware of the purpose of their visit, its outcome, and any information about their host. The incident of the day before still had them on their toes, the reality of being chased away like rabid dogs from their family heritage had hit them hard in the morning when they woke up from a restful sleep. But the one thing that helped them keep their cool was the fact that they were in the premises of the Ngohmbi Royal Palace and the King of Ngohmbi was a childhood friend to Mingo and had met with Muungo on multiple occasions. But this assurance was only minimal, especially because not everyone who had fled with Tahkuh had been dressed up that morning. Solange, Eve, and their mother had not been dressed up.

Only those guests prepared by the boy and the girls of the house responded to the host's invitation and went into the small room. The ladies Nsoh, Mercy, and Irene sat on the bed to the right of the stool, Wilanne and her father sat on the other bed. *Anaa* Nantono sat on the stool and her bare feet rested on the furry side of the leopard skin beneath the stool. Once the guests were seated, *Anaa* Nantono, who had been staring at the fireplace, raised her head and then rose from her seat. She turned around, leaned forward towards the wall behind her seat, and dipped her hand in a sack. From that sack she pulled a pod of kolanut placed it in-between her legs in a calabash lying on the leopard skin. Then she dipped her hand into two other sacks from where she brought out cowries and dried bones; she placed those in a second calabash resting on the leopard skin.

Anaa Nantono sat down and handed the pod to Nsoh and asked her to pass it round. The pod went round and came right back to *Anaa* Nantono who smashed the hard cellulose cell it against the leg of her stool, and then cracked the pod open. She took out a seed, chewed the first piece of the seed and spat the pasty content on the palm of her hand. She then rose from her stool and walked towards the fireplace next to which a short conical-shaped mount of hardened soil guarded the opening to a hole that ran into the depth of the earth and passed the foundation on which the room was build. The host muttered some words and dropped the chewed kola nut seed into the hole. She returned to her seat, and then she passed the kola nut seed to all her guests starting with Nsoh. They each picked a cotyledon, took a bite, and passed the seed to the next person, and eventually the leftover kola nut seeds returned to the old woman. *Anaa* Nantono repeated the same ritual with a gourd of fresh palm wine, and then again with a platter of bits of grilled plantain dipped in salted palm oil. The guests had masticated a variety of items and the twist on their lips signified this combination was not that delicious, but none of them except for Wilanne had had the guts to spit out or refuse any of the food items.

The only boy of the house walked in barefooted, with an egg carried in the cusp of his hands. He stood by the side of *Anaa* Nantono, and then he cracked the eggshell and delicately allowed the egg white to drip down on *Anaa* Nantono's palms. *Anaa* Nantono rubbed the egg white all over her hands. She took the remnants of the egg from the boy and with a loud gulp swallowed the egg yolk. Her guests made faces because they were disgusted by the last scene, but *Anaa* Nantono did not care and would not, in a hundred years, care about those faces. The slimy egg white was still lodged in between *Anaa* Nantono's fingers when she picked the bones and cowries in her two palms, leaned forward toward Irene and asked her to spit on the contents in her open palms. Despite the not so pleasant smell of the egg white, the old dirty bones, and the cowries, Irene lowered her face and spat out a small amount of spittle on the items in *Anaa* Nantono's palms. Standing up, her hands now cusped back together, *Anaa* Nantono shook and shuffled the items trapped in between her hands while speaking simultaneously in very ancient *Chrambo*, so ancient that even Muungo did not understand much of it. Next, she simultaneously shook and moved her hands, still closed together, in a clockwise direction over Irene's head. By so doing, she aligned the colliding cowries and bones trapped in her hands to Irene's invisible aura ring. Then she sat down on her stool, and then cast the cowries and bones in between her bare and painted feet resting on the leopard skin. She kept quiet for a moment, and then used her right index finger to point at, and even at times move, a bone or a cowry. Next, she looked up from the leopard skin in Irene's direction.

"You did well to take the bag. You did well. I will give you a sacred cloth with which you will wrap the bag and travel with it overseas. In the meantime, fetch three bamboo stools, three hens of white plumage, 3 cans of palm oil, and 3 gourds of palm wine, and offer them as peace offerings. Give one of each item to the queen mothers of Ngohmbi, Mighang, and Mendenkye."

Anaa Nantono gestured to Irene to leave the room, and without questioning Irene walked out of the room. *Anaa* Nantono then picked up the cowries and bones and once again she performed her shuffle, align, and cast process, but this time the same ritual of cowries and bones involved Nsoh.

"Mingo! Mingo!" *Anaa* Nantono insisted as she looked in the direction where Nsoh was seated and called her with her father's name.

"*Anaa!*" The young girl replied with a voice barely above a whisper.

"You know what to do, and you are doing it right! you have my blessing to follow through with it."

By the time the last word was pronounced the gesture asking Nsoh to leave was made. Eyebrows curving inward, Nsoh rose feeling more confused than she was at the beginning of the ritual. "Was *Anaa* Nantono referring to her wedding?" she wondered as she went past the doorpost of the small room into a brighter space.

Anaa Nantono then performed the same ritual for Mercy who all this while had been becoming really uncomfortable because the smoke from the fire irritated her eyes. She also had begun gently twisting her body because the camwood and ancient clothes had begun to mildly itch her skin; a skin already darken by the tropical sun and ashen up by the dry harmattan winds. Once the cowries and bones were thrown onto the leopard skin, *Anaa* Nantono paused and stayed seated for over a minute before she gracefully rose from her seat. She stretched out her hands towards Mercy. At first Mercy frowned as she hesitated in holding those hands on which almost everyone had spat on, but *Anaa* Nantono stretched her hands even farther, getting them closer to Mercy, and nodded her head, insisting that Mercy hold them. Mercy mustered the courage and with her eyes closed and her hands barely stretched out she felt the cold hands of *Anaa* Nantono hold hers and gradually pull her up from the bamboo bed. Mercy allowed *Anaa* Nantono to lift her up from her seat. Still holding Mercy's hands, *Anaa* Nantono guided her to the stool resting on the leopard skin. Muungo quietly looked at what was happening. He saw *Anaa* Nantono repeatedly make Mercy sit down on her stool and then stand up ffor nine consecutive times. After rising for the ninth time Mercy who was lost in a reflex act almost sat down one more time. She had lost herself in what seemed to be a game of standing up and sitting down, but the firm grip of *Anaa* Nantono resisted her descent and held her up. Mercy recovered control of her body movement and stood up straight next to *Anaa* Nantono.

"Do not worry about the injunction. It is them, those ignorant, who have to worry because you moved the injunction." *Anaa* Nantono said.

Mercy let go a loud sigh and her shoulders rose and dropped back in relief, she had, this time around, gotten really worried about the consequences of her acts related to the injunction amulet. On the day she picked up the injunction amulet, Mercy had seen people in a mortified state of terror, pale faces, and trembling bodies. The manner in which *Anaa* Nantono ended her phrase, a controlled voice incarnating extra confidence, and her very obvious intentional avoidance of eye contact while speaking to Mercy was quite intriguing. Muungo could tell that *Anaa* Nantono had much to say but chose not to.

Anaa Nantono stepped to the side of the stool and Mercy walked back towards her seat on the bamboo bed. Instead of gesturing to Mercy to leave the room *Anaa* Nantono did what everyone least expected. She stared at Mercy for a while, still avoiding direct eye contact, and let go one of her sporadic but bright smiles.

Then she said, "Only mountains say farewell forever, and only bad fruits do not yield plants; You can stay for the last part if you so wish."

"I would love to but since we are leaving this afternoon I will, with your permission, go get ready." Mercy replied.

The truth is Mercy had had enough of all these mystical practices on her and would rather call Blaise, and why not Brianna, than to assist at some mystical thing where she could once again be forced to touch a forbidden object.

It was then Mungo's turn for *Anaa* Nantono to interrogate the cowries and the bones on his behalf, but what he really wished was to interrogate *Anaa* Nantono herself. Following a ritual like the one used on the ladies, *Anaa* Nantono began her work with Muungo. After casting the cowries and bones on the leopard skin, she looked at them and moved a few items around and then she said:

"Do not worry I see all your questions and I will answer then at the end."

Muungo raised his eyebrows either because he was surprised that she read his mind or because he was extremely curious to hear what the cowries will say about him, Tahfuh, and Prince Ngeu Wowo. *Anaa* Nantono took a broom from behind her stool, dipped the tip of the broomsticks into a calabash containing water submerging some peace plant leaves, a few coins, and a red and black cloth. She then used the broom to sprinkle the water from the calabash on Muungo and Wilanne. Terrified, the little girl clung harder to her dad and began breathing faster in anticipation of a cry for freedom. But even before she was able to let out her first cry, *Anaa Nantono* had handed the broom to Muungo saying:

"Sweep away every dirt they lay on your path, kill every bug that flies in your direction, clear every wood ash that seats in your fireplace. This broom surpasses the induction hat. And so Tahkuh Muungo in the presence of your ancestors and guardians of our people, I make you leader of immortal men of the *Ngumba*, commander of armies of the spirits, protector of the boundary between the visible and invisible realms, and bearer of the insignia just like your brother, your father, your grandfather and his father before him."

Muungo passed the baby on his left side and seized the broom from *Anaa* Nantono's grip. By seizing instead of politely taking the broom Muungo simply meant that he considered the induction into the *Ngumba* a birthright and accepted all the responsibilities that came with it. *Anaa* Nantono nodded her head in approval and turned around to stack her utensils back to their respective positions. With her back facing Muungo, the new heir to the lineage of the Tahkuh family asked her this question:

"Who are you *Anaa* Nantono? Doesn't one have to know the directions of the sunrise and sunset for them to interpret the signs of the sky?"

"**W**ould you come with me?" *Anaa* Nantono asked Muungo while the others were savoring their breakfast. Letting go of the teaspoon he used in stirring his coffee milk beverage, Muungo rose from his seat and walked out of the brick house with *Anaa* Nantono. They began walking the perimeter of the house; *Anaa* Nantono walked with a peace plant in hand which swinging it from side to side while she told him the following story:

Our people still sing songs and tell stories about your ancestor, Tahkuh son of Tasha, and truthful reincarnation of his grandfather Mboronui, who had gone on his last mission. The goal of this mission was to take the queens of Mighang, Ngohmbi, and Mendekye to safety, and unfortunately, he failed. Kidnapped by slave traders, after a very fierce fight put on by Tahkuh and his lieutenant, your ancestor had to broker a deal with the enemies. His captors, the slave traders, agreed to certain conditions in addition to taking him captive. But the greedy captors did not hold on to their end of the bargain. Against Tahkuh's will, the queen of Mighang handed herself and her son over to the captors so that the other queens and princes will be released from captivity. Faithful to his King and heart broken by this let down of his own gods, Tahkuh stayed behind with the queen and the crown prince. The news of this failed mission created so much tension between the three kingdoms that eventually a bloody battle ensued.

Till this day it is the only and the bloodiest fratricide that had ever existed between these sister kingdoms. We are lucky that the battle lasted for only four nights. Those nights are forever remembered in the kingdoms. Every year within a

167

given week, which is chosen by me, the King of Ngohmbi harvests three roots of the peace plant from the burial site of the mother to the first Kings of Ngohmbi and Mighang. He gets stripped of every royal attribute and he walks through the deep dark moonless night to the palace of the King of Mighang. The visiting King spends an entire day and a night over in the royal quarters of the King of Mighang. Both Kings make sure that no one, not even their wives, except their personal guards are aware of this visit. The King of Ngohmbi hands over one of the roots to the King of Mighang.

Then the following night both Kings, temporarily undone of their royal attributes, walk all night to the palace of the King of Mendenkye. They give him the third root of the peace plant and spend their entire stay hidden in the royal quarters of the latter and remain unseen by the everyday citizen of the Mendenkye Kingdom. After spending a day and night at the Mendenkye palace all three Kings go to the battle site and plant those peace plants, share a meal and then walk to the palace of the King of Ngohmbi where they spend the final day and night. On the following night, the Kings of Mendenkye and Mighang walk back to their kingdoms and pretend as if nothing ever happened.

About the damned bloody battle, it was thanks to Nahshieh, Tahkuh's youngest wife that this battle came to a permanent halt. Her sister wife, Mahbangoh, had gone to the fields and had not returned when the war broke out. After many days Nahshieh got really worried about Mahbangoh, whom she loved very much, and so she took a fresh stem of the peace plant, whose leaves were bright green and healthy. With food and water in her basket, she headed out to the fields, cutting through the battlefield. The warriors from the three kingdoms, faithful to their Tikar tradition and to the respect it gives women, were obliged to stop the war. Nahshieh found Mahbangoh trapped in a trench with a broken leg. She helped her out and they returned home.

Few months later in the Kingdom of Mighang, Nahshieh gave birth to three beautiful daughters who would never know their father. The King of Mighang made your ancestor Nkwanui, the son of Mahbangoh—Tahkuh's first wife, heir to Tahkuh's family lineage and custodian of all the powers associated with this position. This transfer of powers was performed right before the King left on an expedition to go look for his wife, his son, and his best friend. The King's decision to abdicate the throne did not make everyone happy, some people had even wished to inherit Tahkuh's family, his rank, and his belongings. But Nahshieh's father, the King's messenger, and the regent King battled hard to make sure that such a thing never happened. Joining forces with the Priestess Mahbangoh and his own daughter Nahshieh, the messenger of the King of Mighang made a promise to the leaders of the three kingdoms. He promised to offer sacrifices that will not only guarantee that the white invader will not overthrow their kingdoms but will also ensure that the rightful heir of the throne of Mighang, the missing prince, would one day return to his people. This sacrifice required that four people be buried alive.

Muungo had been listening keenly to this narration, and even though it had not yet answered his question, he was glad that he was learning an unknown part of his family history— the role Nahshieh had played in ending a war provoked by Tahkuh's failed mission. Muungo walked very close to *Anaa* Nantono as they walked past the fourth pillar located on the facade of the house. He was so close to her that he could smell her strong body odor mixed with smoke from the small room where she had invited her guests earlier that morning.

"In this pillar, the one next to you, Nahshieh's father was buried alive" *Anaa* Nantono announced.

Muungo looked at her with a mix of surprise and doubt. His hand resting on his hips, without uttering a word, and with nothing else but his wrinkle-filled forehead he asked her if she was serious about what she had just said.

169

"I am very serious, Nahshieh's father is buried in this pillar." She tapped the pillar three times with the peace plant in her hand. She stared at the second pillar located at the other end of the facade and then pointed at it while saying "Mahbangoh was buried alive in that one." This time she did not give Muungo the chance to ponder on her words. "In the next pillar Nahshieh was buried alive and on the last one the first son of Tahkuh's elder sister, who is the mother of the ancestors of Tahfuh, was buried alive."

Two streams of warm tears rolled down Muungo's cheek at unequal speed. The left tear tolled down and as it caressed the left nostril the right tear began rolling down. Muungo was not sobbing or breathing heavily but he was crying in an unusual way.

"Who are you *Anaa* Nantono?" He asked her one more time, staring at her, his eyes red with tears rolling down his cheeks with increasing intensity and at a faster rate.

The three daughters of Nahshieh were betrothed to the three kings of the three kingdoms. These three queens and their heirs have each, all through these centuries, given a daughter in marriage to the king of the one of the two other sister kingdoms. In addition, they have also given another daughter up for adoption by this house, where we educate them on their history and responsibility and make one of them the heir of this house and guardian of the truth. In the small room where we sat this morning, that is where the oldest of the three sisters, queen of the Ngohmbi Kingdom, was buried.

As for me, I am a princess from the Ngohmbi Kingdom and heir to a late princess of the Mighang Kingdom. She was, and now I am, the guardian of the sacred bond of three Kings. My sister is queen of the Mendenkye Kingdom. My sister's daughter is queen and mother of the crown prince of the Mighang Kingdom, she is also future mother-in-law to your niece Nsoh.

Muungo turned around and was on the verge of walking away from the conversation when she grabbed his hand. His head still turned away from her he could hear her voice piercing all the way through his heart and soul.

My niece, who is the future queen mother of Mighang, has not been blessed with a female fruit of the womb. The young boy in this house is her youngest son and the crown prince is her oldest son. Because she has no daughter to give in marriage to one of the future Kings of Ngohmbi and Mendenkye, just like she has no daughter to give up for adoption by this home, she is obliged to adhere to the one of the exceptions of the royal bond between the three kingdoms. The exception invoked here is applicable when the queen has not daughter and the Takuh family has a girl of marriage-age. Thus, given this scenario my niece's son must marry Nsoh, because of Nsoh's relation to the throne. Nsoh will become queen and could then give a daughter of hers in marriage to a King of the next generation after her and give another daughter to this house.

Walking out of the brick house through the main door Tahfuh addressed his cousin who was standing next to *Anaa* Nantono.

"Muungo we all thought, at least I for one thought, your westernized ass was going to deny the duty that was yours as the last male and direct heir of the Tahkuh lineage. That is why I had to step in to inherit Mingo's position within the Mighang Kingdom."

"How easy it is for you to justify your treason." Muungo replied as he took his hand off *Anaa* Nantono's grip and turned around to face his interlocutor after he had recognized the voice.

"Your ancestor worked hand in hand with mine. Heck your blood is in one of those pillars, and yet you help banish me from our kingdom." Muungo continued.

"The fact that you reside overseas and Nsoh's quasi indecision on the idea of the engagement allowed Prince Ngeu Wowo to begin gaining grounds. With you not claiming the title of heir to your brother, I overhead Prince Wowo planning to marry Nsoh to his younger brother living in Germany, so that just like you she would be taken far away from the culture and this will make him the new leader of the *Ngumba* in terms of rank and title. And so, I decided to beat Prince Wowo at his game."

Muungo paused for a moment rethinking the justifications from Tahfuh and the explanations of *Anaa* Nantono. He went into the house and moments later walked out with his luggage. Stepping out of the house he noticed that a vehicle was parked at same spot where Musa's van was parked the day before. Parked in front of the brick house was a silver-colored SUV. On the steering wheel was the crown prince of Mighang, he opened his door and hopped out of the car. He greeted his grandaunt with a wide and firm embrace, and then shook hands with all others. After hugging his younger brother last, he looked once more at Nsoh who had a big smile on her face, but as soon as she made eye contact with him, her bright smile disappeared, walloped by her shyness.

"Quit looking at her, you have an entire lifetime for that... take them to the Abakwa Airport." *Anaa* Nantono jokingly scolded the young man who rapidly hopped in the SUV and turned on the ignition while the other passengers brought in their belongings. As they squeezed themselves and their luggage into the SUV, Tahfuh approached Muungo and offered a farewell handshake. Muungo looked at his hand, then looked into his eyes, looked at Irene and *Anaa* Nantono. He wondered what had become of his brother's relics and thought of the text message of the previous night. After thinking very hard on whether to shake his cousin's hand, Muungo slowly, relaxed his jaw muscles, loosened up his clenched fist and with tough taps he patted his cousin, instead of shaking his hand. Muungo muttered some words and Tahfuh's eyes brows rose in reply.

Chapter 5

Panama City Beach, Florida 2017

Jonah could not help it; he burst into laughter at what Brianna had just said. Brianna was adamant, every time a black man made the big bucks his next objective was a white woman. It was a chat garnished with gestures and faces. For example, whenever she referred to people of the black race, Brianna pointed at the melanin-dominated caramel skin on her backhand. On the other hand, when she referred to persons of white race she pointed at her light pink-colored palms. Brianna occasionally used derogatory terms to refer to both the black man and the white woman. But it was not the appellation or the gesture that made Jonah roar with laughter. The fact was that Jonah had often heard accusations like the one advanced by Brianna. He had heard them so many times that he ended up always expecting them from most black females whenever they were confronted with questions regarding interracial dating. And here was Brianna raising up that same argument almost unconsciously. Statistics neither vouched for Brianna's assertion nor discredited it, Jonah thought.

Jonah was a Football agent working for the sports agency which had signed up Dwayne, Brianna's cousin. Following Dwayne's new and lucrative contract with one of the football franchises, Jonah had been invited to attend a family gathering at Dwayne's summer mansion in Panama City Beach. Jonah was a former football player himself; his glorious days of college football and professional football were gone but his big arms, broad chest and mountainous shoulders stood sturdy, intimidating, and captivating.

Jonah had gone through his career without any crippling brain, spine, or muscle injury... but his love life was in its nth overtime. Overtime after overtime, rescue after rescue, back-to-back turmoil for Jonah even after he had *scored two touchdowns* with his wife—giving her a gorgeous first baby and then a sweet second baby. Every now and then Jonah had to do his very best to rescue his marriage from troubled waters. The troubled waters came from all and every direction; on one side his father-in-law prayed for the day when Jonah will not have enough money to look after his daughter and grandchildren, and on the other side most of Jonah's black female acquaintances waited for the day Jonah's wife will leave Jonah for another rich black man. He had to stay afloat above the restless waters around him; he had to keep his bank account full in order to maintain a standard of living that would make him accepted amongst the *whites* and respected by the *blacks.* Having the job of an NFL agent was Jonah's way of keeping the sweet juice of his current lifestyle from fermenting.

It was Jonah's fame and contribution to the game, and his mastery of the game's ropes that had pushed Dwayne to embrace the idea of having him as his agent. Calm and very observing, Jonah always looked at life as being a magnified version of a football game Super Bowl.

"I am dead serious, you are his agent... you are the closest thing to family for Dwayne, and you are a *brother.*" Brianna said interfering in Jonah's laughter and comedy brake.

"He is my employer and I can't tell him who to date and who not to date, I can't force him to be on *BlackPeopleMeet.com.*" Jonah replied in between chokes of laughter as he used the middle finger of his left hand to dap tears of laughter off the canthi of his eyes.

Jonah knew the weight of his last phrase and kept a vigilant eye on Brianna expecting her to react to it.

"I am not successful but my Michelle, even though she's white, is a fine cook and loving partner as any other black woman from the South is. We black people see the devil in every detail related to race, just as Americans we see the devil in every detail on Arabs of Middle East" Jonah jokingly made the analogy.

"If you, a Heisman trophy recipient and two-time Super Bowl champion, are not successful, then I am not alive." Brianna replied before catching the last thing Jonah said regarding black people. "Oh gosh! Another *white wannabe!*" she thought. Then she continued her conversation as if she did not care about those last words from Jonah.

The two continued their conversation on interracial relationships for a moment, raising their voices and jokingly shoving each other as they exaggerated in their testimonies about interracial relationships. Their laughs did not go unnoticed to Mercy, who had drawn her own little crowd around herself. Mercy's audience listened to her as she talked about her trip to Africa. The audience was so curious about how much jungle and wildlife Mercy had come across while in Africa, and how many people roamed the forest trails with pieces of animal skin covering their nudity. Unfortunately, for this audience its curiosity was not being sharpened by stories of Mighang. So, the audience gradually split into smaller groups which created themselves around new conversation topics.

After the very few wows and quick group dispersion around her, Mercy walked through the uneven crowd and joined Brianna and Jonah by the pool. Contributing to the already existing debate, Mercy surprisingly took Jonah's side. She believed that an atmosphere of perpetual comparison between the black and white races made it difficult for interracial dating and marriage to reach their full potentials. These potentials could be fulfilled by making the most out of the diversity add-on. Yet, focusing too much on an add-on instead of the main piece of a relationship made it difficult for one to see life for what it really is —an inexhaustible blessing.

To support her stance on the topic excessive distraction caused by racial disparity, Mercy made a comparison of the consequences of race issues in America to those in Africa. According to her, there was an overwhelming majority of black people in Africa, and a huge volume of personal life problems in Africa as there were in other parts of the world. So, if these problems existed independent of the black versus white race conflicts, then it would be silly to blame all the evils happening in any part of the world on racial diversity and disparity. Most personal problems in America had their mirror images in Africa, and these mirror images that had nothing to do with races. In conclusion, races probably only got invited to the ball of personal problems as a way to hinder critical minds from promoting change based on self-development. Consequently, giving room for an 'I' versus racism development instead of an 'I' versus an 'I' development.

Mercy further elaborated that, in Africa one could clearly realize that all sorts of failures, the broken socio-political systems of Africa and even failed human relationships, were results of individual and collective inefficiency. In the African settings, where skin color was not the focus, relationships and general societal problems similar to those in interracial environments existed. Clearly therefore, racial differences were not and should not be the root cause of failed societies and their many other ills.

Mercy's contribution slowly drifted the debate into a scope wider than the one spanned by interracial relationship. It took a broader socio-political approach. Her deep love for social studies was responsible for that drift.

"During my time in Africa, I observed that almost everyone strives forward without thinking that his or her color will stop him or her from reaching his or her goal. Something we don't have here in America because some of us are made to believe that racism must be addressed first before anything else can work. Nonetheless, I must say nepotism and tribalism are the African's *racism*. The political class brandish them as the problem of problems, and so the people forget to work on developing themselves and end up focusing on fighting or reinforcing nepotism and tribalism." Mercy argued. "So maybe we will be better off if we put racism and tribalism in second place on the priority list of our fight for personal and collective successes.

"So, you see; here in America we have a giant, by the name race, in the room who draws all the attention and makes our everyday problems always have a racial connotation. Even those problems that have a political and governmental policy foundation end up anchoring themselves on race." Mercy continued.

Jonah and Brianna had been quiet for a few moments. Their limited experiences of the world beyond the continental USA bubble, especially for Brianna, had reduced their participation to nothing but occasional head nods and raised eyebrows. Mercy, blossoming in her lecture on the state of the world and after letting Jonah contribute for moment, further claimed that the American system was trying to perform a balance act on an unbalanced equality-justice-freedom tripod. By putting an accent on freedom bordering libertinism, the American system had sacrificed equality and justice in the society. In addition, equality and justice, which are the rungs of the ladder leading to success, were race-color-coded. And all the focus was being put on the color-code instead of grooming those climbing up the figurative ladder. But if, for just one moment, everyone chose to excel without focusing on the racial bullets catapulted in their direction then eventually, the societal dynamics would forcefully gravitate towards them when they reach a certain threshold of indispensability. Mercy took as example to her postulate a former teammate of Jonah's. During the course of his career and by virtue of his talent, the teammate, had forced many professional football teams to commit to long term investments in his quasi-unknown and predominantly black hometown as a condition for of him to join their teams. His name was Spencer Spencer Jr.

As a quarterback "Super" Spencer's athletic capability made him the winner of Super Bowl rings. Initially no professional football team was interested in signing him despite his unmatched record in college football, simply because he insisted on having potential recruiters invest in his quite small poor and black hometown before he would negotiate any contract with them. But, after a few years, when his former college football coach became coach of a professional football team things changed; the coach convinced his employer to hand them a Super Bowl champion title if they let him sign up the 29-year-old unorthodox former top college athlete. For his first professional contract, "Super" Spencer had his new team do the impossible; They built a modern medical center in his hometown in exchange for a lucrative one season contract. SS, "Super" Spencer, Super Sonic, however you wish to call him used his throw, his precision, his vision, his agility, and his speed on the pitch to put an end to the Super Bowl dry run of the NFL underdog that recruited him. After eight seasons and six rings, the legend quit the game before the game quit him.

A damped nodding of the head, the left hand on the left hip, and Jonah was absorbed in the discussion and memories of the game with SS. "Because SS was indispensable, SS forced respect even from those who had counted him out." Jonah added as he nodded to Mercy's contribution.

Feeling outmatched by the solid pair, Brianna excused herself. She headed toward the minibar to go grab another drink. In the meantime, Jonah and Mercy, football fans, continued their discussion and barely noticed Brianna's exit.

From a withdrawn corner of the vast party area came the bubbly sound of water being pumped into the swimming pool; this sound added itself to the voices of Jonah and Mercy. Often nodding his head and twiddling his fingers, Jonah agreed with most of what Mercy said. Granted, in some few cases he did have his own opinion that diverged from Mercy's. One of such discussions was the one about Historical Black Schools.

According to Jonah the labeling of certain schools as Historical Black Schools and Tribal Schools, which could essentially serve as incubators for the type of race-free self-development ideology supported by Mercy, was a problem—a softer version of apartheid. He believed that semantically speaking the labeling was the subtle prelude to historical black jobs and tribal jobs. Jonah supported his assertion by arguing that because every so often these schools did not generally rank amongst the very best in national rankings, the appellation was insinuating that the professional aptitude of graduates from Historical Black Schools and Tribal Schools was inferior to that of their Caucasian counterparts.

Feeling very inspired, Jonah continued onto another remark that was worth mentioning. Jonah also believed that even the term Native America was not appropriate. Unlike African Americans, most Indians knew their tribes of origin and should be referred to as Americans with ancestry from these tribes rather than just Native Americans. He went on to ask Mercy the following question: "Why is it not common for one to say either Seminole-American or Cherokee-American meanwhile it is common for others to say either Irish-American or Italian-American?" To Jonah this categorization of all Americans of Indian descent as Native Americans was a subtle process of erasing the potency of their independent and powerful communities in days of yore, and consequently impeding them from self-development as communities and as individuals. So, while Jonah agreed on race being attributed too much attention to the detriment of other ills of the society, he believed that the process of self-development had to start elsewhere-- somewhere other than the academic system. For a start, each community had to agree to the same terms with respect to their relations to the government and the nation at large. In addition, these communities had to drop terms and expressions that suggested uneven battlefields amongst race communities.

"It is this apparent disparity in the ways races are treated that formed the basis of racial rivalry." He added.

Mercy thought Jonah's stance was off the grid. According to her it was but natural to remember and keep the labeling of these Historical Black Schools which nested civil right activists and educated most black scholars of the post emancipation era. In addition, Mercy believed that the names of the Native American tribes and their geographical locations which were already perpetrated in historical archives made the term Native

American less vague than the term African American. Thus, the specificity of appurtenance to a particular Indian tribe belonged to the individual's choice on details.

Jonah listened to Mercy with much interest. He had met many women of color with a strong character, too strong for him at times. But Mercy was one who defended the black woman and the black community with a certain finesse, the kind celebrated on the media. What Jonah did not know was that with Mercy, that finesse of hers disappeared whenever proper debating was nonexistent: that is, when she fell that either her private space was violated, the history of her ancestors ignored, or that she was being treated as a lesser human compared to others. Jonah was not done listening to Mercy when she was interrupted abruptly.

Michelle had unintentionally slightly bumped into Mercy as she walked towards her husband. Michelle did not care to apologize. After all, to Michelle it was Mercy who had moved in on her path. Jonah's spouse, oblivious to Mercy's need of an apology, coldly requested the car keys from him. Their baby needed some breast milk and his mother wanted to go collect her breastfeeding necessities, breast pump and nipple pad, from the car. So, Jonah handed the car keys to his wife, and that alone would have been enough. But an overzealous Jonah attempted to make introductions. The introduction of Mercy to Michelle and vice versa did not go too well.

"Michelle! Meet Mercy, and Mercy this is my wife Michelle." Jonah said while handing the keys to Michelle.

"Oh, nice to meet you Mercy, and apology accepted for bumping into me." Michelle answered.

Mercy was quite puzzled at the last part of Michelle's response. In the split of a second Mercy thought it was a joke. So jokingly too, Mercy replied saying that she believed it was her, Mercy, who deserved an apology. Michelle who had already gone past Mercy by a few steps immediately turned around.

"May be if a *sister were* not trying to take a *brother* home tonight, she would be more attentive."

Mercy did not find anything comic in this response from Michelle. She closed her eyes for a few seconds; it was an attempt at controlling her inner being quivering with the desire for retaliation. Luckily, Mercy did not respond to this inner demon. Why should she? She did not expect much decency from one whose father was a diehard racist. It was known by everyone in the sport business that Michelle's father had disapproved of his daughter's wedding to Jonah. He had always wanted his daughter to marry someone who was white and of a higher social class than his daughter. Rumor had it that Michelle had fallen out with her father when she had decided to marry the then sex symbol amongst the black males of the Florida panhandle football community--Jonah.

"Sorry for that uncalled for behavior from my wife, I better leave before hell breaks loose on us." Jonah apologized and walked away as he grinned.

Mercy walked a few steps and stopped at another corner of the courtyard. She stood there all alone in that corner of Dwayne's backyard by a calm pond and away from the splashing sound coming from the swimming pool. Holding her glass of wine between her thumb, index, and middle fingers, she rotated it clockwise and then took a sip of the swirling red content. Her isolation gave her the time to revisit the short drama that had just happened

Mercy questioned Michelle's reaction, but even more she questioned the fact that she herself and everyone else did not seem to be able to see Michelle without seeing her father through her. Mercy pondered if that was how she was looked upon whenever she went back home to Atlanta, Georgia. Did people see her as the sister of the once popular drug Lord or as a woman who had forged a new life for herself. She dwelled drowned in her thoughts even though her stare remained glued to the silent fishpond in front of her, giving the impression that she was watching the ducks swim around. It was the sudden loud quacks of these ducks that finally helped Mercy out of her ocean of thoughts.

The get together had not lost its jovial side. Dwayne had kept the ladies laughing and the guys arguing. It was when this fun reached its climax, that Mercy and Brianna left, almost unnoticed. At least they did not know that some of Dwayne's friends had them under their radar and were planning to play the *"haven't we met before?"* card at the upcoming Sports Family Ball in Miami.

Brianna dropped off Mercy at her apartment and once inside her apartment Mercy quickly undressed and hopped into the shower. Vapor from her warm bath rose and clouded the glass door of her shower. Behind the clouded glass, a fine guitar-shaped silhouette scrubbed and clean itself and hummed a series of popular tunes.

Minutes later, she was in her bathrobe holding her dark blue hair dryer above her head. The vibration from her phone, transmitted into the hard-wooden surface of the commode, interrupted her moment of beauty. It must be Brianna who had texted her to let her know she had made it home safely, Mercy thought. Carefully placing the hairdryer on the commode, Mercy picked up her phone and realized the message was from an unknown number.

"Hey, I really enjoyed our discussion! One of my clients is searching for motivational speakers for his youth fan base, let me know if you are interested and I'll send you the details. Good night! Jonah" Jonah had texted.

Mercy did not mind finding a message from an unknown number. The concern was who had given her number to Jonah? Jonah with the crazy and over jealous spouse. She decided not to reply to the text, at least not that night. She connected her phone to its charger and returned to her beauty session with her hair dryer. After applying ointments on her neck, wrist, fingers, and hair Mercy was done preparing herself and went straight to bed.

Saturday morning came with a loud bang. The night before Mercy had forgotten to turn off her alarm clock so that she could sleep through the morning. Here was the result of such negligence; she was awakened by an unexpected early morning alarm. The acute and ear-aching bugle horn ringtone snatched Mercy from a cloud nine morning sleep. Eyes firmly closed and right hand tapping all over her bed commode in irritation, Mercy hit and turned off her alarm, but unfortunately, she was unable to go back to sleep. So, minutes later she jumped out of her bed, and headed for the shower. The hot water trickled down her bare body, making it harder for her to break free from Morpheus' arms. The prolonged shower caused the steam to end up as fog deposited the glass sliding door of her bathtub, and Mercy could not see through the door. Another thing she could not see through was the hidden message, if any, buried behind last night's text from Jonah.

The warm bath and privacy felt good even though the bath had come in earlier than expected; both luxuries were rare to come by during her time in Africa. From her loud humming under the shower it was easy to deduce that she was glad to be back from Africa; she once again realized how much she had missed her place. Hand pressed against the tiled wall of the bathroom, she let the drops of warm water crash against the skin of her bare body. With each crash of a water drop on her skin, impulses were fired, and they traveled from neuron heads on the skin, through the neuron bodies and synapses, and ended up in her brain. The brain then dissipated a strong feeling of relaxation in and all through her body.

Moments after her prolonged shower Mercy stood strong and fully awake next to her couch in a pair of leggings and a sport bra. The bra was stretched by the upward movement of her right hand holding a glass from which she was gulping the last droplets of orange juice. Her head was tilted backwards to let in the juice droplets and still it did not distract her eyes checking out the news headlines on TV.

Among the headlines was a breaking news from the sport rubric: it was the signing of Dwayne by a football franchise. That breaking news and the name Dwayne sure reminded Mercy again of yesterday's late-night text. She immediately put down her glass on the stool next to the couch, picked up her phone and dialed Brianna's number to find out if it was Brianna who had given her number to Jonah. A few rings on the other end of the line and then Brianna picked the phone and they exchanged a series of greetings before diving into the heart of the subject. It was indeed Brianna who had given Mercy's number to Jonah. Mercy, a little bit unhappy about her number being given away without her consent, kept a calm and controlled voice and tried to point out the awkwardness about getting a late-night text from Jonah, a married man who was nothing more than an acquaintance and whose wife was ...

"Gurl! It's not like the boy was sexting you, and more to that, that wife of his ain't nothin' but a white gold digger!" Brianna responded.

For a moment Mercy zoned out of the conversation, the darkness and coldness of Brianna's last words sealed-froze her upper lips to her lower lips. Mercy shook her head sideways and squirmed as she replayed Brianna's phrase in her subconscious. Brianna continued talking on the other end of the telephone line, and her words flowed into a loud provocative giggle. The giggle was irritating to Mercy, so irritating that Mercy jumped into the conversation with a forced clearing of her throat and an indescribable urge to call Brianna back to order. Without letting Brianna finish her caricaturing of Jonah's wife, Mercy barked at Brianna.

The infuriated Mercy questioned her friend on how she would feel if someone came to her and described Mercy as the younger sister of a black drug Lord, a single black *sista* who thinks she is too good for a *brotha*? Brianna was caught off guard and was fully surprised by Mercy's words. She was profoundly surprised given Michelle's attitude towards Mercy the night before. But Brianna's surprise did not last for too long as Mercy continued to sermonize her regarding her description of Michelle. The conversation lost its convivial component, Brianna's voice now had a lower pitch and her participation in the conversation limited itself to listening.

After the conversation, or better still, the one-way heated exchange with Brianna had finally returned to normal, Mercy and Brianna each said goodbye and hung up their phones. Mercy took some time for herself. Immersed in an atmosphere perfumed with the smell of damp red wood chips that lined the flowerbeds in her front yard, Mercy sat on a wooden stool she had brought from her trip to Cameroon. She thought about the multiple scenes filled with stereotypes, the dramas of stereotypes which she had experienced all through her life and especially in the last couple of days. She recalled the most embarrassing of the scenes, with a pound of pain and an ounce of tears.

When Mercy was in ninth grade, she had fought, alongside a bunch of her friends, against a Latina classmate. Dora Sanchez had just arrived from El-Salvador her Amazonian complexion and strong "r" influenced accent had made her the center of attraction to most boys in school. But the other girls accused her of using some Latino candle prayers to cast a spell on their boyfriends. Mercy and co ganged up and fought Dora one afternoon after school. The poor girl was not only hurt but decided not to ever return to that school. All these memories weighed on Mercy's shoulders, and the good versus evil scales of conscience did not balance up. As a grown woman, she now realized the need to overcome stereotypes. Mercy decided she had to make things right; break barriers and build bridges. She hesitantly picked up her phone and texted Jonah. She inquired if the motivational speaking invitation involved a multiracial audience.

Chapter 6

Panama City, Florida 2018

The old gymnasium attracted crowds, and unlike most other gymnasiums this attraction was not thanks to the great membership deals offered every year to their short-lived zealous clientele of the month of January. These days the gymnasium was just a wide empty hall—no workout machines, but most of the mirrors still glued to the room's four walls. Jonah and his crew had ordered thick cardboards to cover these mirrors. Thanks to the funds from some of the football players affiliated to his agency, Jonah had bought seats, tables, projectors and screens, and bathroom lockers. Funds had also been allocated for the renovation of the bathrooms and the games courts inside and outside the gym, the installation of an up-to-date audio system and the complete replacement of the HVAC system. It was in this reawakened splendor and beauty that the gymnasium, *Dinkinesh* as she had been baptized, welcomed young adolescents and children who needed mentoring.

Dinkinesh was the Amharic appellation of the relics of the oldest human remains found near Hadar in Ethiopia. *Dinkinesh* in Amharic signifies "you are marvelous," but to the youth mentor this name was chosen to remind the children that it was a haven, protection provided by the mother of all humans. Here at *Dinkinesh* it did not matter if the children were white, black, brown, yellow, blue or even green, they were all children of *Dinkinesh*. The mentees were taught that they were children of one parent and had to look out for one another the same way players on a successful football team do. It was this message of brotherly love and team spirit that was transmitted to the mentees through brochures, field trips, volunteer work sessions, summer camps activities and exchanges with guest speakers.

On one occasion, when *Dinkinesh* was at the beginning of her transformation, the mentees and their mentors had gathered in great numbers to volunteer with the replacement of tiles, the polishing of door frames and other wooden structures. The volunteering initiative was preferred over outsourcing not because of insufficient funds, instead it was a way to instill civic engagement and community service to the young mentees. During that renovation period, while most volunteers were roaming around in their idleness, a young kid with a bruised left cheek and blackened left eye had made a temporary seat for himself next to a broken fountain of the gymnasium. The little boy lingered in the gymnasium scouting the place in search for a spot to hide himself until everyone was gone. It seemed nobody had noticed him in his hiding place until it was time to the close the doors and go home.

"Hey man! We got your back man!" came a loud statement of support that took the sneaky kid by surprise while he was trying to slide and hide behind a stack of empty boxes gathered next to the gymnasium's half-renovated restroom. Once he heard those words, he knew his plan was aborted. These words of encouragement were from another boy who knew that his young friend was scared to go home because of some serious gang related problems.

This bruised kid was having to deal with a situation involving his former weed wholesale provider whom he was owing some cash. Because of the money owed to this wholesale provider and boss, the kid had no choice but to either work for the boss, and by so doing slowly pay back the money he owed, or to pay all the money owed at once in order to avoid being harassed. This money owed to his boss was payment towards a packet of weed that had been seized from the kid during his last arrest and sentencing to a juvenile correction center. Following the time at the correction center, the once weed seller chose to turn his life around. This decision was bad news for his former boss, who insisted the kid pay him for the packet of weed that had been confiscated by the police during his arrest. Thus, with every night that went by without him paying his former boss, he was beaten and ridiculed by bullies, and because of a very high interest, the money owed kept accruing at an unbelievable rate.

The other kids at the center had heard of the story and had pitched in money together to pay back the weed dealer's $3,263. The mentors could have helped pay for this when they found out about the story a few days earlier, but the other kids decided to stick together like one family and take care of their own. An initiative which they led with success and bravery, and the best part was that they had kept it a secret from the victim until this night when they had put all the money together. Unfortunately, they could not get the police involved because *Black Phantom*, the wholesale weed dealer, was more than just a person, he was an entire enterprise, the kind you do not confront if not well equipped. It is even said that *Black Phantom* had customers and partners in the local city and county police forces. *Dinkinesh* was home to many other stories and testimonies like this one, but today was about something different. Tonight, *Dinkinesh* was reserved for an illustrious guest speaker.

The weather forecast had predicted a cloudy evening, but the stubborn night sky luminaries joined the sodium lamp of the parking lot to illuminate the tarmac surrounding *Dinkinesh*. A Volkswagen beetle crawled into the parking spot between a SUV and a minivan bearing the logo of the C.O.O.L. Foundation. Out of the Volkswagen beetle came Ms. Lewis, one of the newest mentors of the Courage, Openness, and Overcoming Limits Foundation. She was first introduced to the mentees about six months ago and from that time on, she had been very involved in creating a stronger bond amongst the foundation's mentees. At every opportunity she reminded them that the only way for them to overcome stigmatization from outsiders was to crush any form of stereotypes within the group. But tonight, she had driven to *Dinkinesh* for a completely different reason. She was not going to be the guest speaker; instead, she was going to be part of the audience. Paul Peyton, a bestselling author and renowned host of a nationwide radio talk show was expected to address the members and mentors of the C.O.O.L. Foundation.

Chapter 7

Ellicott City, Maryland 1984

Paul Peyton grew up in Ellicott City--Maryland. His mother rented a two-bedroom apartment in this small town in the outskirts of Baltimore. His father, just like the fathers of his other four siblings, was nowhere to be found—at least that's what he had concluded. At the age of 14 Paul was arrested together with two of his friends on car theft charges. In fact, beyond the motif of the arrest, the incident was some sort of prank that ended up in bad note for Peyton. Following the arrest on charges of car theft, Paul's two other friends got off with what could be described as mild taps on their wrists, while Paul spent two years in a juvenile detention center. Every single detail of this unfortunate ordeal was engraved in his mind.

Before the arrest, the then teenage Paul and his friends had spent most of their weekends idling on a steep slope covered with vibrant green turf. This green turf stretched over the space between the backyard of their apartment building and a shallow bushy valley. At times they would slide down the valley's slope into a small water course caressing the roots of the bushes as it flowed through the bottom of the valley. They did this so that they could escape from their boring and *unnecessary* chores. But an idle mind is certainly the devil's workshop.

So, on one evening of one of those many Saturdays, the boys had come up with the insane idea of driving to Arundel Mills Mall. It had always been a plan of theirs to someday go to the malls to roam whatever aisle they pleased for as long as they pleased. After puffing a few marijuana joints and having the illusion that they had grown longer beards, that their biceps had grown bigger, and their testicles had dropped lower, they decided to stroll through parking lots in search of a car left unlocked. Blake, one of Paul's friends, had claimed it was a common mistake for tired drivers to forget their car keys on their car doors or to simply forget to lock their cars. So, Paul and Claudio were on the lookout from either end of the parking lot while Blake zigzagged between parking spaces testing the door handles on the driver sides of parked vehicles. Well, on that day the trio was out of luck, no driver was tired enough to offer them an opportunity to go for a joy ride around town. Disillusioned, the boys sadly walked away and slipped back down the slope to the banks of the small river running through the valley.

After returning to their hangout spot and puffing some more herbs, they once again climbed out of the valley and revisited the parking lot. Only this time they were hovering on their feet, their conscious being was at an all-time high sensation, and they proceeded without the least concise plan in mind. Two was indeed a charm, for it was during this second exploration of the parking lot that Blake, under the heavy influence of cannabis, walked towards a car that had visibly just rushed into a parking spot. With his head all covered by his hoodie and walking past the smoke oozing out the car's exhaust pipe Blake poked the driver in the back with black car jack handle he had found abandoned in the parking lot. Pretending that the car jack was a gun, Blake seized the car keys, cell phone and wallet of the driver. The assailant guided the driver towards a slope and asked the terrified man to run down the hill. To run without looking backwards and counting out loud from one to five thousand or else he was going to shoot the driver down. The horrified driver heeded to the warning; he took off while counting out loud as ordered, and Blake rapidly got in the car and sat on the driver's seat, took his hoodie down and with his leg on the gas pedal he accelerated as he drove out of the parking space. Immediately, Blake drove to the other parking lot where his friends had been walking in between the cars and they hopped into the vehicle.

The three boys had been in the stolen car for over 10 minutes, and their minds and reasoning were still clouded by the smoke from all the marijuana they had inhaled. None of them had been smart enough to adamantly inquire where Blake had gotten the car from. Who cared after all? Didn't Blake say he had borrowed it from his uncle? The silver-colored Toyota Camry had barely zigzagged pass other cars moving through the averagely dense traffic of the Baltimore-Washington Parkway when a State Trooper lit his rotating roof light, turned on his siren, and pulled over the Camry. It is funny how the boys went from being just high to being high and aware of the mess which they had gotten themselves into. On the steering wheel of the car was the 14 year-old Paul Peyton; Blake and Claudio had convinced him that the law did not condemn underage white drivers. A Black or Latino underage driver was a whistleblower, something Paul had also heard from his friends. Paul was charged with illegal possession of weed, armed car theft, reckless driving, underage driving, and driving under the influence.

Usually, for Paul Peyton, Saturdays and their sunsets ended with a great unique touch. The great thing was that after hanging out with his friends he would walk home, and his mother would have left for work and would not be there to nag him. But that particular Saturday was an exception to that trend. At that instant of trouble, Paul wished the setting sun had helped the driver identify his assailant as being of Black race like Blake. He wished he did not know where his mom stashed her weed. He wished he had a father to school him about underage driving, DUI (Driving Under the Influence), and reckless driving. Too late! Paul ended up only in a Juvenile detention center thanks to vital information provided by the car owner who was a close friend to his mother.

Paul's stay at the Juvenile detention center was, at least at the beginning, the worst nightmare of his young life. His involvement in the carjacking incident had led cops to search their apartment and his mom's weed stash was discovered. His four younger siblings were found at home alone with no adult guardian. Following the investigations, the cops concluded that the weed probably belonged to Paul and social services took his siblings away from their mother. Paul's newly earned criminal record and the fact that his siblings were not properly looked after had also led to the conclusion that it was not safe for the children to live with their mother and so they were given up for adoption. Extremely saddened, their mother eventually ended up depressed, suicidal, and bottom-line schizophrenic and was finally admitted into a mental facility.

At the correction center Paul Peyton often sat at the very edge of the topmost bed of one of the bunk beds in his dormitory zone, he let his feet dangle as he reminisced the events through which he had destroyed his family. The first few nights, tears ran down his cheeks and he only went to sleep when those lachrymal glands of his red swollen eyes were empty and the eyelids too heavy to remain propped open. After weeks without visitation and weeks full of altercations with fellow delinquents, he stumbled on something special. It was the autobiography of Malcolm X which he came across while finishing up his punishment for picking another fight with an older delinquent. He read through one page of the book every night, right before the staff cut off the lights, and because of it he resolved to make the most of his stay at the center. He still had sporadic clashes with those around him, that earned him cuts, bruises, fractures, and even an attempted murder by hanging once. But he read and reread the autobiography and sharpened his decision of becoming better.

Thanks to his close ties with the employees of the juvenile detention center who had rescued him from being hanged by the other juveniles, Paul got books on regular basis, read them and learned a variety of things. One of the books he laid his hands on was on communicating beyond words, and that book was a game changer for him. He came up with the idea of writing to a newspaper, providing its readers with pieces of advice from a detained teenager. It took a couple of months before the local newspaper gave him an unused space of their weekly paper, mostly because they found themselves short of ideas. Over the next weeks he was awarded a column in the local newspaper entitled *Stay Free or Become Free*. In his column he talked about his story before and during his time at the center. He used his experiences as words of caution to those who read his column and used his writing as way to heal from the pain he harbored inside him. When he ran out of personal experiences, fellow delinquents and even inmates from other facilities sent him letters so he could tell their stories as well.

Two years later, under the blue sky and surrounded by a pollen-filled breeze of the spring season, when Paul Peyton walked out of detention center he decided to give a positive twist to his life. He continued receiving letters from detainees and writing for the local newspaper. Thanks to this freelance writer job, a few academic grants, and untaxed cash from a Disc Jockey job in the hood Paul managed to make some change and pay his way through college. He graduated with a Bachelor's Degree in Journalism after having minored in communication. He later became the host of a popular talk show that aired all over the USA, but he still bore the feeling that he had not written out all of his pain.

Because of this deep pain he decided to spend part of his time and huge fortune in search of his siblings, their mother, and the father of each of his siblings. He had successfully found them, but more importantly he had maybe found a way to reconcile himself with his past. One step at a time, as he tracked down each of his family members a chapter of his personal story was concluded; the ends were not always pleasant, but they were curative. From foster home to foster home, hidden family secret after hidden family secret, he discovered the chains that he needed to break to set himself free of his pain and those unbreakable chains that shackled him to his identity. It was this story that he shared with *Dinkinesh*'s audience on that evening when he was invited as guest speaker. Most of the members of his audience easily related to the story and they could not help but dream of the day when they too will be free.

Panama City, Florida 2018

Paul Peyton's voice, narrating his life stories, flowed through the already packed gymnasium; like water flowing through grains of sand tightly packed together in a recipient. Paul's words found room in every corner of the tightly packed multiracial audience. Tears and cheers alternated amongst members of the audience, especially from one of them—Mercy. The guest speaker paused and gulped some fresh water from his glass and continued inspiring the kids whose eyes were wide open staring at the orator's beautiful redeemed and gleaming soul.

Mercy never knew her father and when her mother was still alive, she barely visited her mom at the retirement home because she avoided family drama with her middle sister. Even weirder, for the last four years she had been financially assisting her late brother's daughter without wanting to make herself known to the little girl's family. There on the stage was a middle-aged white man who had been a victim of stereotypes and who had made every mistake in his past count for a thousand positive things in his life and the lives of others. She had read, more than once, Paul's Peyton's autobiography and the *New York Times* bestseller entitled *When Being White was a Crime*, but listening to him was a completely different experience in itself.

After the talk the young mentees rushed towards the pizza, sandwiches, cookies, and sodas that populated the table at the back for the room, Mercy gradually moved towards the front stage. She intentionally walked at a slower pace hoping to reach the front stage when most people would have spoken with Paul Peyton and cleared the stage. Then shock waves from her phone vibrating in her purse reached her hand as she kept walking. With a reflex act, and her eyes still tracking Paul Peyton's slow darting movement across the stage, Mercy pulled her phone out of her purse. She quickly glanced at the phone's screen, its backlight gradually fading, and she kept guiding her steps in the direction prescribed by her brain's nerve cells. On the phone's screen she noticed a recent missed call from Brianna and another missed call from Muungo, but she did not care very much about those two that instance.

Before she even noticed it, there she was standing next to Paul Peyton. She was so close to him that she could easily tell he was wearing *Essence* fragrance by AXE. No surprise that she could make that remark; she was a big fan of male fragrances. In front of her was a Caucasian in his mid-fifties, with a black beret on his almost bald head on which survived few red hairs evenly spread on the sides of his head. His blushed face blended with the red hair from his moustache and beard. A white man with a very strong African American fraternal way of acting, she thought to herself. Maybe it was the beret which he wore in the Ernesto "Che" Guevara style and the colorful dashiki that made his African American persona so conspicuous, Mercy imagined as she stretched out her hand to greet him.

"Powerful speech Mr. Peyton," Mercy said.

"Speeches are for political promises and ethical talks; I do testimonies and lessons. Please call me Paul." Mr. Peyton responded as he tenderly held out his hand and shook Mercy's.

Chapter 8

Panama City, Florida 2018

The crowd at the Festival of Nations was very diverse. Like multicolored ocean debris being washed on and off the golden white sandy beaches of Panama City Beach, the participants at the festival walked away from, while others towards, the parking lots. The barricades that had been set up to block off vehicle traffic seemed to delimit a space for the air and energy of the festival. When those heading towards the place of celebration went past the barricades, they immediately got hit by the air filled with aromas and refined musical tunes from different food stands and improvised music stages respectively. One band seemed to attract more people than others, it was the Latina band. The Latina band was performing old school Salsa dance acts. Despite the rough and hard texture of the dance floor, the three pairs of dancers were executing delicate and complicated Salsa moves with great dexterity. The tarmac that served as dance floor did not seem to matter to the dancers as they swap partners time and again as part of their choreography. It was during one of these swaps that a toddler ran onto the stage. Watching her run gave the impression that she was jumping on springs, obviously her motor skills were not completely developed. Once she got close to the dancers, the toddler froze with her right thumb in her mouth. She hesitated in her young mind on whether to join the dancers or rush back to her parents who were calling her and slowly approaching the toddler. Without her permission, one of the male dancers picked the little girl up, held her tight against his torso, and finished the last couple of dance moves. A storm of claps escorted the dancers off the stage, and the toddler, Wilanne, was returned to her father, Muungo.

Muungo took Wilanne back to the African Stand which he managed alongside his wife. From a distance one could recognize a cluster of silhouettes. The silhouettes grew more visible as they moved towards the African stand. Brianna, Mercy, Jonah, Paul, Michelle and two other people stopped by the African stand. Mercy took the responsibility of introducing her friends to Muungo. Brianna who already knew Muungo, and did not need any further introduction, simply picked up Muungo's daughter and started talking with her. Though everybody's attention was focused on the little girl, Paul Peyton's attention quickly drifted to the objects displayed in the stand.

"So, what part of Africa are you from?" Michelle asked.

"Geographically I am from West Africa, but politically I am from Central Africa." Muungo replied as he reached out for a mask that was out of Paul's reach.

"How can that be?" Michelle asked with much astonishment in her bright smile.

"Mercy would you please tell Michelle what you know about the history of Cameroon?" Muungo asked as he tried to sympathize with another guest who had just stopped by his stand.

Michelle and Mercy had not exchanged many words since their last encounter at Dwayne's cookout. Michelle and Mercy had come across each other during the C.O.O.L Foundation events, and even though one could sense a desire of reconciliation between the two, Jonah did not want to take any risk and so he kept them far apart as much as he could. But with Muungo's offer the two ladies were given a chance to talk to each other. Mercy turned towards a world map at one end of the stand and invited Michelle to join her. Michelle hastily got there and began listening attentively to Mercy's lecture on Cameroon.

Muungo was done talking to a couple of folks visiting the African stand about the twin-headed snake—totem of the Bamoun Sultanate, he turned around and saw Paul discussing with a man dressed in a black jacket over a white shirt, a knee-length skirt made of checkered cloth, and a lone pair of socks ending in a black pair of shoes. The man was dressed in the traditional Irish attire. It seemed to Muungo that Paul was lecturing the visitor on a calabash resting on one of the tables in the stand. Muungo drew closer to Paul; he wondered what Paul was saying about the calabashes. He was worried that Paul could be misinforming the man. To his greatest surprise Paul was very informed on the role of the calabash in the West African culture.

Calabashes are made out of matured melon, preferably long matured melon. They are harvested, dried, and their inside diligently carved out. The outside of the calabash is either left smooth and untouched or beautifully decorated with paint or sculpture. When the calabashes are intended to serve as dishes they are cut in the form of hemispheres. They can also be used as receptacles for beverages, in that case they are modeled in the form of gourds. The quality of the decoration on the calabash increases its value and at times defines the purpose for which it was designed.

Paul paused for a moment to listen to a question from his interlocutor.

Paul then continued explaining more about the calabash as Muungo walked away to attend to other visitors of his stand. One after another, guests succeeded themselves to hear Paul or Muungo talk about the calabash, masks, clothes, and other items. On the other corner of the tent, Mercy and Michelle were very much at ease with each other. They had chatted over the map of Africa and about the ambiguity in Muungo's answer regarding his origins. Their conversation had even continued into expressions of apologies regarding their first encounter. As the two ladies got to know each other better, Brianna sat at one corner not too happy about what she considered their growing complicity. Brianna tried to ignore the ambiance between the girls; she created her own fun with the toddler, Wilanne. Brianna and the toddler were immersed in games installed in Brianna's cell Phone.

The Festival of Nations was drawing to an end. Stands were being emptied and tents being taken down. A few food stands were still crowded as people swung by to buy plates of food for the evening. The ultimate signs of the end of festivities were the groups of people from different nationalities joining in the final parade. The Mexicans, the Russians, the Israelites, the Irish, and many other nationalities joined in the march past. Each group marched with their flag and their members. Made up of children and adults, the groups marched graciously and waved their flags under the ovation and applauses of the few remaining spectators. Jonah and Paul were helping Muungo fold his tent and tables, when all of the sudden Paul suggested that they interrupt the packing and join the parade.

"We don't have the number and the choreography to go that far." Muungo who was bent over, looked up and replied.

"I say we do. You, me, Mercy, Jonah, Michelle, Brianna, and your wife and daughter." Paul insisted after temporarily pausing in his task.

"You are funny but let us keep that for some other festival" Said Muungo as he resumed packing his items.

Paul insisted again and again on having the African team participate in the parade. In normal circumstances Muungo and Jonah would have resisted the invitation. But how often in the south of America or elsewhere across the globe did one see a white man so passionate about black cultures. Despite the temptation to resist the idea, the two fellows and the ladies joined Paul in improvising a group for the parade. Irene quickly wrapped pieces of cloth on the heads of the ladies in the form of headscarves tied with an African touch; Jonah picked up a *Djembe* and carelessly forced a traditional Tikari hat on his head. Paul and Muungo were already wearing dashikis. Muungo hurriedly adjusted Jonah's hat and then he turned and walked towards Paul. The two men dressed in dashikis each picked a mask and a calabash. The improvised African group hurried and took a spot behind the Irish orchestra, the last group of the parade.

One of the coordinators of the parade approached them and asked them to position themselves in front of the Irish orchestra instead. Initially, the African group did not really have a show going on, as such they simply marched to the sound of the Irish orchestra behind them. The melodious sounds from the uilleann pipes and drums of the Irish orchestra overshadowed Jonah's erratic beats of the *Djembe*. But as the African group reached the halfway mark of the street on which the parade was taking place, the representatives of the Brazilian group joined them. The Brazilian drummers introduced a beat of samba and in the blink of an eye the Brazilian girls went ablaze. Burning with the rhythm and the yodeling, the Brazilian girls, dressed in colorful carnival attire, hopped onto the street and set it on fire. As these ladies threw their feet forward and sideways and moved their arms as if swimming through the frenzied atmosphere, their hips swung rhythmically and sensually causing the crowd to whistle and clap passionately. Without any notice the ladies from other Caribbean nations' groups also joined the African group. The original members of the parading group, caught somewhere between admiration and participation, joined in the spectator's applause and sailed with the samba dancers down the street. Paul nodded at Muungo when they made eye contact as they danced alongside the other groups. Paul also mouthed something like "Africa is in the blood, not in the numbers!" Muungo did not quite understand the words but he smiled back at him.

The beautiful evening kept her sunset glow on everyone's smiling face; Jonah and his wife wished the others goodnight as they stood up ready to leave the dining table in Mercy's apartment. Between sips of some good French wine, Muungo made fun of Jonah.

"You should have listened to Jonah's beat of the *Djembe*." He chuckled.

"Muungo I heard that!" Jonah replied as he pulled the door closed behind him.

The door reopened as Michelle rushed back and gently pushed the door open right before Mercy had reached it to turn the lock. Michelle whispered something in Mercy's ear and both ladies burst out in laughter.

"Oh *Gurl!* I see you there on Tuesday then, and don't forget!" Mercy said in between smiles as she closed the door and turned the lock.

As soon as Mercy sat down, Brianna looked in her direction and slightly shook her head in disapproval. In her mind she felt as though Mercy was diving headfirst into a friendship pool that seemed deep enough, when it was filled with rocks sleeping quietly at the bottom of the water. Muungo and Paul did catch a glimpse of the head shaking. Muungo, not being a big fan of Brianna, immediately flipped the attention switch.

"I must say your mastery of West African culture is one that warrants admiration." Muungo said as he looked in Paul's direction.

Paul did understand that the purpose of the new topic was not just to stay off Brianna's and Mercy's little girl's fight, it was a question that had been burning Muungo's lips all through the evening.

"When you look at me, would you believe if I tell you that I am Cameroonian?" Paul asked with a smile stretching across his face as he admired the puzzled look on Muungo's face.

He had seen all sorts of reactions, coming from black and whites alike, each time he said he was of African descent. Paul did enjoy those reactions from each and every one of his auditors.

"I bet you are joking... you must be joking." Muungo replied as he recovered from his astonishment. The frown on his face fading away slowly.

"Do I look like I'm joking? I represent 237, *rio dos camaroes.*" Said Paul.

"Wait, wait, hold on!" Muungo raised his hands to the chest level, his palms facing Paul and placed in quasi-vertical position with the fingertips oriented towards the ceiling. His hand gesturing a halt signal he then said: "Do you mean you have a Cameroonian parent, lived in Cameroon before, or may be married a Cameroonian?"

"None of that; it is a long story" Paul tapped Muungo on the shoulder, raised his glass to his mouth. And as he drank its content, he kept his eyes focused on Muungo, admiring the effect of the suspense.

Paul took the time to explain to Muungo what he meant when he said he was of Cameroonian origin. As he narrated his story, his audience gradually increased in numbers with the ladies joining Muungo in listening to another breathtaking anecdote from Paul Peyton.

According to Paul, after making it in the Television industry he decided to mend his broken relations with his family. He went searching for his siblings and tried to make peace with them. It was not an easy task because Paul's youth mistakes had snatched away from his younger siblings the only biological parent they had ever known. Out of his four siblings, the two youngest had landed in the same foster home. The other two siblings, older than the youngest, were sent to two separate foster homes. But these two older siblings did not stay in either one of their foster homes for too long. One of them ended up in jail while the other became a member of drug gang. Paul used every possible conventional and non-conventional approach to track down his siblings. From social service records on adoptions and foster families, to private detectives, to gathering information from guys buried deep in the hood's life game. It was this wide array of leads that aided him in finding each of his siblings.

Having found his siblings, each in their own decor, Paul decided to make it up to them by finding their fathers and reconnecting his siblings with their mother. As Paul recounted this story to Muungo, he resisted giving details on the story of some of his siblings. Maybe it was out of concern for their privacy or maybe their stories were not quite interesting; we may never know the real reason why Paul made this choice.

Nonetheless, he spent more time on the story of the oldest of the four siblings, Leah. Leah was four years younger than Paul and it was with her story that the first lines of his Cameroonian origins were written.

Chapter 9

Washington, D.C. 2000

The Metro Center metro station located downtown Washington DC was getting busier as the hour hand of its immense wall clock courted the Roman numeral digit four. The beauty of clock's digits, made of fake marble and inscribed in Roman numerals, and the elongated diamond shape of the clock's hour and minute hands were a major attraction to metro riders who stopped at the Metro Center station for the first time. Paul was not one of those new riders but he always took pleasure in admiring that clock. It reminded him of the clock at the juvenile detention center which was smaller but had same color and numerical patterns. He gazed at the clock at the juvenile detention center, day after day, as he lived through his sentence. Here he was today, free from the barbed wire, the metal bars, group fights and the risk of confinement in what served as a Secured House Unit; yet despite that freedom he was still a prisoner of the chaos which his reckless acts had created in his family.

To get his "get out of jail free card" he had decided to find Leah, help her to get back on her feet by reconnecting her with her father and mother. He also planned to do the same for each of his other three siblings. That day was Leah's turn.

Staring at the wall clock Paul was busy imagining what his reunion with his younger sister will be like after 16 years of separation. His daydream was suddenly interrupted when he noticed the faint distant light of a train emerging from the abyss-like darkness of the tunnel housing underground rail tracks. The squeaking sound produced by the steel tires making contact with the brake system, merged with the humming sound from the revving engine of the locomotive, grew louder as the chain of train cars drew closer. The illuminated display on the top of the locomotive became visible and it read

"Greenbelt Metro." This indicated that the final destination of the chain of train cars was Greenbelt Metro station, implying that its departure station was probably Branch Avenue Metro Station. The series of train cars approached, and a handful of commuters agglomerated at various spots on the quay where they anticipated the metro cars' door would open. Contrarily to the crowd, Paul moved away from the quay and headed towards the spot underneath the clock.

The clock was also the arranged meeting point for Leah and her brother. This meeting point was maybe symbolic... at least it was to Paul He considered it as yet another gaze at a clock while revisiting his past and awaiting his release from another jail. This other jail was the psychological snare in which he was trapped, and which was created by the effects of his actions on his sibling's life.

The Metro train conductor issued the last warning, asking riders to stand clear as the doors of the metro cars closed. The Metro Center's quays got relatively emptier with riders heading for the station's exits, yet one could see a young lady with blond hair walking towards the wall clock under which a red-haired Caucasian stood twiddling his fingers out of anxiety.

"Leah... it feels good to see you after all these years. How are you?" Paul began after a noisy gulp accompanied saliva down his dry throat.

"It does feel good to see you, I was not sure of how this moment was going to be." Leah replied.

The two hugged each other and kept that posture for a moment that lasted more than a few seconds. They went from a full hug to holding each other's arms around the elbows for a few more seconds and finally both let go of each other's arms. Then Paul led Leah towards an exit escalator; they walked slowly and talked about the respective anticipations they had while coming to their reunion. Once they got out on the street, the two siblings rode off in Paul's car going to his home where their mother and Leah's father were calmly waiting for them. As soon as Leah walked into the house, her mother began crying uncontrollably. Occasionally, insignificant amounts of spittle and catarrh forced their way out of her facial orifices. Leah did not care about the nastiness that accompanied the emotions, she hugged her mother even more tightly, because in the absence of her mother she had seen more nastiness and horror than anyone in that room could ever imagine.

After the tears had either dried away, or better still after the tears had been pushed away, and Leah had exchanged some sweet reunion words and kisses with her mother, Paul introduced Leah to her father. Sluggishly unburying his head out of the pages of a newspaper, he looked in Leah's direction and stretched his lips to force a smile. It was clear that he was not very enthusiastic about being part of what he considered a melodramatic event. Leah, like everybody else, had noticed his attitude—his reluctance to be part of this special moment. Leah did not spare her words in telling him off.

"Dear sperm donor, your job was done decades ago; get the fuck outta here before I …!" Through these hard words, Leah traversed from one end to another of the sadness bandwidth on her emotion spectrum. She felt extremely saddened and deeply infuriated.

It was in reaction to these mean words from Leah that the old man responded rudely, doing nothing but confirming that he initially had no intention of attending this reunion.

"For real? I did not want to deal with this siesta mistake, I said this before!" he said looking in Paul's direction.

Leah's father, infuriated, continued ranting. He revealed that he had accepted to be at this reunion because of a deal he had stroke with Paul. A deal!

In that deal Paul had promised him a job interview, possible work, with the jazz band of a renowned pub in downtown Washington D.C. The job interview was going to be arranged for him in exchange for his accepting a meeting with Leah. As soon as the revelation about the deal surfaced, poking its uninvited face into the party, Paul felt sick and feverish at the same time. Cold sweat ran down his back, spread over his forehead, filled his palmar creases and moistened his armpits. He felt as though he was being dragged down to the Secured Housing Unit of his emotional prison. This revelation from the oldest man within the four walls had completely devastating effects on Leah.

Leah went from being simply very angry to being extremely aggressive, Paul had never seen this side of his younger sister. Spittle splashed out of her mouth as she scolded Paul and screamed at her father. She pushed furniture off her way as if the household gears stood in the way of her anger, stopping the emotion from reaching Paul and her so called father. Her older brother moved a couple of steps towards Leah hoping to calm her down, but at almost the speed of light Leah grabbed a kitchen knife and pointing in his direction she warned him that she would hurt him if he came any closer. Leah was burning and shaking with anger. It seemed as if it was anger that had come into existence days, months or even years before that moment. Otherwise, why was she so upset at her brother for doing all and everything to reconnect her with her father?

"I have dreamt and prayed for this moment for many years, a day to tear you into pieces... just like you both tore my life and that of our family to pieces." Leah said as she pointed the knife at Paul for one moment and then the next moment she pointed it in the direction of her father.

Once again Paul tried to negotiate with Leah as he moved towards her. But it was a waste of time, Leah ordered him, once more, not to take one more step in her direction else she was going to gut him, cut him open and spill his black blood to the floor.

"That's right I said black blood! Fake white man that you are! You are nothing but a Mulatto! Leah uttered as she looked into Paul's eyes desperately searching for some form of pain in the man standing a few steps away from her.

The smallest sign of emotional hurt in Paul's eyes would have meant she had broken his ivory throne from where he gave orders to everyone else telling them to save the elephants.

Paul's communication skills may have failed him in that moment but his savoir-faire as a journalistic investigator had not. He felt a strong urge to ask Leah what she meant by professing all those racial slurs. Instead, Paul fought hard with himself not to ask her any question, if need be, he was going to investigate these claims without her help. Paul stepped away from Leah, picked up his home phone and dialed the emergency service number to get the police to intervene and avoid any irreparable damage. Leah did not stop spitting racial slurs, letting herself be controlled by venom-filled with anger. In the meantime, Paul's mother was in a state of shock, she had turned pale, was rooted on her seat and all this while she had not said a thing. As for Leah's father, he had moved a significant distance away from Leah, and it was certainly not the first time he had walked away from her.

The tension in the room had not really subsided even though its occupants were relatively quiet. In this heavy atmosphere, the police showed up and escorted Leah out of Paul Peyton's residence. Paul did not want to press any charges and was glad that no journalist from the local media had been tipped off about the mess happening in his home. Moments after Leah had been escorted, it was her father's turn to leave, once more he left, leaving behind no sign of either a father or a family man.

When no one but Paul and his mother were left in empty but emotion-filled house, Paul decided to ask his mother why Leah referred to him as black, fake white, and Mulatto? Paul himself was not sure if he expected an answer from his mother or if he expected her to avoid the topic and just go home. A pair of watery eyes followed by rapid successive blinks of both eyes. These uncontrolled eye movements preceded a torrential flow of tears on Paul's mother's face. The tears flowing down Jessica's cheeks were the prologue to a story that was going to change Paul's life forever.

Chapter 10

Jacksonville, Mississippi 1967

Jessica was far away from thinking she was going to give birth to a baby, Paul. She was young and still dependent, but even more so, her family did not like the idea that she was dating a negro, an African immigrant. Jessica was from Mississippi and it was in the then radically racial Mississippi that she had spent her entire life. On the other hand, Paul Samba Yenyi was an international student who, thanks to an international scholarship, had been admitted into the same college as Jessica. It was not too long ago that James Meredith had broken the proverbial glass ceiling by getting enrolled at the University of Mississippi, but the pressure coming from the U.S. Federal Government Officials was without parallel and so Yenyi's school had not real option but to take him in.

Yenyi's accent and his mastery of the French language easily singled him out amongst the other few black students of his college. He was not only shunned by some blacks for having too many white friends, he was also shunned by most whites for not having blue eyes, curly hair and a lighter complexion. Amongst the few white friends he had was Jessica; he had met her for the first time at the school library. The two students were part of the same group in a sociology class project, and from that moment on Jessica and Yenyi started hanging out together.

One thing led to the next and the two started dating secretly. Right around the time of their graduation Jessica had discovered that she was pregnant. Jessica's parent demanded that the creature in her womb, the affection in her heart, and relation in her life be terminated. Threats of all kind were issued to Yenyi. Threats of lynching, deportation, exclusion from the college did not scare Yenyi. It was not until an anonymous letter, claimed to be from the Ku Klux Klan, was dropped on Yenyi's bed at night while he was asleep that he began to seriously consider the threats.

The threat letter was dropped next to him, on his bed, and in his bedroom even though he had recently changed the locks to his bedroom door and his apartment's main door. In this last threat the authors promised to kill Jessica and the baby, if the later had the least black features. Yenyi tried relentlessly to reach his point of contact in the Federal Government who had assured him that his scholarship program was short term the time for him to be assigned to a U.S. consulate in Africa. When he finally got hold of the former diplomat, who was his point of contact, the man told him things were spinning out of control, a number of fellow scholarship recipient had been relocated up north or simply allowed to return to their home countries. Frightened and desperate to live their love and give their baby a chance, Yenyi and Jessica attempted to elope. The couple hit the road one very dark night in an old van, drove across state lines and along state roads for miles and miles. With every mile came a brighter smile for they smelled an even stronger odor of freedom's fresh air and heard an even louder sound of freedom's strong waves. They drove all night along the interstate, until one time during the early morning hours, they got intercepted by the police somewhere in the outskirts of Atlanta, Georgia.

The couple was pulled over because of excessive speed. Yenyi got in to trouble with a police officer as he attempted to make sure that Jessica, who had taken over the driving responsibilities on the early morning, was not held accountable for the speed infraction. What started like a minor misunderstanding over an almost negligible verbal exchange, one which would have gone unnoticed if the passengers were both white, took a turn for the worst when the radio in the police car relayed a missing person alert issued from Jackson Mississippi. Jessica's father had used his influential position to launch a search order less than twenty-four hours after it had been noticed that his daughter and her boyfriend were nowhere to be found. The underlying orders of the missing person alert were clear: make sure the black immigrant is kept in custody for as long as possible but do him no harm for fear of diplomatic ramifications.

After prolonged questioning around false charges, the couple of travelers understood the officers were doing everything in their power to hold them back and if possible, push Yenyi to commit a mistake worth locking him up. The drama slowly but surely unfolded into a tragedy; Yenyi was detained under false charges of assault and rape on a fellow college student in Mississippi, and he was taken to the police precinct. Conscious of his fate, he asked Jessica to run away for her safety and that of the unborn baby. Anchored by love, Jessica was not able to run away that time; but later, after Yenyi had been deported, Jessica ran away from home one more time, but this time for good. She moved to Maryland.

Jessica lived in Maryland where she gave birth to Paul Peyton, a biracial baby who looked just like every white baby boy. Disowned by her father because she had refused to come back home even before the baby was born, Jessica never returned to her family, to the people who had threatened to take away her life and that of her son—the same people who had deported the father of her son. This was the story Paul Peyton learned from his mother on the day his sister called him a mulatto.

Weeks after his mother told him this story, Paul successfully reinitiated reconciliation efforts with his siblings and also decided to take an ancestry DNA test to be sure that the snow powder over the ebony soul was real. The result of the ancestry DNA test from African Ancestry, the records of Jessica Peyton and Paul Samba Yenyi at the University of Mississippi, and many other proves which Paul Peyton could lay his hands on proved his father was Cameroonian from the Babungo Kingdom.

It was during his maiden journey to the land of his paternal ancestors, which finally became an exploratory visit to the

Kingdom of Babungo, that Paul discovered the Babungo Museum. He spent an entire month studying the culture of the people and searching for his father. That was how he became very acquainted with certain things about West African culture. Paul also found out that his father, fondly called *professor*, had succumbed to a witchcraft attack, even though research revealed that poorly treated typhoid fever was the cause of death. His father had lived a life that had been characterized by selflessness, just like his epitaph read:

"Here lies a man who every day from birth he practiced dying, now that he has perfected that craft... he leaves you all his wealth and health, we shall meet on the other side."

Chapter 11

Panama City Beach, Florida 2018

The guests had just left Mercy's apartment, clearing the stage of a fun-filled day and taking with them an exclusive experience of the story of Paul Peyton's life. Tired limbs, aching back muscles, and the semblance of a migraine got Mercy dragging her feet. A scrubbing sound followed her as the thread-filled soles of her flip flops rubbed over the wooden floor. She turned and glanced at the pile of dishes in the sink and half-filled cups of drinks on the kitchen counter. Overwhelmed by the thought of the effort required to clean the place, she exhaled, sighed loudly, and sluggishly made her way to the door of the refrigerator. Her hand slipped across the refrigerator door then stopped as she picked up a magnetized business card bearing a local maid service agency. She read off the number, repeated them in a barely audibly voice to make sure she had memorized them correctly and stuck the card back onto the door of the refrigerator.

She picked up her phone and called the agency, made arrangements for them to send someone to clean her apartment the next day. As she dropped her phone on the breakfast station, she noticed a folded piece of leather designed with a checkered pattern. She took a closer look and noticed it was a wallet. She picked it up; it felt unusually light she thought. She decided to flip it open, hoping to see a picture that will help her guess which one of her guests had forgotten their wallet. The feel of the rough texture of the leather reminded Mercy of the souvenirs she brought home with her from her visit to Africa.

"This must be Muungo's." She thought.

Inside the wallet where two pictures, one picture of a baby and the other the picture of a young boy around the age of ten. She looked intensely at the young boy in the picture, and then gasped in surprise. The young boy in the picture was none other than Blaise. Yes, Blaise the adolescent she had met in Cameroon.

"Men! Men! Men! Muungo denies he is not the father but here he is carrying the boy's picture all over the place." Mercy whispered to herself.

The words had barely fallen off her lips, colored red by the wine she had sipped moments ago, when he phone vibrated. It was Paul calling.

"Hello Paul, everything alright?" Mercy picked up the call.

"Yeah. Everything goo! Hey thanks for the impromptu get together; it was a success." Paul ended with a soft chuckle.

"I enjoyed more than anybody. Thank you guys for not complaining about my untidy crib."

"Could you please take a look around the bar? I think I dropped something of mine there." Paul asked.

"Sure, what does it look like?"

"A brown, checkerboard pattern decorated, leather wallet made of viper skin, it is of great value to me, a souvenir from my visit to Cameroon."

Pulling the chair backward produced a soft but irritating sound as the wooden feet of the chair rubbed against the hardwood floor. Muungo rapidly lifted the chair to stop the irritating sound and once it was at a reasonable distance from the table, he placed the four legs of the furniture on the ground. Then he gently shook the furniture to assess its stability, and then sat.

"Are you ready to order?" A middle-aged waitress asked as she approached the table hesitantly. She must have been forced to go carter for someone else's table. *Atlantic Seafood Diner* was always short of staff once the spring break was over.

"Few more minutes, we are waiting on a third guest," Mercy responded.

"Sorry, I am so sorry. I thought it was for two" The waitress replied wearing a fake smile, which exposed her yellow teeth,

218

as she tried to cover up her embarrassment. She turned around followed by her long blond hair blown sideways by the air current from the ceiling fan.

"Who's the third person?" Muungo asked.

Mercy had asked Paul to join them for brunch. She had not told Paul that Muungo was going to be present, she also had not told Muungo that Paul was going to be joining them. She had hoped they will arrive at almost same time, but with Paul lagging behind Muungo was easily going to become too curious.

"I have something important to discuss with you two and that is why I asked you both to come for brunch today." Mercy answered. She had made sure she was not looking at Muungo straight in the eyes. Her eyes, avoiding to meet Muungo's, met those of the waitress. Instantaneously, Mercy raised her hand and beckon to the waitress.

"Let's order something while waiting on Paul," Mercy said. This was her way of trying to take Muungo's mind off the idea of questioning the reason for this unplanned and rather restrictive brunch.

A sip, a smack of the lips, then another sip and another smack of the lips. Mercy's lip dried up fast or at least that's how she felt. This was a sensation induced by her mind spinning on how to evoke the reason for their brunch to her guests. Muungo had chosen to play the game, he kept his patience by browsing through the menu. His decoy became useless, so he raised his head to place his order but first he looked at the door. Paul had finally arrived and as he walked through the door, he instantly noticed Muungo and Mercy's table. Paul joined them at table a little bit surprised to see Muungo, even though he knew the closeness that existed between the two friends. Paul sat down, just as the waitress was taking the first two orders. In no time, all three had ordered something to eat and off the waitress went.

The waitress had been gone for a while from the time she had brought beverages for the three, and Mercy was becoming

219

quite clumsy. She had a tough time taking her drinking straw out of its package, and then inadvertently dropped a sachet of sweetener in her cup of iced tea. Muungo immediately pushed his glass of iced tea across the table towards Mercy, and he then took hers to the counter for a replacement.

"If you don't mind my asking, is everything okay?" Paul asked Mercy while tilting his head sideways and staring intense at her.

"Not really Paul. Not really," Mercy braved the answer out of her guys.

Mungo returned with a fresh glass of iced tea and sat down. Mercy cleared her throat once, twice, and then a third and longer time as if she were subtly calling out bids at an auction. Then she began talking to the two men seated, equidistant from her, her hand laid palms down on the light brown table covered with whitish circular shaped stains. These stains were caused by prolonged exposure of the table's wooden surfaces to water condensing and dripping off the outside of cold cups, glasses, and pitchers.

"Guys, I have much respect for you both. Muungo is literally my brother now and you Paul, you are such an inspiration."

Then she sighed as she launched into the crucial part of her speech. "I recently stumbled on something that had bothered me for quite a while. I had resolved to let go of it because it fragilized my relationship with Muungo but then I realized it somehow involved Paul that was when I chose to have you guys talk it out. Paul, do you remember the wallet you forgot at my house last week?"

Paul nodded in acknowledgement.

"Do you have it with you?" Mercy continued.

Paul pulled the wallet out of his pocket and held it out for Mercy to see, all this while he had kept looking at Mercy trying to discern what was going on.

"That evening when I found this wallet at my place, moments before you called me, I looked into it trying to

220

deduce who the owner was and I saw the picture of a boy whom I know quite well."

Paul seemed surprised, he sat up in his chair and folded his arms to listen to every detail of this saga. Mercy stretched out her hand and open her palm. Paul unfolded his arms and then dropped the wallet in her palm. She whispered a thank you and then handed the wallet to Muungo.

"Please open it," Mercy told Muungo.

"What?" Muungo questioned in astonished.

"Please open it," Mercy insisted.

Muungo looked straight into Mercy's eyes for more than a second, then turned and looked at Paul. The later nodded his head in approval. So Muungo grabbed the wallet and flipped it open. He starred for while at the picture in the wallet and then let go of a loud sigh of surprise.

Upper Nun Valley, Kamerun 2000

Another group of students had just walked past Muungo and his friend Justine. The two walked slowly; Justine walked even slower because she was not feeling too good. This was not the first time that week since she had begun complaining about fatigue and nausea. Muungo proposed to wave a taxi-bike for Justine to ride home, but the later shook her head sideways in firm refusal. She wanted to make sure she got home after her mother was gone for choir rehearsal. If she met her mother home, she would not have the time to rest, yet she was extremely tired.

A distance away a pickup truck drove heading towards Muungo and Justine.

"Your brother's car! Look Muungo!" Justine exclaimed fearfully, her voice becoming feeble and shaky.

"Climb in, let me drop you guys home." Mingo proposed to the two teenagers. "Brother, we have to stop at a friend's place for some few minutes, I think we will just walk." Muungo

221

uttered an improvised alibi trying not to let Justine's plans go to waste.

"You guys are very young, keep walking, it is good for your health" Mingo responded as he pressed down on the clutch, shifted his gear from neutral to first and accelerated. The car's engine roared as the treads of its four tires clung to the dusty road and took off.

"Are you my friend?" Justine asked interrupting a moment of silence that had installed itself as the two teenagers calmly watched Mingo's pickup disappear under a cloud of dust.

"Of course! Actually, we are more than friends we are family. I can't believe you will even ask such a question" Muungo replied.

Justine broke down in tears without any warning. Muungo rushed towards her and with a big hug walloping her, he let her use him as support. The crying went on for a while, Muungo inquired countless times about what had happened but all he got as response were louder sobs. Then unexpectedly between two sobs she said:

"I think I am pregnant." Justine went right back to crying.

"Oh my God! That's not good!" Muungo retorted. "Not that the pregnancy is not good, but the fact of being pregnant without being married," Muungo rapidly corrected those words which emotion had forced out of his mouth. "Did you take a pregnancy test? Did you tell your mother? Did….?" Muungo asked a thousand and one questions.

An avalanche of questions that only triggered a matching avalanche of tears. Justine slowly released herself from the hug that had transformed itself into a grip. Her panting vigorously shook her shoulders as she sobbed; it was so powerful that it was noticeable as she walked away.

Justine was a month or two pregnant; she told Muungo. Being pregnant was not the deal breaker, the deal breaker was informing her parents--her father. He was a very angry and violent man. Whenever he laid his heavy muscular and scarified hands of a farmer on anybody, tears and screams were bound

222

to prevail. Justine, her mother, her siblings, and even other villagers had been served a piece of this man's fury. Muungo had once heard that Justine's mother had had a miscarriage and a deformed index finger because of her husband's violence. Yet, strangely enough Justine's father, *the Olympic gold medal winner in bully sports*, bragged so much about his daughter and her qualities of a great kid. He bragged so much so that this pregnancy gotten while attending school and out of marriage was not something he could ever fathom.

"When did you realize you were pregnant and who is the father?" Muungo asked Justine who continued walking in tears.

In the back of his head the young Muungo began running different scenarios of who could have made his friend pregnant. Only one person came to his mind, their Physics professor, a man whose thirst for carnal pleasure reigned king in his heart and mind. A married man who ran after high school girls, after single female professors, and after every skirt in town. "The goat feeds off the grass closest to where it has been tethered" and "one needs to feed off different food items if one wishes to have a balanced diet" were two of the educated lecher's slogans.

A suspect in mind, Muungo caught up with a disoriented and broken Justine, and asked if their Physics teacher was responsible for the pregnancy. Infuriated by the question Justine's tears stopped flowing abruptly and her confusion cleared away for a moment. She got close to Muungo, so close that bits of spittle flew out her mouth and ended on his face as she angrily refuted his assertion.

"All this while you've thought of me as one of those cheap women who will go with any and everybody; and you call yourself my friend? Well dear friend he is not the author of this pregnancy!" At these words the girl turned around and walked away pulled by her anger; long strides and curses under her breath as she walked away.

Justine looked at the picture in her hands. How could she be this naive? She wondered. She had fallen in love with someone even though deep in her mind she knew their love was impossible. He seemed serious; at least that's what she told herself in order to excuse her naivety. They had spent twelve weeks of romance like none she had ever experienced, and just like that he had come up with a reason to travel back to his homeland.

"So, the guy is the father of your child?" Muungo asked.

"No other possibility." She replied. "He went back to America, and I am not there, there is no way we will ever meet again." She sighed expiring the last ounces of hope that were logged in her being.

"Your father is going to burn this village to ashes if we do not produce this guy. You know that right?"

"I know, I know. I have a plan, but I am worried it might not work." She added slowly moving her head from side to side

Those were not reassuring words to say the least. Justine's plans were seldom the best option in any situation. About 4 months ago when a bloody fight broke out between her father and mother, leading to her mother deserting their home for some months, Justine had come up with the great idea of going to live with her elder sister who lived in Ongola City; one of the biggest and wildest cities in the country. Against every advice from Muungo and all of her friends, the young girl moved to Ongola City. Three weeks ago, she had returned home from Ongola City, not because her mother had come back to her husband--as was always the case, but because her sister was gravely ill. So ill that everyone in the village was awaiting the news of her death. But this sad news was not the bad part of Justine's plan of going to Ongola City; the bad part of the plan was the fact that her short stay in the city had earned her a pregnancy. Had she heeded to advice, she would not have been roaming the village with a baby in her womb.

In a passion deprived voice, made of slurry words dragged to the ground by doubt and confusion, Muungo asked what the plan was. Justine looked at him straight in the eyes for a moment but said nothing.

"What is the plan?" He insisted with the same passionless voice.

"You could say..." she paused. "You could say you are the author of this pregnancy." she said.

Then she followed with a very rapid flow of words to inhibit any interruption. "The time for me to find a way to handle my father and all this drama, and ..."

"No!" Muungo shook his head vehemently in disapproval, "That's not going to happen." Muungo interrupted Justine with a strong and resolute voice that carried well-articulated words and that sounded like a shout.

"Your mother and mine have always talked about us ending up being married to each other, and you have told me more than once that you love me in more than just in a friendly way..." Justine's tender voiced struggled out through her constricted windpipe as tears rolled down her cheeks.

"Oh really? So, you know of my affection for you only when the boat is sinking; huh? Do I have to hold the drum for someone else to play it? No, thank you." "No, thank you," Muungo repeated as if he made sure his answer was concise, precise, and final.

Both remained silent for a moment, one could hear bugs buzzing, the wind cutting through the grass, and the sound of the students' breaths. The silence was not because one expected an answer from the other, but because they both hopped that it would help each of them better understand their interlocutor.

"When I got home yesterday, I told mom that I was pregnant. As it turns out my father wants to repudiate her and get her exiled from this village and so they both have to appear before the village on the next *contri-sunday*."

"What did your mother say when you told her you were pregnant, what did she say?"

"Well, believe it or not, she asked if you were the father of the child.

Muungo eyeballs bulged out their orbital in astonishment.

"Then she said she cannot bear another humiliation in addition to what my sister has brought upon her, so she wants me to either get married with the father of my child or go and abort the unborn baby."

"What did you answer her when your mother asked if I was the father?" Muungo asked while drawing even closer to Justine; the sound of his racing heartbeat sounding almost louder than his voice.

Chapter 12

Upper Nun Valley, Kamerun 2000

The sun had gone past its zenith, the shadows of trees were regaining in length and the harmattan wind's breeze helped dissipate the heat and disperse the dust. The population of Mighang had respected the *contri-sunday* by staying at home and getting involved in light domestic chores. One of these chores was gossiping with the neighbors. Women and girls were fond of this chore. They will trek for distances, with the pretext of going to purchase or borrow some kitchen spice, or even learn a new recipe--one they had already mastered, when their real and unspoken intent was to debate over the gossip of the week. This week the headline of every gossip session was the meeting of the village council of elders, following a convocation from the King, to discuss the tension existing between Justine's parents. In kitchens, at the village spring, in village shops, and even under tree sheds where women were having their hair braided, every conversation was about Justine's Parents.

Because the problem was a family one, the audience was limited to the family involved, the village elders, and the King. Instead of holding the hearing in the marketplace, as it would have been if the issue were a village problem, the hearing was to take place in the royal courts under the shade of a centuries-old palaver tree. Still, the queens welcomed unexpected visitors in their private quarters whose real intent was to spy on the court sessions and deliberations.

The village elders, proudly adorning different models of their traditional regalia made from *toghu* and armed with their tiny old but sacred bags, formed two parallel rows as they sat on their stools. Each row of stools ran on one side of the oldest baobab tree. The large trunk of the tree bore a wide opening leading into the darkness-filled guts of the tree. Screeching and flapping of wings by bats living in the baobab tree were occasionally heard. But even more audible were the village elders' chit-chats about the different cases scheduled to be examined on that day.

Justine, her mother, and father, and all others having to appear before the village council of elders had long arrived at the palace but were left out in the open air, under the not so hot sun, waiting to be summoned to the palaver tree of the palace by the King and his advisors.

A calabash containing garcinia kola, kola nuts and a bottle of snuff circulated from hand to hand amongst the village elders as they chitchatted and awaited the arrival of the King. A couple of royal guards rushed under the shade of the palaver tree, stretched out a tanned leopard skin on top of which they placed the royal stool. This arrangement meant the king would be coming out any moment from then. The village elders rapidly gulped the palm wine in their drinking horns, masticated and then swallowed the kola in their mouths, ran their tongues over their incisors and canines clearing off all debris left behind from the chewing of the kola nuts and garcinia kola. Using the thumb and index fingers of their right hands they cleaned their noses and their moustaches—wiping off the snuff that had clung to their nose hairs and moustache. They slipped their drinking horns in their bags and adjusted their hats, bearing bird feathers symbolizing their status, on their heads. As soon as they saw the King approaching, a big umbrella over his head and a scepter in his right hand, swinging in sync with his left foot, the elders all rose from their stools. Like one man, they all bowed to their leader, and waited for their King to seat on his stool.

His Royal Highness the King of Mighang, sat down on his stool after which the elders held their hand next to their mouths, and clapped three times while saying "Mbeh! Mbeh! Mbeh!"--saluting their ruler. Then they each stood up straight and then sat down on their stools. By order of rank and seniority, the King saluted by name and made small talks with each of his advisors. Each of the elders kept his face down and answered the King with his hand close to his mouth and his eyes fixated to the ground. Once the greeting formalities were over, the court was in session, presided by the Lion of Mighang, the slayer of sea monsters, the killer of white ghosts, the immortal amongst mortals, the King of Mighang.

"This not the first time your Majesty! It is not the first time he has laid hands on me" Justine's mother said.

"Do you plead guilty to the accusations of unfaithfulness towards your husband and of casting a love spell on him?" The King asked.

"Your Majesty, Elders of the village, I have not been unfaithful to this man, and I have never cast a spell on him. All I did was..." Justine's mother responded.

"Woman the question did not ask for any explanation, simply for your pleas." One of the elders interjected with authority pointing his staff at the woman and repeatedly stabbing the still air between him and her with his staff as he spoke.

"Why will he accuse you of such crimes then?" The King asked.

There was a murmur amongst some of the elders as the woman bowed her head trying to recover from tears streaming down her face.

"Silence!" The oldest elder commanded stumping his left foot and his staff to the ground when he noticed the King's discontentment over the murmurs or childish attitude of the elders.

"Your Majesty, he blames me for not giving him a male child, an heir. He blames me for his lack of sexual prowess every time he lies with another woman and for the barrenness of his two other wives." Justine's mother replied between sobs.

At the mention of sexual prowess, the murmur amongst elders almost resumed; this time the King's guard hit hard on his gong to warn the elders. But before the sharp and imposing sound of the gong silenced the elders one could hear the question "How can he only impregnate and be sexually prolific with one of his three wives? There must be some *juju* involved."

The King spoke to his guards and one of them escorted the woman and returned with her husband. Justine's father stood a distance from the King and next to the elders furthermost from the King. He bowed down to greet the King and then got back up and greeted the elders.

'You tell everyone in the village that Jinwi Justine and her sister are your daughters, rightly so. But you have to tell this court the truth lest the gods of the land curse you with infirmity for life." Began the King. The man listened to the King and began giving his account of the story. His shaky voice, his sweaty palms and forehead, and his occasional stutter were not compatible with his heavily build arms and torso and his legendary physical strength and charisma. His physical strength did not save him of the fear every citizen had towards the King.

".. my King, the witch doctor told me all that. He warned me that ill will befall my supposed children if they are not really mine. Recently the oldest daughter came back home sick as a dog and she is probably going to die any day from now. I also suspect that the second one is pregnant, her stepmothers have noticed some important changes on her body." The man concluded his account.

The question-and-answer session over, the case of Justine's parents lasted for more than an hour. Justine's stepmothers were called in as witnesses and so too was Justine. The young girl, dressed in a loose gown that concealed her engulfed breasts and protruding belly, approached the presence of the King, saluted and stayed silent waiting for the King to ask her questions.

"My daughter what is the problem between your father and mother?"

"*Mbeh*! My father believes that my mother does not want to bear him any male child. He also believes that my mother has made my stepmothers barren and that my sister and I are not his biological children." The teenage girl replied in a faint voice.

"Why is your elder sister not here today?" The King continued.

"She is very sick your Majesty, she is suffering from cancer of the bone and it is in its terminal phase." She replied, her already faint voice barely audible, as she had begun crying.

"Daughter, I command you to stop crying"

"Yes your Majesty" She replied still in tears.

"Young lady the King has ordered that you stop crying!" A King's guard reiterated with insistence.

"I see your pregnancy is controlling your emotions. Who is the father of that child?" The King asked as he adjusted his traditional regalia.

The council of elders went silent, every ear in the assembly of elders and withing a hearing distance stood erect in anticipation for an answer.

"His Majesty has asked you a question. You do well to answer." The voices of some elders and the King's guard fused as they propounded the same request.

The girl struggled to stay calm, hold back her tears and her fears. Her fingers fidgeting and her lips trembling, she tried to muster enough courage to answer the question.

"Your Majesty…" she began.

"Your Majesty and the great elders of Mighang!" Mingo interjected. "May I speak to the question?"

The King nodded in approval while the other elders looked in astonishment at their colleague, the highest ranked village elder—Mingo—standing up next to the King, wondering what he had to say concerning the King's question.

"May the gods bless this land and its people. May we have reason and compassion in our judgment. May the King live forever." Mingo continued. After which the other elders responded in dissonance as they hesitantly approved those wishes which they thought was to flatter the King.

"About the pregnancy of Justine Jinwi, there is a saying amongst our people which says: without the hands of the weaver, the raffia shall not know the beauty of its fibers. My younger brother Muungo and I plan on doing the rites and traditions for this child to bear our family name."

A wind of confusion blew over the assembly of elders, leaves fell off the baobab tree, birds flew off its branches, bats flapped their wings from within the tree's trunk, and the elders whispered as they exchanged comments amongst themselves.

When the King raised his hand and clenched his fist, absolute silence settled in the assembly.

"You can leave my daughter." the King dismissed Justine and then began listening to his advisors input about the case at hand.

Chapter 13

Panama City Beach, Florida 2018

Peyton looked down at his empty plate on the table, he picked up his fork fumbled with it for a while and then raised his head. His eyes watery and his face blushed, he could not hold back the tears that rolled down his cheeks. Muungo handed him a tissue. He took some few minutes to regain his composure and then looking at Mercy and then Muungo he began to speak.

Thank you Muungo. Thank you from the bottom of my heart. Two days before Justine had travelled with her sister to the village, I unexpectedly travelled back to the States because my mom was scheduled for an urgent open-heart surgery. Back in those days without any cellphone or email, Justine could not feed me with any information on what had happened during my absence. So, when I returned, Justine and her sister no longer lived in their apartment. I was not aware of the fact that she was pregnant. I spent 4 more months in Cameroon trying to find her in vain.

Last summer when I took my mom with me to Cameroon, a friend of mine at the U.S. Embassy in Cameroon invited me to a seminar about cancer and cancer survivors. That is where I recognized Justine's sister, who had miraculously survived her bone cancer. I asked about Justine. At first, she did not trust me, and rightfully so. But eventually she gave me Justine's contact. I later travelled to Mighang where I met Justine. It was a very difficult moment for me and her. She was convinced I had abandoned her and had moved on with her life while on my end I was convinced she was never into something serious with me.

She introduced me to the boy, but we haven't told him I am his father. We are still working on that. But this meeting right here, right now is the best thing that ever happened to me after finding out that I had a son with Justine.

Mercy was filled with emotion as she stretched her hands out and grabbed Paul Peyton's hand and then Muungo's. Both men hurried up to her as she began sobbing and smiling simultaneously. A group hug followed and then the trio sat back down, with smiles of relieve slowly spreading over their lips.

Peyton pulled out his phone and dialed a number. The phone rang for a while with no one picking up. Peyton's face shrunk with wrinkles; he seemed a little uneasy but still he attempted the call one more time. A voice answered from the other end of the line.

"Hi baby." the voice amorously responded after a soft giggle.

"Hey sweetheart, how are you?" Peyton asked.

"Tired! Oh my god I am tired. I have been shopping for the wedding again and it's not been easy at all."

"I can imagine, I too I have been busy with trying to free my calendar. I'm glad things seem to be working out just fine so far." Peyton said.

"Good for you... can't wait to see you. Can't wait for you and Blaise to get to know each other." Justine replied.

"Hey! Hey baby" Peyton insisted as the network momentarily got disrupted. "I would like to introduce you to my best man, that is if he is fine with it and of course if you are too."

"Ooookaaay" Justine responded with a long hesitating pronunciation of the word.

Peyton rose from his chair, stood behind Muungo and placed the phone in front of him.

"Hello Justine!" Muungo began.

"Oh my Goooood!" the sound of Justine's scream gushed out of the phone.

The Volkswagen Beetle had been standing on its parking spot for quite a while now, but Mercy had not noticed the number of steps the minute hand of her watch had made. All

234

this while she had been sitting in the car holding an envelope in her hand. On multiple occasions she had made up her mind to rip open the envelope and read the content of the folded mail. And each of these times she felt the envelope's content with her fingers, detecting the rigidity of the paper in the envelope. Yet, she somehow managed not to open the envelope. Her mind was still kidnapped by this seemingly endless dilemma, when her phone began ringing.

Peyton was returning her call, but it seemed to Mercy that Peyton was a *too late Hewett*. She wished he had returned her call minutes after her voicemail, and why not even picked the phone up when she had called the first time. But she was also aware of the fact that with Justine and Blaise in town for the American wedding, which was a follow up to the traditional wedding ceremony that had taken place in Mighang, Peyton and his family were certainly very busy. The only reason she had tried calling him despite his probably busy schedule was that Peyton's story about his skin color and his origin had not only deeply touched Mercy, but had brought them closer to each other. Peyton's life story was way more complicated than Mercy's, and so if he had managed to deal with that excess baggage, she could learn one or two tricks from him.

Some months ago, the months after Peyton had told his story to Mercy and company, things had gotten complicated for Mercy. She found herself caught in a maze, tons of questions without any clear answer. She wondered: "what if her experience in Cameroon was more than just some other African folklore?" Yet, within that same period Brianna had introduced Mercy to a plethora of stories about African scams based on folklore; Brianna had convinced her that whatever had happened in Mighang was to stay there. What will some story of royal blood lineage add to her life in Panama City? Her friend made her wonder. After all there were many stories of how Africans had claimed royalty just to extort money from people more fortunate than themselves--especially westerners.

There was the internet trend about the Nigerian prince scam. In addition, Brianna had dug deep, passed the mantle of the internet, in order to support her assertion that nothing good could come from too much attachment to Africa. She even had come up with the story of a Cameroonian conman who had rose to global prominence. Dorian Nkongman, the Cameroonian con artist, claimed to have the power of transforming blank papers into real banknotes. Beyond his reputation of money multiplication, it was said that Nkongman had made people believe he was a King in Cameroon and eventually walloped the naive and gullible into investing into his fake business and life. He successfully collected huge amounts of money and objects of great value from his victims without any resistance of any kind. Amongst his victims were world class political leaders and business gurus.

Brianna's stories and warnings had helped calm Mercy's ardor of finding out if she was a descendant of a Cameroonian princess. But this semblance of oblivion lasted just the time for Mercy to meet Peyton, and when that happened she once again was confronted with the questions: who was she, and what was her real past like--where had her family come from before landing on American soil? And these questions tormented her more and more every day.

Agonizing in silence, Mercy simply vacated to her daily routine with the questions about her past and her existence agitating in her mind; each question scrambling for attention like a snake whose head had been cut off. In her new office, lighted by a window facing the restless ocean of Panama City Beach, Mercy sometimes found herself searching videos on YouTube about the Mighang people, and about the transatlantic slave trade. Like a black hole all the information she found never really brought her any satisfaction.

Barely contenting herself with her American life and an exhilarating experience of the real Africa, Mercy carried on with her life. She kept telling herself she was neither the first nor the last African American not to know of a river called

236

Kamby Bolongo and an ancestor called Kunta Kinte. But then, about two weeks ago as she read through her personal emails, she stumbled on a correspondence from Dr. Shengweh, the sister to the King of Mighang.

A couple of years ago, after their meeting in Mighang, Shengweh and Mercy had exchanged email addresses, but they had written to each other a few more times after that. In those last correspondences, Mercy had agreed to provide Dr. Shengweh with her results of a radioallergosorbent test. The test had proven that Mercy indeed was allergic to a chemical contained in the secretion of the sacred plant of *Pa'ah Nguong*. This result had intrigued Mercy but she had held herself back from emailing Dr. Shengweh to discuss the socio-cultural and historical connotation of this positive results. Time flew by and the mirage of familiarity that had appeared in their social sphere rapidly had faded because of their lack of communications. So, it took a minute for Mercy to recall who Shengweh was. Luckily enough, for Mercy, the content of the email was more than a clue of how they had both met and what experiences they had shared.

Sitting at her desk at home and caught somewhere between fear and hope regarding her sweet-sour African adventure, Mercy began to read the email from Dr. Shengweh. According to this email, the dermatologist had continued in her quest for a scientific answer to the mystery behind the sacred plant found in *Pa'ah Nguong*, the sacred forest, and the sacred quarters of Mighang Royal Palace.

This research was rekindled around the time when Dr. Shengweh was part of an international colloquium on Albinism and the marginalization of Albinos in sub-Saharan Africa. The colloquium was held in the booming, exotic, traditional, and yet exquisite and historic town of Addis Ababa, Ethiopia. After hours of conference and presentations during this colloquium, Dr. Shengweh had invited some of her peers for dinner at her hotel of residence, the Lalibela Hotel of Addis Ababa. There the scholars dined over a plethora of delicious colorful African

237

cuisine. The menu consisted of recipes originating from the Mediterranean coast to delicacies enjoyed at the banks of the Orange River in Cape Town, South Africa. Munching and chatting became one when they began a discussion on the history of Ethiopian's emblematic figure Emperor Haile Selassie and his Solomonic ancestry. They evoked Makeda, or Sheba as some called her, and her African origins. The conversation, like a thread ended up passing through needle eyes, carefully evoked the royal ancestry of Dr. Shengweh, and then it sewed its way into the fabric of the story about the sacred plant in the Kingdom of Mighang.

Amazed by the claims made about the sacred plant in the Kingdom of Mighang, a hand full of dermatologist, of different racial backgrounds, decided to plan a vacation trip to Cameroon alongside their peer and potential tour guide—Dr. Shengweh. During their trip they visited the Kingdom of Mighang and her sacred rock in the marketplace, but most importantly they put the sacred plant to test by collecting sample of the sap and the bark's secretion.

It was the result of this test that had prompted Shengweh to write to Mercy. As it turned out, the plant did grow only in Mighang and its capacity as an allergen was not widespread across planet earth. Prof. Yeung, Dr. Kahn, and Prof. McClure, experts in the field of dermatology, could not find a test subject with radioallergosorbent test result the same as Mercy's, that is any one allergic to the sacred plant. Thus, it was almost conclusive that an allergic reaction to the sacred plant was a *sine qua non* condition for anyone to belong to the original missing royal family of Mighang.

The email and the news it contained had certainly left Mercy worried, it seemed as though her peace of mind was always made too ephemeral by the happening around her. After hearing about the news in the email coming from Africa, Brianna had reiterated her suggestion that Mary should simply forget the sacred plant incident and move on, while on the other end Peyton encouraged Mercy to take an African ancestry DNA test. Clearly, her visit to Cameroon had not only resulted in a suspense-filled drama about being a crowned princess of the Mighang Kingdom, but it had certainly raised questions about her past. It had given her an opportunity to reconnect with an unknown part of herself—the African root in the appellation African American. So why not take the African Ancestry DNA test anyway?

Trapped in the dilemma of either giving up or carrying on the quest for precision and accuracy on her African identity, Mercy took the decision and the time to seek advice from her newest friend Michelle, Jonah's wife. Michelle, Jonah and Dwayne all had the same advice for Mercy. Dwayne and Jonah even confided in her that they both had searched for their ancestral links. Dwayne was a descendant of the Igbo people of Nigeria while Jonah was from the Ashanti people of Ghana. This was good and encouraging news for Mercy, but more importantly it was the peace that emanated from the faces of these two men when they talked of what they had learned about the culture of their ancestors that made Mercy to want to discover more about her own ancestral links. The magic was beyond any logic, Jonah and Dwayne felt free by being chained to a past they almost never knew existed until then. An experience that Mercy longed to live. In this very old world filled with young souls every experience may have existed before, yet it was lived differently by everyone

Mercy knew for a fact that Brianna was never interested in the whole African lineage thing, so Mercy decided not to talk anymore about it with Brianna, not until everything was all settled. Mercy was not going to tell Brianna, Michelle, Jonah, or Dwayne that she had decided to research on her ancestry. The only person who knew of her secret plan and who had referred her to the best in the field of ancestral lineage search was Paul Peyton. She feared telling Jonah and Dwayne because eventually Brianna could be informed of her decision. Fast forward, two weeks later here she was with the result of the ancestral DNA exam and Paul Peyton, her primary motivator, was not picking up his phone.

Mercy's car still had not moved and the streetlight would be coming on anytime soon. Peyton called one more time. When he had called the first time all he heard were multiple rings and then a beep which sent the caller to Mercy's voicemail, but he chose not to leave a message. this next attempt Mercy picked up the phone. But it wasn't Mercy who spoke; it was confusion that was on the other end of the line.

"God, I don't know why I took this test; I don't even know why this whole *African roots* thing began. Here am I with an envelope in hand unwilling to open it and yet dying to know what the content says." Mercy managed to say between the urge to cry and the desire to hug someone very tight.

She could not fulfill either one of these desires, and Peyton knew exactly what that feeling was. He had opened up and told most of his friends how he had discovered his identity, but he did not tell them how nerve wrecking the experience had been. Peyton asked Mercy to calm down and drive to Muungo's home and once there she could open the envelope.

"I have observed how well Muungo and you interact, and you two are nothing less than a brother and a sister. You'll need someone like that next to you when you read the results." Peyton encouraged Mercy.

"You are absolutely right. Goodbye, I'll call you later." Mercy hung up and then dialed Muungo's number as she pulled out of the packing lot of her office space.

Muungo was at home with Wilanne, his daughter, when he picked up the phone. The little girl's voice reminded Mercy of Nsoh, Muungo's niece. Nsoh always referred to Mercy as auntie and was a big fan of the idea that Mercy may be a princess of Mighang. Mercy's little car was almost at the exit lane of the lot, and the idea of this little magical girl, Nsoh, whom she met and with whom she had built such a genuine love relationship seemed to squeeze all her body organs towards the core of her body.

"Muungo; let me open this envelope and read the content, I will drive to your place whatever the results. We have shared so much together, even more than we should have, that I feel I am a part of the Tahkuh family no matter what this piece of paper says." Mercy said in a relatively controlled voice, revealing a great deal of dominion over her emotions.

At the sound of these words, Muungo's ears momentarily tuned off his daughter's semblance of whining.

"You are and remain dear to my heart... no matter what." He replied.

A moment of silence followed, and then came the rustling sound of an envelope being torn open and a letter being unfolded. Mercy cleared her throat and read:

"Dear Mercy Lewis,

Thank you for contacting Kemite African Ancestry Services. Every tree has roots, and we are here to keep the great tree connected to the roots. In response to your request regarding your ancestral lineage amongst the peoples occupying Africa, our laboratory results based on your Mitochondrial DNA indicate, with a 93% accuracy DNA match and 99.99% precision laboratory results, that on your maternal side you are related to the Tikari people of Cameroon, precisely the Mighang people in the Northwest Region of the Republic of Cameroon situated in West Africa..."

Mercy stopped reading as the news made her break in tears and as emotions seemed to grab her by the neck—the sensation of a lump in her throat. On the other end of the phone line Muungo kept quiet with his mouth agape in response to his amazement at what he had just heard. As soon as he was about to close his mouth and gather the breath to express his joy, he heard a loud deafening sound of metal crashing against metal, followed by the squeaking sound of rubber in hard contact with coal tar and a deafening endless car honk. The horrific sound of a car accident was the last thing which Muungo heard on the other end of the phone line.

Panama City, Florida 2018

Sitting in the waiting room of the Emergency ward of Bay Medical Center Muungo held his cup of coffee while waiting on Brianna. Brianna had walked to the vending machine to grab some cookies. Jonah had just driven in and was responding to a text from Peyton. Brianna walked in the next second and sat next to Muungo, offered him some cookies as well as offered him an opportunity to let go off their unexplained feud. Muungo raised his eyes looked into Brianna's eyes, her pupil flooded with tears that broke bounds with every blink of her eyelids. Muungo grabbed a tissue and handed it over to Brianna. While she was dabbing her teary eyes for the millionth and one time, the doctor walked into the waiting room. The group of three friends promptly rose and walked to meet the physician halfway.

The lady in her white lab coat looked exhausted as she took off her pair of glasses. Initially, she asked to speak with a member of Mercy's family; the three friends explained that they were the closest thing to family for Mercy that was present at the hospital. Hesitantly Dr. Priya Takumala, a woman of Asian descent with a British accent, told them she did not mind updating them while awaiting family members.

"The surgery was complex but successful. I will say she has a fifty percent chance of surviving the accident; the next hours, from now till dawn, are critical and are going to determine the final diagnostics. If, and when she wakes up, there is a high risk of amnesia due to brain injury: that is, she might not recognize either some people or everyone, and she might not remember either anything or everything about her past. This could be temporary, permanent, or might not even come to be."

A short moment of silence fell upon those listening to the doctor. Because of the long stare through her glasses and the prolonged folding in of her lips, it seemed as if the doctor was expecting a specific reaction from Mercy's friends. A reaction she did not get. Her beeper went off and the voice on Public

Address System requested the doctor's presence in one of the post- theatre ward's recovery rooms. Hurriedly, she silenced her beeper, tossed it in the right pocket of her white coat and once again spoke to the speechless, and confused group of Mercy's friends who stood frozen in front of her.

"Have you contacted anyone from her family? I really need to talk to them; right up to this instance I have violated protocol because I have no other choice. But huh... By the way do all you can to get Muungo Takuh here as soon as possible. Did I say that right?"

"I am Muungo Takuh!" Nodding his head vehemently, Muungo responded strongly and rapidly. So rapid that he said it before the doctor had finished her words.

"How come the receptionist did not get you registered in with that name? Any way we've got some serious details to discuss about Mercy and you are her emergency contact." She began walking away in the direction leading to the recovery room as she finished her last sentence. "Get your registration squared up, if you really are who you say you are, and I'll see you ASAP.

As the surgeon walked away, Muungo turned to the others and said: "I registered with my *American first name:* Maurice, I bet that's what is causing this confusion."

"It's okay. Just get it fixed and let's see what important information the surgeon has concerning Mercy. Oh! My! God! I hope she ends up okay" Brianna said and lowered her head and her lacrimal glands engorged with salty tears, as her eyelids flapped in rapid succession.

Muungo instinctively opened wide his arms as Brianna crashed into him and burst into tears even before the medical doctor who had explained details on Mercy's condition had made a right turn and disappeared from the field of vision. Once the doctor had walked away, Jonah returned to his seat feeling demolished by the relatively sad news. Muungo and Brianna remained standing for a moment hugging each other as their sorrow and hope overtook their differences. They were different in origin and vision but united in sorrow and hope; shackled to a past of war, a present of sorrow, and a future of hope.

The apparently late morning finally took over the presumably very long night. Muungo was not sure of exactly when he had fallen asleep. But the early ringtone announcing an incoming phone call for Brianna, a returned call from the mother of Mercy's niece, woke them both. Jonah, who could not stay overnight, mostly out of fear of Michele's worrisome nature, had gone home the night before and had promised to start working with some brain specialist of the professional football industry to have their opinion and why not their expertise in case subsequent brain surgeries were prescribed. Brianna walked from the waiting area toward a glass window as she spoke on the phone. As soon as she was beyond the maximum audible distance for a moderate voice call, a nurse approached Muungo.

"The doctor is with your patient; she woke up moments ago" the nurse announced.

"Will the doctor let me talk to her? Because yesterday she would not let anyone, except direct family, see the patient." Muungo asked as he hastily got up from his seat and approached the nurse.

The doctor opened the door to Mercy's room and signaled Muungo to come. Muungo looked at Brianna's direction, but she never noticed him waving, she was busy on the phone trying to get hold of Mercy's niece.

There was the beeping sound of the heart monitor, the hissing sound of the oxygen dispenser, the ticking of the clock, the low volume of the TV hung from the wall, and then there was Mercy laying lying inert in bed as Muungo and the doctor walked in.

"She's awake. Go close to her and call her by her name please!" the doctor pleaded. "If she recognizes you then that will be great" She continued.

"By the way the baby is just fine, no issue detected." She said as she signaled at Muungo to seat on the chair next to Mercy's bed.

"Baby? The Baby?" Mungo asked as he hesitantly sad down.

Then came a long and weak sigh of pain from Mercy who opened her eyes and looked at Muungo.

"Mercy, Mercy... it is me?"

Mercy opened her eyelids and looked at Muungo. Her top and bottom lips parted. Her finger clamped to the clip of the heart monitor rose and managed to point towards her the belly.

"I kept the baby. I kept the baby. I kept the baby king."

Printed in the United States
by Baker & Taylor Publisher Services